GOT NO FRIEND ANYHOW

A MAXX MAXWELL MYSTERY

GOT NO FRIEND ANYHOW

PEGGY EHRHART

FIVE STAR
A part of Gale, Cengage Learning

GALE
CENGAGE Learning™

Detroit • New York • San Francisco • New Haven, Conn • Waterville, Maine • London

GALE
CENGAGE Learning

LIBRARY OF CONGRESS CATALOGING-IN-PUBLICATION DATA

Ehrhart, Peggy.
  Got no friend anyhow : a Maxx Maxwell mystery / by Peggy Ehrhart. — 1st ed.
    p. cm.
  ISBN-13: 978-1-59414-932-0
  ISBN-10: 1-59414-932-1
  1. Women singers—Fiction. 2. Women blues musicians—Fiction. 3. Blues musicians—Crimes against—Fiction. 4. Murder—Investigation—Fiction. 5. Manhattan (New York, N.Y.)—Fiction.
I. Title.
PS3605.H746G68 2011
813'.6—dc22   2010041696

First Edition. First Printing: January 2011.
Published in 2011 in conjunction with Tekno Books and Ed Gorman.

Printed in the United States of America
1 2 3 4 5 6 7 15 14 13 12 11

To my husband, Norm Smith, the sweetest man of all time.

ACKNOWLEDGMENTS

Tremendous thanks to my Five Star editor Deni Dietz and to my friend and fellow Sister in Crime, Kathleen A. Ryan. Kathy is a retired Suffolk County police officer whose help with police procedure was invaluable.

CHAPTER 1

Blues has been the soundtrack of my life. I sing about things, and then they happen. Take "Another Man Done Gone"—that one has happened a lot. It might even be happening tonight, because somebody's supposed to be here and I sure don't see him.

I'm not singing "Another Man Done Gone," though—not yet anyway. I'm singing "Little Red Rooster."

Belting it out in my best Big Mama Thornton voice, in fact, and the audience is really into it. Beer bottles have paused halfway to mouths, and every face is turned toward the stage. Even the guys hanging around the bar are paying attention. Or maybe they're checking out my gold snakeskin pants and my 36C bustline, courtesy of Zazie's Lingerie Barn.

Next to me, Stan's bobbing dreamily over his guitar, eyes half-closed behind the wiry tendrils of dark hair escaping his ponytail. At the keyboard, Neil's punching out chords, while behind him, Michael works the strings of his bass, and Mitzi holds everything down with a solid shuffle on the drums.

This song seems pretty safe. I don't think I'll ever own a rooster. "Little Red Rooster" is a great blues tune, a tune we worked up for the CD that's going to propel Maxximum Blues to greater heights of glory. Not that we don't appreciate gigs like this one. So what if the Basement only holds about fifty people, on an assortment of sofas and chairs that Willy collected by hitting the streets one step ahead of the garbage trucks? It's one of the most happening clubs in the East Village.

But the festival circuit is where we'll make our name, starting next month with CityBlues. New York will be full of blues lovers and we'll play the gig I had to fight like crazy to get and our CD will be on sale right up there with CDs by some of the biggest blues names in the country. Besides that, once we've got a CD to show what we can do, I can hustle every festival organizer on the East Coast.

As Neil launches into his solo, I scan the audience more carefully, searching for the face of Rick Schneider. It's an ordinary face—brown eyes, nondescript nose, a smile with a little gap between the front teeth. But I wasted five years of my life with Sandy Wilkins, a guy that any woman would drool over. And even though I'll never forget Sandy, that experience taught me to appreciate somebody who'd rather look at me than in a mirror. Besides, Rick Schneider is the genius at Prowling Rooster Records who's capturing the definitive sound of Maxximum Blues—yeah, we put "Little Red Rooster" on there as a kind of thank you. And tonight Rick's showing up with the master for us to check out before he puts in the order to burn the CDs.

Neil is winding up his solo, so I glance over at Stan. As his gaze catches mine and his eyes widen, I nod. He snaps to attention, tosses his head back—and loses his balance. His guitar slips from the eyelet at the end of its strap and he grapples with it to keep it from hitting the floor. He's on one knee, clambering up with a hand braced on his amp while the other hand clutches the guitar. But when he's almost on his feet again, he stumbles, mutters, "Oh, shit," and reels backward.

Everything that's plugged in dies at once—guitar, bass, keyboards, vocals—and the room is suddenly pitch black, except for spots of blurry light cast by candles scattered on low tables. Mitzi keeps drumming for a few seconds, then stops, her taps replaced by a sudden burst of alarmed chatter from the audience.

I force myself to take a deep breath, trying to ignore the panicky clutch in my throat. "Stan?" I hear my voice, for some reason whispering. "Are you okay?"

No answer.

Down in the audience, candles are blotted out as dark shapes shift restlessly. Chair legs scrape the floor, the chattering becomes more intense, and it's punctuated by nervous laughter. A woman calls, "Frank? Frank? Are you still here?"

"Hang on, everybody," says a voice from the back. It's Willy, the owner. A flashlight sweeps the room, revealing people clumsily poised to dash for the steps that lead up to the street. The flashlight's beam reaches the stage, momentarily dazzling me. I blink and put a hand over my eyes.

Somewhere near where Willy's standing, a second flashlight clicks on. Whoever's carrying it makes his way toward the stage. As the flashlight plays over the equipment, I strain for a glimpse of Stan, notice him huddled next to his amp.

The flashlight guy threads his way between Michael's amp and the drumkit and fumbles with the curtains at the back of the stage. He disappears with the flashlight and we're in the dark again. In a few seconds, he reemerges and the flashlight's beam resumes its nervous dance over the equipment.

"It's just a fuse," he says. "You guys blew a fuse. Lights'll be back on in a second." The flashlight picks out Stan's and Michael's amps. "Switch those amps off though, will you?"

Suddenly, it's bright again and we're blinking at each other like we've never seen light before. The flashlight guy is kneeling next to Stan's amp holding up a cord that looks like a dog chewed it. "You shorted out, man," he says. "It must have been about ready to go and then you snagged your foot on it when you lost your balance."

Stan mumbles something and reaches to switch the amp back on.

"Oh, no you don't," the flashlight guy says. "Want to blow everything out again?"

"But how can I play?" Stan says, tucking a stray bit of hair behind his ear.

"I guess you can't," the flashlight guy says. Out of the corner of my eye I notice people leaving.

"Don't you have a backup amp stuck away somewhere?" Stan says hopefully.

"No point in hauling it out now," the flashlight guy says. "You guys only have about ten minutes to go."

Stan picks up his guitar and slouches dejectedly off the stage, apologizing to anybody who'll listen. We finish the set without him, for what's left of the audience—about five people.

And when Willy hands me a couple of folded bills, I unfold them to discover that only the one on the outside is a twenty. It's wrapped around a couple of tens.

"What's this?" I say. "The bar was doing great business tonight. Forty bucks for three sets?"

"Did you see how many people left when you guys fucked up the lights?"

"The third set was almost done by then," I say. "The place was full of people drinking until nearly two A.M."

He shrugs and walks away. I'd run after him and argue, but it wouldn't do any good. Club owners will use any excuse they can find to beat you on a gig. This is why we need the CD.

Respect, like Aretha Franklin would say.

"So where *is* Rick, anyway?" Michael says, fastidiously pouring the rest of his beer into his glass. His bass, neatly zipped back into his gig bag, leans against his bar stool and his thin face wears an expression somewhere between annoyance and disgust.

But that's nothing new for Michael.

"He'll show up," I say, trying to act less bothered than I feel. "He probably hit a little traffic."

"At two in the morning?"

"Maybe they're doing construction on the bridge. Sometimes they wait to do it at night. Give me your cell phone and I'll call him."

Michael hands me his cell phone. "Where's yours?"

"I owed them money so they turned it off. I can't get it back till payday at the restaurant." I punch in Rick's cell phone number, and after four rings I get his voice mail.

"No luck," I say, handing the phone back to Michael.

"He doesn't leave his phone on all the time?" Michael says with a frown, his enunciation as precise as if he was giving a lecture.

"I guess not."

"Some businessman." He snorts. "How about the number for the studio?"

I try it but I only get the machine.

"Maybe he's waiting for us at Stan's place," Michael says.

"He said he'd come here."

I purposely look away, hoping Michael will get the hint that I don't want to talk—at least not about that.

At the other end of the bar, Mitzi is exchanging high-fives with a couple of women that look like her—short hair combed like guys, flannel shirts, blue jeans, and sturdy boots. Just past Mitzi and her friends, Stan is sitting on the edge of the stage, noodling around on his unplugged guitar, plucking out whispery versions of his favorite licks. When he notices me looking at him, his head droops so low that all I can see is hair, and his nervous noodling speeds up. Neil is nowhere to be seen.

But Michael doesn't get the hint. "Even if he showed up right this instant, we wouldn't have time to listen to much." He takes a careful sip of his beer.

"Sure we would. Stan won't care how late we stay."

"And even if he does show up and the master's okay, which is unlikely, I doubt the CDs will be ready in time for the festival."

"They will," I say. "Rick's been doing this forever and he knows how long things take. Burning the CDs is nothing. Getting the master the way you want it is the hard part."

I look away again, tap my fingers in time to the taped music as if I'm really into it. Michael stays where he is, but at least he doesn't say anything else.

Minutes pass, lots of minutes. The few remaining people wander out. Willy turns off the taped music and turns on the overhead lights. The barmaid roams around collecting glasses and empty bottles. Mitzi's friends take off. Neil drifts back from wherever he was hiding out, probably smoking a joint.

Stan scoots off the stage and edges toward me, nervously, like a dog that expects to be scolded, head bowed and bony shoulders slumped.

"I'm really sorry," he says from under the cloud of shaggy hair that hides most of his face. "You won't fire me again, will you?"

He looks so pitiful that I grab his hand. "No," I say. "Our destinies seem to be interwoven, for better or worse."

"I consider you a friend, Maxx."

I nod and pat him on the shoulder. Being friends can be a complicated thing. Maybe there's a song about that.

We're the last people left in the place and Rick's still not here. Everyone in the band is looking at me—everyone except Stan, that is. He's gone back to his noodling, busy with some complicated pattern he's repeating up and down the fretboard, one fret at a time. But everyone else is looking at me. And I don't know what to say.

In my mind I'm revisiting the last time I saw Rick, our clothes in a pile on the studio floor, except for the T-shirt that he wouldn't take off even though I asked him to, sinking back onto the sofa whose leathery smell mixed with the smell of Rick's skin.

Michael holds out his cell phone. "Here. Try him again," he says. "This is ridiculous."

But there's still no answer on the other end, except for an impersonal voice telling me I can leave a message. Michael nods, not at anybody in particular, but kind of smugly to himself, like he's confirming something he suspected all along. "I told you this was a bad idea," he says.

"You think everything's a bad idea," I say. "So what's new?"

"This involves money."

"You have to spend money to make money," I say. "Bands without CDs almost never get booked at festivals. We only got into CityBlues because I knew somebody who could pull strings. And besides, we can sell copies of the CD and make all our money back and then some."

"There isn't going to be a CD. *Your friend* took our money and vanished."

The "your friend" part comes out as sarcastic as Michael can make it.

"Oh, come on," I say. "You think he left behind his house and his studio and all his gear to make off with a thousand bucks?" I pull on my fake leopardskin jacket. Usually the jacket cheers me up but it's not working tonight. I try to summon a smile anyway. "Everything will be fine. I'll get in touch with him tomorrow and find out what the story is. See you at rehearsal Thursday night?" I head for the stairs and the band follows me. I try to stay far enough ahead that Michael's voice is only an unintelligible whine.

Out on the street, an East Village street of six-floor walkups with narrow stoops angling from the sidewalk, Mitzi hangs back as the guys troop off.

She's about a head shorter than me, a sturdy woman with a fresh, makeup-free face, straight dark brows, a well-shaped mouth. "How come you let Michael give you such a rough time?" she says.

"Ever looked for a bass player?" I say.

"Hard?"

"Almost impossible."

"What do you think happened to Rick?" The worry in her face makes her look kind of gentle, despite the careful toughness of her image.

"There's probably a message on my machine at home," I say.

"Why wouldn't he call the club?"

I shrug.

My car—an ancient Bonneville, seafoam green like the classic old Strat color, but with one dark green door—isn't as out of place down here in the East Village as it is, say, in my parents' rich North Jersey suburb, not that I visit them all that often. The car's waiting right where I left it, in front of the vintage records shop, snugged up close enough to a big Harley to clear the yellow curb that marks a hydrant.

I open the passenger side door and slide across the seat. The lock on the driver's side got messed up a long time ago when somebody broke in while I was parked outside the place where we rehearse.

I drive back to New Jersey trying to convince myself that everything is going to be fine, but somehow deep inside I know it isn't.

CHAPTER 2

"Didn't you hear me say I wanted it unbuttered?" The woman has hair the color of well-polished brass and a face as lean as her well-exercised thighs.

"No, actually," I say. "I didn't."

"Well, I do." She hands me the plate of toast. "Please take this away." I nod. She looks suspiciously at the omelet I've set down in front of her. "Are you sure this is whites only?"

"That's how I put the order in." I gaze at the mural on the opposite wall. It shows a group of cowboys lounging around a campfire while their ponies munch grass in the background.

She squints and leans closer to the plate. "It looks so *yellow.*"

I shrug. "That's what came out."

She looks up at me with a frown. "Why isn't Martha here?"

"She had to take some time off," I say. "I'm filling in on her shift."

Usually I don't serve breakfast. I show up late in the afternoon and work till closing time, serving the shrimp scampi and fried calamari that give Aldo's Seafood Chalet its name. The cowboys and ponies date from when it used to be a barbecue place, before Aldo bought it.

Many omelets and waffles and short stacks and tall stacks and coffee refills later, Susanne tells me I can have a break. I help myself to a mug of coffee at the coffee station, take a few hot sips, and make my way to the pay phone, where I punch the number of Rick's studio—which also happens to be his house—

17

into the keypad. Needless to say, there was no message from him on my machine when I got home from the city last night.

The phone responds with a series of variously pitched chirps, and a voice tells me to deposit a dollar fifty. I dip in my apron pocket for some tip change.

Now I've got the receiver to my ear. It's ringing, and, hoping for the best, I'm phrasing some kind of a casual greeting like, "Hey! I guess we got our signals crossed about last night," though what I'm afraid of is that something bad happened with the CD master and he's embarrassed to face me.

All I get is his machine again, and when I try his cell phone number I get the voice mail. Disgusted, I drop the receiver back into its cradle and head for the break room, where I work the combination on my locker and pull out my bag.

Slipped between the pages of my address book I find the card Rick gave me the first time we discussed the CD. "Prowling Rooster Records," it says, in a flamboyant scrawl that shadows each letter's shape with a red outline. Prowling Rooster Records has some pretty heavy bands on its roster, and Maxximum Blues wasn't an official project. Rick was producing and recording our CD on the side, for money, yeah, but also because he's a friend of a friend—Nathan Danzig—and an all-around nice guy. At least I used to think he was an all-around nice guy.

Further down on the card three names appear: Rick Schneider, Ben Darling, and Steve Bernier. But there's only one number, Rick's home number, and only one address, Rick's address. In a way, that's Steve Bernier's address too, because he lives in an old trailer parked on Rick's property. Though he's supposedly a partner in Prowling Rooster Records, I've never met him. He doesn't seem to do much, and Rick gets embarrassed when his name comes up.

I flip through my address book till I find Nathan's number and pull another handful of change out of my apron pocket.

Maybe Nathan knows how to track down Ben, or has a separate number for Steve—though Steve might not be all that helpful. But all I get is Nathan's machine, and his recorded voice, as raspy as if his vocal cords were made out of old bicycle chains, telling me he can't come to the phone right now.

Later, at home, I try Rick and get the machine and the voice mail again.

He could be there, though. He could be there and trying to avoid me. I head back down to my car.

Too bad what's taking me up to Nyack isn't a pleasanter errand, because the ride up the Parkway is gorgeous on this bright fall day. Patches of the Hudson, smooth and blue, gleam between stands of reddening trees, and on the opposite bank, Yonkers is far enough away for the random buildings that dot the shore to look romantic.

I take Route 303. Then, just past the Day'n'Nite Limo Service I make a sharp right onto a narrow road of pitted asphalt that climbs a gentle hill. After a quarter of a mile, I come to a wooden sign with Rick's address on it. My car sways and creaks as I turn off the asphalt onto rutted dirt.

As I approach Rick's house, I feel myself leaning forward, straining to see—what? But there's only the dusty road, tree trunks, and patchy grass dotted with a rusty fall of autumn leaves. The car sways over a few deep ruts and the road curves to the left. I pass Steve's trailer, looking like a giant silver jelly bean, and soon the screened porch that forms the back of Rick's rambling wood frame house comes into view.

Usually Rick's pickup truck is parked a few yards from the back door. Now there's only an empty spot, bare dirt strewn with a few recently fallen leaves.

He's not here now. But I am. I decide to leave a note.

As I drive into the cleared area around Rick's house and pull

19

up to park where the truck is usually parked, I notice something. It's a black truck, Rick's truck, but parked in a different place, over near a thin stand of trees at the edge of the thicker forest.

So he *is* home. Now while one part of me is matter-of-factly shifting into PARK, twisting the key in the ignition, and listening to the engine shut down with a whining moan, another part of me feels like I'm about to go onstage. My heart has expanded up into my throat while a busy little drumbeat clicks away in my chest.

Am I a pissed-off customer or a jilted girlfriend? And do I have to decide that before I pound on the door and ask the son-of-a-bitch why he didn't show up last night?

I take a deep breath and climb out of the car. A gust of wind makes my hands reach for the pockets of my jacket even though I'm wearing gloves. By the time I expel the breath, I've climbed the steps to the door that leads into the screened porch. The breath disappears in a frosty wisp and I replace it with one that's a sudden lung-chilling shock.

The flimsy screen door squeaks on its hinges as I pull it toward me. The door is never locked, because the porch holds only a daybed covered with an Indian-print bedspread, a few old wooden chairs, and a small table with music catalogues scattered here and there.

A low moan makes me catch my breath, but when it's followed by the rushing sound of leaves heaving in the wind I realize it's a branch rubbing another branch.

I step toward the door that opens into Rick's kitchen, and I begin to knock, lightly at first, then harder and harder and harder, till I almost forget that I'm trying to rouse Rick, that it somehow isn't the door's fault that we might not have our CD in time for the festival and that when I finally trusted a guy again, he let me down.

When I finally unclench my fist and let my hand fall slowly to my side, my knuckles are throbbing. Is he in there or not?

I turn, push back through the screen door, and make my way down the steps. Out in the yard, I wander along the side of the house, standing on tiptoe to look in each window, tapping and calling, listening for any faint response. My steps stir up dark mossy smells as I kick leaves out of my way. On the front porch, long windows look into the old living room, now the studio, but they're masked with heavy drapes, never opened.

Finally, I've circled the house and I'm standing in the backyard again, staring at the truck. I wander over to it, kicking leaves out of my way, asking myself why it's parked here and not in its usual spot.

I peer in the windows. Everything looks normal, like it always looked—except the seats aren't aligned. Either the passenger's seat has been slid way back or the driver's seat has been slid way forward.

I open the driver's side door and start to ease myself into the seat, but I can barely fit behind the steering wheel—and I'm a skinny chick. I'd be a total beanpole if not for the Zazie's Lingerie Barn bra. Some tiny person with really short legs has been driving Rick's car.

I finally get myself wedged into the seat and I'm squirming around trying to figure out if *anybody* could actually drive with the seat like this, when I feel something underfoot. I bend over and twist my head around the steering wheel to see what it is and realize that it's dirt. Lots and lots of dirt.

Rick's not the tidiest guy in the world, but he loves this truck. Could he possibly have climbed in with shoes so muddy that they left big clumps of dirt like what I see now?

I ease myself out of the seat and lower my feet onto the ground. Then I bend over and scrape up a handful of the dirt. In my hand it almost looks like some weird kind of pasta, super-

21

healthy because it's made out of whatever they make that dark-brown health bread out of. The parts that didn't get squashed because I didn't step on them look like little squiggles carefully molded in squiggle-shaped molds—or like bits of mud that dried in the treads of some very heavy-duty boots and then popped out.

But if his truck is here, he's here. There's no place around here that you can go on foot. Maybe he's sick or hurt. Even if he's trying to avoid me, he doesn't seem like the kind of guy to cower inside while somebody pounds on his back door.

I head back to the house and check the window that opens from the screened porch into the kitchen. I could climb up on the daybed and squeeze through, but the latch looks pretty secure and I don't want to break any glass unless I have to. So I circle the house again, hurrying, because the sun is already near the horizon, staining the sky the color of a mango smoothie. The side windows are too high, even if one of them happened to be open, and the windows that look out onto the front porch are tightly latched.

But as I cruise along the other side of the house, I notice a pair of old cellar doors, almost flush with the ground, butting up against the rough stone that forms the house's foundation. I bend down and grab the handle on one of them, give an experimental tug, and the door opens a few inches then falls closed again when I release my grip.

I brace myself against the side of the house and pull harder. The door swings all the way back and flops onto the ground. I peer into the darkness then run back to the car for my flashlight.

Wooden steps lead down into the basement. I take a deep breath and creep slowly down them, balancing myself by holding onto the edge of the other door. Once I've reached the bottom, I let the flashlight's beam wander here and there, trying not to inhale the musty dampness, cringing as the basement's clammy air chills my skin.

I follow the flashlight's beam across the floor till it picks up another set of stairs. In a few seconds, I'm pushing open a door and stepping into Rick's kitchen. It's chilly too, and shadowy, with the blinds on its one small window closed against the fading afternoon light.

"Rick?" I call. "Hello? Rick? Anybody here?"

A soft scratching pulls my attention to the table against the right-hand wall. A wire mesh cage about the height of a laundry hamper but wider sits on top of it, and inside the cage a rooster with a sleek dark-feathered body and a bright red comb shifts uneasily. The whole rest of the table's surface is taken up with a phone, a bag of something called "Farlo Boonton Chicken Feed," and a pile of mail, some opened, some not.

The rooster is Red, Rick's pet and the mascot of Prowling Rooster Records. Usually he roams around in the yard during the day, wandering in and out of an old chicken coop the earlier owners of Rick's house left behind, and he only comes in at night.

"Awrk?" Red cocks his head to stare at me. I look back at him. His stare seems somehow aggrieved. I look closer and notice that his food and water cups are empty.

"Okay," I say. "I'll feed you. Just let me look around for a minute."

I continue through the kitchen and into the dim hall that leads past what was once a dining room but is now an office, though the tall windows with their ornate Victorian moldings are still curtained in heavy rose brocade, somewhat the worse for wear.

"Rick?" I call softly, stopping in the doorway. No answer.

I continue on till I come to the studio, once the living room, its walls hung with spongy gray soundproofing. An old upright piano stands against one wall, an assortment of guitar and bass amps are pushed against another wall, and a jumble of mikes on mike stands fill the corner like a thicket of bare metallic trees.

I flip another switch, and brightness bathes the piano, the amps, the mikes in the corner, the monitors, and the table where the 32-track sits, cables snaking out from it and drooping to the floor like coils of rubbery rope.

"Rick?" I call. "Rick? Are you here?"

No answer.

I've never been upstairs before. Rick was all business until those last few sessions, when I stayed behind after the band left and Rick and I wound up on that leather sofa.

One hand on the banister, I creep up the steps, feeling as breathless as if I'd already climbed twenty flights. Old houses make strange noises—a gurgling clank that could be a radiator, a creak that could be the wind buffeting an ill-fitting window.

At the head of the stairs I face the bathroom, door ajar, white tile walls shimmering with an inner ghostly glow. I step inside, easing the door further open till it bumps the end of the tub. The shower curtain, with a jaunty pattern of musical notes in every shade of the rainbow, is drawn closed, just skimming the lip of the old claw-footed tub.

"Rick?" I whisper. I fumble for the curtain's edge and, quickly, before my brain can summon up an image of what *might* be lurking behind it, besides an expanse of porcelain that would be whiter if a guy didn't live here by himself, sweep it open. The sound of the shower curtain rings scraping along the rod sets my teeth on edge.

Nothing's behind the curtain but an empty tub.

I back out of the bathroom, feeling strangely relieved, and advance along the hallway. The sun has sunk so low that inside the house, shadows like grayish gauze soften the angles where wall meets wall and wall meets floor. For some reason I'm tiptoeing.

24

I reach the door to Rick's room and step onto the threshold. I can make out a double bed covered in something dark, with a pale rectangle at the head. A shape against the wall, a shade between dark and pale, is probably a bureau. A tall stripe of paleness adjacent to a dark rectangle is probably a closet with the door half open.

I feel along the wall till my fingers encounter a light switch and suddenly detail replaces shapes softened by shadow. The bed is covered with a puffy dark-green comforter that's pulled up far enough to partly hide a pillow in a white case. The surface of the dresser is a jumble of clock, magazines, a sock, a baseball cap. A T-shirt dangles from the closet doorknob, and the half-open door reveals a few flannel shirts, a few pairs of jeans on hangers, and a pile of sneakers.

Yeah, Rick always wore sneakers. It occurs to me that even if he didn't mind getting his truck dirty, sneaker bottoms wouldn't produce anything like those curlicues of dried mud on the pickup's floor. Just to make sure, I step into the room and grab a sneaker off the pile. I run my finger over the sole. It's nearly smooth. Somebody else has been driving the truck for sure.

As I turn to head back downstairs, my gaze sweeps the walls but stops when it encounters a photograph hanging over the bed. It's a photograph of a woman, a beautiful woman. Maybe that's the reason Rick never invited me up here. Maybe there's another woman in his life. But she looks much too young to want to be with a guy Rick's age—though maybe she's not young now. Her hair and makeup suggest the photo dates from at least twenty years ago, maybe more.

I certainly hope she's not a current love interest because she'd be stiff competition, and then some. Nobody could look at that face and not be fascinated, drawn to the haunting dark eyes, the perfect sculpted cheekbones, and most of all the soft

25

mouth made so human by the tiny asymmetry of its upper bow.

"Awrk?" Red blinks at me in the sudden wash of light as I flip the switch inside the kitchen door. His glossy feathers ripple as he twitches his wings. "Awrk?" His head with its gaudy comb darts toward his empty food cup, darts back up, and his bright eyes look at me accusingly.

Poor guy. He must really be hungry.

"Okay, okay," I murmur. "I said I'd feed you, and it looks like you need some water too." I reach for the bag of Farlo Boonton Chicken Feed, and as I pull it toward me, it skims the untidy stack of mail, knocking about half of it to the floor.

I stoop to collect it, and as I'm retrieving junk mail and bills and catalogues, my attention is caught by a letter scrawled in careless writing across a dog-eared sheet of paper. Above me, Red is pacing in his cage and my eyes are drifting over the scribbled words while my heart is sinking.

"Sweetheart," the letter reads. "I'm doing a show in Westchester Nov. 7th. Call me Friday A.M." The letter goes on to give the phone number then says, "Let's get it back like it was," and it's signed "B."

Today's the 9th. I stand up, feeling kind of sick. Red shifts in his cage and fixes me with a beady eye. I turn the page over and see what looks like a tour schedule: the Westchester gig, something in Chicago on the 9th—today—some other stuff all over the place, and another local gig—the Last Chance on the 14th.

I sink into one of the kitchen chairs and punch the Friday A.M. number into the phone. After four rings, a chirpy voice says, "Sleepy Time Motel. How may I help you?"

I ask for Rick Schneider.

"Is he a guest, ma'am?"

"I don't know. I don't know what he is. He's staying with

somebody, somebody named—" I reach for the letter. "Somebody named B."

"Excuse me?"

"Never mind. I'm sorry."

I hang up, but I don't stand up. I call Manhattan information and ask for the number of the Last Chance. For an extra 75 cents, I let them connect me.

The "B." who signed the letter to "Sweetheart," who wants to get it back like it was, who's playing at the Last Chance November 14, turns out to be none other than Brenda Honeycut, one of the most happening singer-songwriters on the current scene. I jam the letter into my bag.

If Rick was going to hang out with his old girlfriend for a few days, couldn't he at least keep me posted on what was happening with the CD? And leave enough food for his rooster? So the pickup is still here because she came for him. And she'll probably be delivering him back home soon, unless he's going to Chicago with her. According to the tour schedule, she should be on her way there about now.

Red's sudden "Awrk?" brings me back to reality

"It's okay, Red," I say. "Here's your food. Coming right up."

I scoop a cup of feed out of the Farlo Boonton bag and unlatch the door of the cage. "Awrk! Squirk!" In a flurry of distress, Red flings himself into the air, hanging suspended inside the cage for a minute, wings flapping frantically as they churn up bits of shredded newspaper. Landing on his feet again, he bustles back and forth until, suddenly, he's pecking my fingers. His beak is like a sharp thorn lodging itself in my flesh and tearing away, again and again.

I jerk my hand away, but I can't dislodge my fingers from the latch on the door of the cage, and the cage comes along as I try to pull loose.

Now it's hanging over the table's edge, and as I free my

fingers, the cage lands on the floor with a crash, another flurry of newspaper bits, and an irritated burst of squawking from Red.

The next thing I know, Red is scurrying down the hall toward the studio.

"Wait, wait," I call, running after him. "I'm trying to help you."

He looks back at me and suddenly swerves into the first doorway he comes to, Rick's office, the house's former dining room. I bolt past him, almost tripping over Rick's desk chair, grab the door that leads into the studio, and slam it shut. I run back the other direction and slam the door that leads to the hallway.

So where is he? A soft cluck and the sighing sound of wings settling into place draws my attention to Rick's desk. Red is lurking underneath, seemingly content to stay put now that he thinks he's found a safe haven.

If I can throw something over him, bundle him up, and stick him back in his cage, everything will be fine. I scan the room and see nothing promising. I could rip down one of the drapes— but they're so long and wide, they'd be too unwieldy to wrap a rooster in. Half a pair is already missing from one of the windows though. I wonder what that's all about.

I don't see anything else that would work to wrap a rooster in, so, okay, it's got to be done. I shrug my way out of my silver thrift-store trenchcoat. Red regards me with his beady eye, clucking quietly to himself, as I come near, holding the coat in front of me like a bullfighter confronting a bull.

"Okay, fellow." I try to sound soothing. "I'm just trying to help you."

I kneel and swoop toward him with the coat. He clucks, louder now, and backs further under the desk. I creep forward on my knees, and as I look into the shadows, something catches my eye, something that doesn't have anything to do with Red.

I'm distracted long enough for him to squeeze past me, half-running, half-flying. But I let him go, for the moment at least, because I'm looking at one of Rick's prize possessions, and it doesn't belong down here on the floor.

I pull it toward me, carefully because the glass is broken. It's a framed album cover that used to occupy a special spot on the opposite wall. I remember asking Rick about it once and he said it was the only thing in the whole place he'd ever care about losing.

"Why?" I asked.

"That music was what my youth was all about," he said.

I study the picture on the front. Four guys, their faces shaded by jaunty fedoras, are lined up against a brick wall. Above them, the word "MEAL" is spelled out in heavy, droopy letters that look like they're melting.

I lift it up and put it on the desk. When I turn my attention back to Red, he's crouched between the side of the desk and the wall. As I swoop toward him and bundle him into my coat, I notice that on the floor in the corner is a big stain that looks like dried blood.

CHAPTER 3

The police station is in the town hall, a modern building that could pass for a mall if the big windows interrupting its creamy facade were filled with mannequins wearing belly button–baring jeans.

Around a corner and up a short flight of stairs, a broad pane of probably bullet-proof glass protects a fluorescent-lit command post manned by absolutely no one. Through a half-open door in the far wall I can make out a slice of a blue-clad back.

I wait a minute or two then tap lightly on the glass. A muffled peal of laughter drifts through the half-open door, but in a few seconds I'm looking into the business-like face of a middle-aged black woman.

"My friend is missing," I say. "He's disappeared. He lives up that hill along Route 303 by where the Day'n'Nite Limo Service is. I guess that's your territory, right? He was supposed to meet me in the city last night, and he didn't come, and I tried to call him today and nobody answered—so I drove up here and he's not here, but some tiny person with really dirty boots moved his truck and when I was in his house I found—"

Her hands make a motion like they're pushing down a mound of dough that's rising too fast.

"Whoa," she says. "Take it easy. When was the last time you saw him?"

"Four days ago," I say. "But I talked to him on the phone yesterday."

She raises her eyebrows and gives me a closed-lipped smile that isn't really a smile. "He's not missing."

"But he's disappeared, and I found—"

"Sometimes people *want* to disappear." She tightens her lips into the odd smile again. "Know what I'm sayin'? They want to leave things behind. Entanglements."

"But I found something at his place that makes me think something really bad happened."

"What is it?" The look on her face says she's not going to be impressed no matter what I say.

"There's a puddle of dried blood on the floor."

"A puddle of blood?" I nod. "Not a body?"

"No," I say. "Not a body."

"You're sure it's blood?" she says. "If somebody removed a body, there'd be a trail."

The drapes. That's why one was missing. "One of the drapes is gone," I say. "Heavy old-fashioned drapes that you could wrap a body in."

"And when did you say you talked to him?"

"Yesterday. A couple of hours before I was supposed to meet him in the city. Then he didn't show up."

"He's about your age?"

I nod. "A few years older."

She chews on her lip for a second and starts to turn away, looks over her shoulder, and says, "Take a seat. I'll be right back." She points to a bench covered in olive-green Naugahyde.

The next thing I know, a door is opening and a guy in a sports jacket is giving me the once-over. At first, I don't know if he's a cop or not, but then he says, "I'm Detective Carlson. Step back here into my office, please." The look on his face is sort of a cross between worry and respect. I'm wondering what's up.

Once we get to his office and I'm settled in a chair that's also covered in olive-green Naugahyde, he asks me the same things the lady cop asked me and some other things too, like how tall Rick was and what color of hair he had and what my relationship with him was.

As he's asking me these things and I'm answering, my gaze drifts around the room, taking in the framed certificates, the bulletin board covered with everything from official-looking notices to greeting cards, the half-empty mug of coffee next to the computer monitor.

But then I hear him say, ". . . body found by a jogger and his dog in Green Forest Park this morning . . . needs positive identification . . ." I start to get that unreal feeling you get sometimes when something bad is happening, like you're not yourself but a character in a play, and you're watching that character from somewhere else, somewhere quite distant.

The cop's voice sounds like it's coming from far away too, even though I'm sitting across the desk from him. Fuzzy black spots start to gather in the air right in front of my eyes and my body sways.

He gives me a card with an address on it and tells me that the county morgue opens at eight A.M. Monday.

I'm about to head south on 303 when I remember Red. He never did get his food and water and maybe now there won't ever be anybody coming home again to take care of him. I swallow back a big lump in my throat.

I'll take him home with me. Maybe this is all a weird mistake and Rick is fine and if he is I'll give Red back.

But as I'm bundling Red's cage into the back seat of my car, trying to keep my fingers away from that sharp little beak, I'm struggling to block out the images crowding into my mind: a violent encounter knocks the album cover off the wall, Rick ends up on the floor bleeding, somebody drags the curtain down—

I slam the car door, which sends Red into a frenzy of wing flaps, and I'm about to get behind the wheel and drive away when I think of something important. Let's say the pickup truck was parked in its usual place Saturday night, about where my car is now. Somebody drags a body wrapped in a curtain out the door and across the few yards that separate the steps from the back of the pickup. Wouldn't there be a trail in the dirt?

If there's no sign of anything like that, maybe it means the body I'm going to look at tomorrow morning won't be Rick and everything will turn out okay.

I stoop and examine the ground, pushing handfuls of leaves aside to expose what's underneath. There's no trail, but it occurs to me that that doesn't mean anything. The carpet of dead leaves would protect the ground from contact with the body and even probably help it slide along better. I head over to where the pickup is parked now and stare into the truck bed. It's got a carpet of dead leaves too, and surely new ones have landed in there since last night, making it impossible to tell if the ones that were originally there have been compressed by the weight of a body wrapped in a curtain.

Back in my car, I'm about to start the engine when I remember Red's food. I locked the back door, so I have to go in through the basement again. I'm hauling the bag of Farlo Boonton toward the back door when I think of something else. The album cover might be a clue, something the cops could use. But it might not. On impulse I dart into the old dining room, Rick's office, and retrieve it. But how to carry it? The frame is wrenched out of shape, and jagged cracks run through the glass, making the broken bits shift and grind against each other as I handle the album cover. I'll have to wrap it in something. Once again I take off my silver thrift-store trench coat, this time to carefully wrap Rick's souvenir of Meal, broken glass and all.

My brain is sending an urgent message to Leon: please be home, please be home, please be home. But the words are getting tangled up with the Lynard Skynard tune blasting out of my car radio. "Gimme three steps . . . please be home . . . gimme three steps . . . please be home—" I put the radio on to try to distract myself on the drive back down to New Jersey, but it's making me feel more on edge.

I click it off and discover that I'm mumbling the message to myself: "Please be home, Leon, *please, please, please* be home." From the back seat, I can hear Red scuffling around in his cage.

But when I pull into the lot behind my building, Leon's accustomed spot is empty.

Red seems to be sleeping now, so I decide it would be better not to try to take him upstairs yet. Besides, it's going to take some extra energy to climb the stairs carrying that cage. So I leave him in the car, but I roll the back window down a tiny bit so he can have some fresh air.

I hurry around the building to the front door—chilly without my coat, keys jingling in my hand, still mumbling "please be home" even though it's useless now. At least it distracts me from the images of Rick swirling in my mind: Rick laughing, then turning serious as he leans to kiss me. Rick pushing my hands away, but gently, as I try to ease his T-shirt over his head. Rick collapsing on top of me with a moan of pleasure.

I fit my key in the lock, give it a twist, and push my way through the heavy glass door, cradling the album cover, wrapped in the silver trench coat. I should probably have left it for the cops, but I didn't. It was really important to Rick and I feel like I owe it to him to preserve it. And besides, it might turn out to be the only thing I have to remind me of him. As the thought goes through my mind, it occurs to me that I'm already reacting like he's really dead.

I can smell the remains of somebody's dinner leaking from their apartment. Even out here in the foyer I can tell it was something with lots of onion and garlic.

My mom hates this place. Not enough to never visit, unfortunately, but enough that I can't spend more than five minutes with her before the subject comes up. And from the topic of my apartment, the conversation ranges to the neighborhood in general, and then to the theme of what am I going to really do with my life. If there's time, she drifts on to the subject of my sister, my *younger* sister, who's now a postdoc in biology at the University of Toronto.

The smell gets stronger as I head for the stairs, then fades out as I climb to my floor, where the apartments generally leak sounds instead of smells. Nobody's fighting tonight, but the 24-hour sports channel guy has his TV turned up even louder than usual.

I let myself into my apartment and gently lower the album cover onto the bed—my whole apartment's one room, aside from the kitchen and the bathroom. My gaze wanders toward the red light blinking at me from the phone machine. My mother? I'd almost welcome a conversation with her. Anything to take my mind off Rick.

I pull my boots off and kick them across the room, toss my bag on the bed next to the album cover, and head for the kitchen. I come back out with a can of Bud and push the PLAY button.

"This is Michael," says a voice I'd recognize even without the ID. It's annoying and precise, and the tinny effect of the phone machine makes it sound even higher pitched than it really is. "What's happening with the CD? Did you get in touch with Rick? Please give me a call. We've got to get this resolved because CityBlues is only three weeks away."

I know that, Michael. I say this to myself as I settle into the big chair—Mr. Rush's chair—debating whether to call Michael and tell him about my trip to Nyack and that I'm going to the morgue tomorrow to look at a body that's probably Rick's body. And that I don't have a clue what's happening with the CD, and furthermore I'm not sure I really care anymore.

I lean back and the chair creaks as it rocks on its big springs. It's ancient. All the furniture in this place is ancient. It was here when I moved in because the previous inhabitant, an elderly black man named Mr. Rush, had just died, and when I asked if I could keep everything, his son and daughter laughed in amazement and said sure.

The wallpaper was probably here even before Mr. Rush—big bunches of huge roses, faded brown, and linked by a ribbon that forms a bow for one bunch then flows along to the next bunch, where it forms another bow, and on and on all around the room.

I finish the can of beer and reach for the phone. Michael may be the most annoying person in the world, but he's in my band, and I've got to keep my band going. I formed it after I broke up with Sandy, and no matter what else happens, it's the one constant in my life.

He answers on the first ring, like he's been sitting there waiting to pounce, his precise voice announcing, "Michael Scott here."

I describe my trip to Nyack and my visit to the police station and the errand that awaits me tomorrow. When I get to that part, my throat starts to tighten and my voice gets squeaky. Michael listens without interrupting, which is a novelty for him. But when I'm all done, he says, "So I guess the CD's going to be on hold for awhile."

I'm so stunned that for a minute I can't speak. He couldn't

even come up with a sentence or two, something to make it seem like he actually has feelings? Okay, the band didn't know I was romantically involved with Rick too, but we all worked with him.

He interjects another thought into the silence. "Didn't he have some kind of partners? You could get hold of them and ask them what's going on."

"Sure, yeah," I say in kind of a numb daze. "I'll do that." Maybe.

"Call me when you know something."

I put on my Big Mama Thornton album and drink another can of beer, listening all the while for the sounds in the hall that will tell me Leon has come home. But there's no sign of Leon and when I open my eyes to discover the CD has ended, I realize that I was sleeping. I peel off my clothes and throw them on the big chair, turn off the light, and cross the room to my bed, tripping over my boots on the way.

Once I'm in bed, I can't sleep, not right away. But sooner than if I'd lain there awake all night, Julio's music starts in with its lively Latin rhythms and I open my eyes to discover that the sky is the gray color of a November dawn.

I can't imagine working a whole shift worrying and wondering about what I'm going to discover when I go to the morgue, so I call the restaurant to say that I've got personal business to take care of. I tell Aldo I'll try to show up in time for the lunch rush.

"What kind of personal business might it be?" Aldo asks. "I can't run a restaurant with people reporting for work whenever they feel like it." I can picture him at the other end of the line, his pudgy face with the silly mustache that migrates to the right or to the left when his shaving gets careless.

"It's personal," I say. "*Personal* personal business."

★ ★ ★ ★ ★

I have a quick shower and put on the same clothes from the day before, grabbing them off the big chair and shaking out my jeans to try to get rid of the wrinkles. This isn't an errand that calls for makeup and I'm too nervous to eat or even drink coffee, so I'm on my way down the stairs in ten minutes.

When I get near the car, I remember Red—because he's crowing, doing his best to greet the feeble sun from the confines of his cage on the back seat of my car. He stops in mid-crow to gaze at me reproachfully. Sure enough, his food cup is empty. I could carry the cage upstairs now and get him fixed up with food and fresh water, but he'd probably keep crowing and people in the building would notice it. I'm not sure what I'm going to do about the crowing problem once I get him installed in my apartment, but I can postpone having to think about it by leaving him in the car while I drive up to Rockland County. I manage to fill the food cup without having him escape. Then I run upstairs and come back with water for the water cup.

The first thing I notice is something like a loading dock: a concrete platform with a wide metal door like a beat-up garage door. The sign on the smaller metal door next to it says "Morgue—Authorized Entrance Only." Aside from the garage door and the ominous sign, the building could be a nondescript grammar school dating from the fifties.

"Help you?" The receptionist is a heavy middle-aged woman with a sympathetic face. I tell her I'm supposed to identify a body, still feeling like I'm not real, but a character in a play. "Have a seat," she says. "Dr. Fogarty will be with you in a few minutes."

Angular chairs, seats covered in orange Naugahyde, are lined up along a cinderblock wall painted lime green. Their ranks are broken by a small table holding a plant and a pile of magazines, things like *Modern Maturity* and *Health News Today.*

"Elizabeth?" says a voice behind me as I'm bending over the magazines. I turn to see a well-groomed woman about ten years older than me. "I'm Ellen Fogarty," she says, holding out her hand. "The police think you might be able to help us."

I give her my hand and nod kind of numbly. "Everybody calls me Maxx," I say. "M-a-x-x."

"Maxx," she says with a small smile. "Short for Maxwell?"

"Yeah. My mom doesn't like it that I call myself that, but . . ." My voice trails off and I try to swallow around what feels like a guitar pick lodged in my throat.

"These situations are very hard," she says, leading the way past the row of chairs, toward a door at the far end of the room. Then, like a doctor who wants to distract you when he's about to give you a shot, she says, "Detective Carlson tells me that you're a musician."

"Yeah," I say.

"What style?"

"Blues," I say. "I'm a singer."

"A singer?" she says. "I sang with a band in college." She laughs, but gently, like she's trying to keep the occasion solemn. "Then I went to medical school."

I nod. "Probably a wise decision."

Now we're in a little office, fluorescent lights emphasizing the no-frills effect of the simple wooden desk with a chair behind it, small sofa along one wall, shelves of books with dark bindings.

Opposite the wall with the sofa, drapes are drawn closed over what must be a window. But what does it look out on? This is one of those buildings where once you're inside, time is marked only by clocks in a windowless 24-hour fluorescent noontime.

"You might want to sit," Ellen Fogarty says as she reaches for a cord hanging at the edge of the drapes.

"He's behind there?" I say, pointing at the window.

"Yes," she says. "Shall I open the drapes now?"

"I can stand up," I say.

With a soft swish that incongruously reminds me of the curtain opening for a show, the drapes part and I'm looking at a gurney like you see on those TV hospital dramas, the ones where bashed-up people are wheeled into emergency rooms while doctors and nurses bark out orders in some secret medical code.

On top of the gurney is what looks like a human-sized cocoon, a cocoon made out of plastic cloth like they make cheap tablecloths out of, except it's pure white, not red and white checks or dotted with little flowers. Down the front is a long zipper.

At one end the zipper has been unzipped far enough to show a face, a bruised face. The eyes are closed, but I know what color they are anyway, and the lips, though relaxed and a little swollen, aren't parted far enough to reveal the little space between the two front teeth.

I back slowly across the floor while some other part of me watches from somewhere near the ceiling. For a few seconds I'm huge and everything around me is tiny, then I shrink until, as I sink backward onto the sofa, I feel like I'm almost not there anymore.

"Let me get you some water," says Ellen Fogarty, as she pulls the cord again and the drapes swish closed.

She returns with the water and I drink it while she sits next to me on the sofa and looks at me with sympathetic eyes. Finally, she says, "Feeling better?"

"I guess."

"There's some paperwork to do."

"What happened to him?" I say.

"A gunshot wound to the head. We cleaned him up. It went in behind the right ear and exited behind the left. Whoever shot him was only a few feet away, almost an execution-type shooting."

"The bruises?"

"It looks like he was attacked. Did your friend own a gun?"

"I think so," I say. "Living way out there in the woods, you know. And he had a lot of expensive equipment." He probably kept the gun in the desk drawer, so it was right there when whoever killed him came after him in his office.

"He may have been trying to defend himself and the assailant grabbed the gun."

I drink some of the water and let my head sink back against the wall. "Oh," says Ellen Fogarty. "There was something else worth mentioning. It could have helped with the ID but I guess you saw enough."

"What else?" I say.

"He'd been shot before," she says. "He had several bullet wounds to his torso, healed a long time ago."

"I never saw them," I say. "Even though we were . . . you know . . ."

"Lovers?" she says kindly.

"He never took his T-shirt off. I used to tease him about it."

"It looks like there might have been something in his past he didn't want you to know about."

After I leave the morgue I figure I might as well go to work, rather than sit around my apartment and feel miserable. It'll be lunchtime when I get there and I'll be so busy I won't have time to think.

I can swing by my place, carry Red upstairs, and change into the black pants and white shirt that we have to wear at the Seafood Chalet. All Aldo supplies is the special Seafood Chalet vests. But when I pull into the parking lot behind my building, the super is in the alley rearranging the trash cans. He catches sight of me and gives a big wave, so I decide it will be better to move Red to my apartment later, maybe after it gets dark.

I'm dying to talk to Leon, but there's no sign of his car in the parking lot when I get home from the restaurant. Red is clucking to himself in the back seat and doesn't seem too unhappy. Good thing too, because now the super is raking leaves along the path that leads from the lot to the front door of the building.

Upstairs, I grab a beer from the refrigerator and throw myself into the big chair. Out in the hall, a door opens and then closes, but gently, so I know it's not Julio or the 24-hour sports channel guy. I'm on my feet in a second, out my own door, and tapping on the one next to mine.

"You're a sight for sore eyes," I say, as the door swings back and he greets me with a smile.

"Yours are sore too?" He lifts a shapely black hand, shifts his horn-rimmed glasses to the top of his head, and rubs his eyes. "I've been studying all day. Torts are no picnic. I thought I'd read for awhile, but . . ." He rubs his eyes again. In his other hand, he holds a paperback copy of *Othello*.

"You know what I mean," I say. "It's such a relief to see somebody that's so . . . so—" I grab him and let my cheek rest against the comforting softness of his sweater. "So *alive*." One of his hands makes a little rubbing motion on my back. "Oh, Leon, Rick is dead. The cops found his body in a park up by where he lives and I had to go to the morgue and look at it. Somebody shot him."

His hands move up to my shoulders and he steps back, holding me at arms' length. The expression on his handsome dark face is so sad and worried that I almost feel like I should be trying to cheer him up. "I'll bet you could use a beer," he says.

"I brought my own."

"Let me grab one." He gets me settled on his sofa, and heads

42

for the kitchen, stopping by his stereo on the way. In a few seconds B.B. King's voice fills the small room.

"Do you ever listen to that when I'm not here?" I call after him. Leon isn't a blues fan, but he always puts B.B. King on when he thinks I need to be cheered up.

Then he's back, holding a glass and a bottle of Heineken and taking up his accustomed place at the other end of the sofa. I tip my head and take several swallows of my own beer, close my eyes for a minute, and take a few more.

"Somebody shot him?" Leon asks. "On purpose?"

"Apparently. The doctor at the morgue said it looked like there'd been a fight first—he had bruises on his face. But he was shot from up close, almost like an execution. And the doctor said he had old bullet wounds too, all healed up from a long time ago. I didn't see them. They only let me see his face. They had him all zipped up into a thing like a white plastic sleeping bag."

"What was he up to?" Leon says. "It sounds like he was hanging out with some seriously mean characters."

"I don't know. I thought Prowling Rooster Records was on the level. But maybe it's not. There are three partners but Rick's the only one I ever met. One of the other ones hangs out on Rick's land in one of those old-fashioned silver trailers and doesn't seem to do much of anything that's useful. In fact, the way Rick talks about him makes him seem sort of crazy. But Rick is the real thing. He loves the blues and he goes out of his way to track down guys that haven't recorded in years. Old black guys that could use the money. And he really understands what we want to sound like—"

I stop myself, close my eyes, and let my head fall back against the granny-square afghan that Leon keeps draped over the back of his sofa.

"Are you okay?" Leon asks.

43

I straighten up, sigh, and drain the rest of my beer. "I was talking like he's still alive," I say. I set my empty beer can on the coffee table, being careful to center it on one of Leon's coasters. "I don't know what's going to happen with the CD now, and Michael's furious and I've got to figure out what to do with the rooster."

"Wait, wait, wait." He holds up his hands like he's fending something off. "The rooster?"

"It was the mascot of Prowling Rooster Records. I didn't want it to starve."

"How'd you end up with it?"

"I went back to his house after the cops told me they'd found a body that could be Rick. I got in through a trapdoor that goes to the basement."

Leon raises his eyebrows and lets his tongue click against his teeth in an expression of mock disapproval.

"I'd already been in that way once before . . . before I knew he was dead and I thought he was hiding out because something happened with the CD or he didn't want to see me for a while. But that time the rooster got loose—" And I tell him about finding the album cover and the blood stain.

"Where's the rooster now?"

"In my car. I left the window open a little. I had to take him to the morgue with me, and the restaurant because I didn't want to carry him into the building with the super watching. Luckily it wasn't too cold today because the rooster was out in my car for hours. Of course, they sort of live outside . . . but I guess I'd better bring him upstairs now. I have to find a home for him."

"He's flapping around in your car?"

"No, he's in a cage."

"I'll give you a hand carrying him up," Leon says. "And you

should talk to Julio. He might know somebody that could use a rooster."

Leon hefts my empty beer can. "It looks like you're about due for another round," he says. "Or maybe we should go down and get that rooster first." He stands up and heads for the closet. "You should probably put something over the cage or he'll be crowing first thing in the morning," he says as he pulls on his coat.

"So that's how I can keep him quiet," I say. "What made you think of it?"

"I am an expert on the avian character. My mom has parakeets."

"Do you think it's evil of me to still be thinking about my band's CD when Rick is dead?"

Leon shrugs. "Maybe not. You said he put a lot of time into the project. He'd probably want people to hear it. Keeping the blues alive and all of that." He buttons his coat meditatively. "You told me once that everything's digital now."

I nod.

"Rick must have had a system to make sure he didn't lose a whole recording session just because he touched the wrong button on his computer."

"Duh!" I slap my forehead, remembering the boxes of carefully labeled disks on the studio shelves. "Sure. I'll go in through the basement again."

He takes off his glasses, polishes them with a crisp handkerchief, and puts them back on. "Do you think that's wise?"

"Probably not. But I think I'll do it anyway."

CHAPTER 4

The sound of ringing bores through the blissful silence of my dreaming unconscious, the way a laser beam cuts through darkness. I open my eyes. The room is light. I fumble the covers away and reach for the phone, my body still weighed down by sleep. Julio's music usually wakes me. I can hear it through the wall now, waves of overlapping sound and jaunty voices singing in Spanish. I must have been exhausted.

"Hello?" The phone has disturbed Red. I can hear him rustling under the bedspread that drapes his cage.

"Maxx? Why haven't you called me back? This is Michael."

I would have known anyway, by the voice. "What time is it?" I mumble.

"After seven. What's going on? Have you found out anything about the CD?"

I retreat to the bed and pull the covers back up, all the way over my head. "That body at the morgue was Rick," I say. "Somebody shot him."

"I guess that means the CD idea is totally fucked," Michael says.

"That's your reaction?" I say. "Somebody's dead and all you can think about is how it affects you?"

"Not just me," he says. "The band. You have to follow up on it. We gave Prowling Rooster Records our money and—"

But I punch the button that cuts off his answer and throw the phone across the room into the big chair.

Michael's a jerk but Rick loved the blues, says a voice in my brain, as I burrow into the pillow and pull the covers back over my head. The time he put into that CD was worth much more than the money he asked for. He did it because he dug the band. So maybe I am going to follow up on it—but not just because of Michael.

Across the room, Red clucks gently under my bedspread, unaware that it's morning and he should be crowing.

I'm still on the breakfast shift so my visit to Rick's place is going to have to wait till I get off work this afternoon. I make a cup of instant coffee, eat a piece of toast, and pull out the ironing board to iron a shirt for work.

On the way to my car, I run into Julio in the parking lot. He's on his way to his orderly job at Hackensack Hospital. I tell him about the rooster.

He looks at me through the granny glasses that, together with his thin face, make him look like a Hispanic John Lennon. "He's gonna be crowin'," he says. "Super's gonna hear about it—unless you put somethin' like a blanket over the cage."

"I already thought of that," I say. "Leon said you might have an idea about how I can find a home for it."

"My cousin, man," Julio says. "My cousin would like to have a rooster."

Rick's house is a crime scene now. I hadn't thought of that.

"This yellow tape is here for a reason," the cop says in a bored voice after I ask if I can get through. "The reason being that the only individuals who can enter are individuals who are authorized to enter."

"But I left something in the house," I say. "I need to run in and pick it up. I was Rick's friend."

"Oh?" For a minute he looks less bored. "Did we get a statement from you?"

The yellow tape, brighter than the leaves on the ground but somehow blending with the autumn color scheme, stretches from bare tree to bare tree. It curves around the side of the house, disappears briefly, reappears, and ends up back here, where this cop, snappy in his Park Police uniform, stands guard.

"Yes, you did. And I'm the person who identified the body. Please let me run in for a minute."

"Sorry." He folds his arms across his chest.

"But I knew him really well."

"Here's a tip. You might want to forget that."

"What?"

"Forget you knew him."

"Why?"

"The FBI's working on this one. It was more than just a murder."

As I walk back to my car, pondering this disturbing statement, my stomach rumbles and I realize I haven't eaten anything since lunch, and that was just scrambled eggs and toast.

Back out on Route 303, I pull into a Donut Delite and order a glazed doughnut and a cup of black coffee. I'm sitting near the giant window that looks out on the parking lot, chewing on the doughnut and waiting for the coffee to cool, when a pickup truck pulls in. A bulky guy in a plaid shirt lowers himself to the pavement, hauls the door open, and lumbers inside. I raise my coffee to my lips and take a scalding sip.

"What's new with Rosie?" he greets the woman behind the counter. Overweight, with pale, doughy skin, she looks kind of like a doughnut herself.

"Not much, Del. The usual?"

"Just gimme the medium today," he says. "Doctor says my cholesterol's climbin' up there again."

As she turns to reach for a cup, he says, "Heard about the big doin's up the hill?" Even though she's not looking at him, his thumb reflexively jerks toward the window.

"That murder? Cops've been in and out of here since yesterday and—" The words are blotted out by the sound of hot milk whooshing into the cup.

"Know what I heard?"

"What?" She turns and deposits a tall Styrofoam cup on the counter, crowns it with a crest of whipped cream, and adds a large pinch of sprinkles.

"I heard that guy had ties to the mob."

My hand jerks and hot coffee sloshes over it. Before I realize what I'm doing, I'm on my feet. "That's crazy," I say. "I knew him. Who told you that?"

He looks startled. "I wasn't talkin' to you," he says.

"But I heard you anyway," I say.

"It was a private conversation between me and Rosie."

"Come on," I say. "That guy was my friend. I'd have known if he had something to do with the mob."

The woman behind the counter cuts in. "Del's done work for everybody around here and he's lived here forever. There's just about nothin' he don't know about nobody." She looks at him shyly. "That's true, isn't it?"

What on earth am I doing? I must have buzzed right past my building. Now I'm cruising past a row of grand but faded houses at the edge of a once-fancy neighborhood a few blocks west of where I live. My brain is churning with what the guy at Donut Delight said, and even the drive from Rick's place all the way down to Hackensack hasn't been long enough to let me sort everything out.

I turn into the first driveway I come to, my headlights picking up the sagging porch that sweeps across the front of a huge white-shingled house complete with a turret. Heading back in the direction I came from, I still can't turn off my brain.

How could Rick have possibly been involved with the mob? That's like something from a TV show, not real life. And even if it was real, it wouldn't be Rick. He was the most honest guy in the world, so totally committed to music that he didn't even think about money. And isn't the mob all about money?

Not many places left in the lot behind my building, but here's one that's probably empty because nobody wanted it. Thanks to the crummy parking jobs on both sides, it's barely wide enough to squeeze into, but I manage.

Fortunately, the lock on the driver's side lets me unlock it this time. I'm much too close to the car on my right to squeeze out that door.

I ease the car door open, trying not to scratch the brand new BMW that's barely a foot away, wondering why anybody with such a fancy car would do such a bad job of parking. I'm squeezing myself through the door when—*crack!* The sound is sharp and sudden, like a branch breaking nearby, but with a deeper echo.

What was that? Crack! There it is again. Bing! Something hits the BMW. Crack! Bing! Somebody's shooting a gun. Somebody's shooting a gun at *me*. The brain haze that made me overshoot my building by three blocks vanishes instantly, the way steam vanishes from the bathroom mirror when you aim your hairdryer at it.

I crouch as best I can, shoving the car door open further, hearing the scrape as it rakes the side of the BMW. I let myself slip back into my car till my forearms rest on the seat, and I lower my head till my nostrils fill with the smell of dirt and cracked vinyl. Now my brain is totally empty, as if swept of every thought by the blood urgently thumping in my veins.

Crack! Bing! Did that one hit my car? I can't be sure. Above me, the wind shakes the trees, rubbing bare branches together with a creaking sound, and it whistles among the parked cars, stirring random patches of dead leaves. Or does that whispering sound come from something else? Maybe from the slow, stealthy progress of the gun and its owner across the parking lot?

For once I'm thankful that, if my car ever had a light that came on automatically when the door opened, it long since stopped working. Maybe whoever's out there won't be able to find me in the dark.

CRACK! It doesn't *seem* any closer, but would the sound be different if it was? I let my cheek rest against the seat and close my eyes. I'm praying that somebody in the building will hear the shots and call the cops.

The most beautiful thing I can imagine at this moment is the sound of a siren. Then bright lights—red, blue, white—dancing off the rows of cars, off the wall of buff bricks that faces the parking lot—

Crack! Bing! Crack! I shudder and start to inch my way across the seat, eyes still closed, pulling my legs inside the car, huddling with my knees pressed to my chest, listening to myself breathe. From time to time a gust of wind shakes the car, sets the tree branches creaking. There's that low whispering again, like something making a stealthy progress across the parking lot.

It's blotted out by the sound of real footsteps, urgent, bustling footsteps, coming closer, coming toward where I'm huddling in the front seat of my car. Near me—very near—a car door opens. Then it slams shut. The next thing I know, a female voice is yelling, "What the hell is going on here? If somebody fucking scratched my car, I'll kill them!"

Still huddled, I warily turn my head in the direction of the voice. A woman is peering in the door of my car. I can't see many details, but she's got big hair, a huge bushy halo of blond ringlets. "Who's in there?" She's still yelling, and, along with the in-your-face New Jersey accent, she's got that raspy kind of voice people get when yelling is something they do a lot. "Who's in there? What are you doing?"

I ease myself into a sitting position. "Somebody was shooting at me," I say. "I was getting out of my car when I heard gunshots, so I crawled back in."

"Are you out of your mind?" she says. "It was probably a car backfiring. This is a crummy neighborhood all right, but not that crummy."

"I think you may have scared the person away," I say.

"What's that supposed to mean?"

"Somebody was really shooting. I heard bullets hitting things—"

"Hitting? Oh, God. My car!"

The next thing I know, she's got her cell phone out and she's chattering away to somebody named Hiram, telling him to come down to the parking lot with a flashlight.

After she gets done with Hiram, I say, "Would you mind using that thing to call the cops?"

Hiram's in the middle of an inch-by-inch inspection of the BMW, his flashlight illuminating one circle of its gleaming finish at a time, when the cops pull up. No sirens or flashing lights, and really just one cop at first, a paunchy middle-aged guy.

"You the people who called?" he asks as he climbs out of his car.

"Somebody was shooting at me," I say.

"What's he doing?" he asks, gesturing toward Hiram.

"Checking her car for bullet holes."

"I found one." It's Hiram, pointing to a spot on the front fender on the side of the BMW that faces the street.

"Oh, my God," the woman shrieks. "My car."

The cop says something into his walkie-talkie and in a few seconds we're joined by another cop. As I'm describing what happened, somewhat calmly, and the other woman is interrupting, less calmly, we hear sirens.

"No," I say. "I guess the person was shooting from a car, but I didn't see the car." The cop looks at the woman. "No, nothing," she says. "I couldn't see nothing."

"No description," the cop mutters into the walkie-talkie.

Soon a second cop car pulls into the parking lot, lights on the roof popping off like flashbulbs, illuminating the nearly bare trees, the shabby houses across the street, and the random assortment of down-market cars. The siren modulates into a sullen growl and two more cops get out.

I'm not there to watch them put the yellow tape up—I only see it later—or to observe as they search the parking lot for bullets. I'm on my way to the Hackensack police station to give an official statement, wedged into the back seat of the first cop car along with Hiram and his lady friend, who has now begun to cry.

For some reason I don't tell them about the mob. I guess I don't want to believe that's true. I do tell them that my friend was shot in Nyack a few days earlier but that he and I knew very few people in common and I can't imagine why anyone would want to be after me.

When we get finished, the cop double-checks all of our names and addresses and another cop drives us back to my apartment building. It turns out the BMW woman is Hiram's girlfriend and lives in Bergenfield.

When we get back, the parking lot is as bright as if it was a movie set and a very long strip of that yellow crime scene tape winds all the way around it. Cops—I guess they're cops though they're wearing regular clothes—are picking their way among the cars and occasionally stooping over.

By the time I get up to my apartment, it's all starting to sink in, and my legs are so shaky that I barely make it to the big chair before I collapse. I didn't tell the cops about the mob connection, but I can't get it out of my mind. I top up Red's food and water, and grab myself a beer out of the refrigerator. Red's the only other living thing in the room, and I find myself appreciating his presence, the pleased clucks that accompany his attentions to his newly replenished supply of Farlo Boonton.

The first thing in the morning I call Walt Stallings, the retired cop who used to be our drummer. And when he tells me he's got an old pal on the Park Police and he'll see what he can find out about Rick, I tell him I feel like kissing him right over the phone line.

"Kiss me in person," he says. "Come on down to the Blues Bar tonight. Zachary's trying out the stuff he's worked up for the tour and it should be a great show. I'll squeeze in some phone calls before I see you."

What did Walt find out? I ask myself as the crowds surging down Broadway carry me into the neon glow of Times Square. Bright signs stretch three, four, five stories above the sidewalk. This one's a frenetic slide show; that one's a neon waterfall. The air is filled with the smells of chicken kabobs, soft pretzels, and sugary roasted nuts.

The Blues Palace has two venues, the Big Room and the Blues Bar. Tonight some rap star is playing in the Big Room, and a long line of restless kids stretches along the sidewalk. A purple velvet rope keeps them in the single file that feeds impatiently past the skinny black guy letting them one by one into the lobby. "The Blues Bar?" I say, catching his eye. He nods briskly and lets me slip past him.

A curving staircase, thickly carpeted, leads down to the Blues Bar, where hidden lights bathe everything in a uniform moody gloom and the atmosphere is 1940s nightclub.

"Dinner?" asks a slim blond woman, all in black.

"Not tonight," I say and head across the room.

Up on the stage, silhouetted against a wall-sized screen bathed in reddish light, a guy in a snappy dark suit squats next to a guitar amp, one hand fiddling with the knobs while the other hand plucks faint sounds from the streamlined guitar dangling around his neck.

On the other side of the stage a willowy Asian guy turned out in a silky shirt and black leather pants is adjusting the knobs on a big bass amp. Between the two amps sits an impressive drum kit, its chrome gleaming in the reddish light. No sign of Walt though.

But then a voice from the bar calls out, "Hey, Maxx! Over here!"

Walt still looks like a cop—a stocky guy with ruddy skin and a practical haircut. He reaches out to give me a hug. "Thanks for coming down," he says. "I think you're going to like the show."

"I'm sure I will," I say. "And I wish that's all I was here for. Did you find anything out for me?"

His face turns serious. "I'm afraid so," he says.

"They really think he was mixed up with the mob?"

His face turns more serious still. "Russians," he says. "They make the Mafia look like model citizens."

But just then we're joined by the snappy-suit guy. "We hit at eight-thirty," he says to Walt, in a voice that sounds like he's drunk his share of whiskey and smoked his share of cigarettes. He raises his arm to peer at his watch. "It's twenty-nine after." Then he notices me. "Who's this?" he asks.

"Maxx Maxwell, meet Zachary Crane," Walt says.

He shakes my hand and turns back to Walt. "Let's get going."

In kind of a daze, I order a shot of Jack Daniel's and a beer. The Russian mob? I sip the whiskey, hardly noticing the way its smoky bite numbs my tongue and etches a warm trail to my stomach. How on earth could Rick have been involved with *any* mob? He was such a nice guy.

Up on the stage, Zachary Crane, bent almost double over his guitar, squeezes out a series of melting cries that on any other occasion would have me riveted.

"Down the hall is a lonely woman," he sings, and Walt cuts the line off with a rim shot. "She always stays out all night." Rim shot. "Doesn't have too much money." Rim shot. "That's why she has to wear her clothes so tight." His fingers move on the guitar strings and a few notes shimmer briefly then die away.

I finish off the whiskey and start on the beer as Zachary launches into "Just a Little Bit." As I sip the beer, my mind keeps returning to the image of Rick's bruised face sticking out of that white plastic cocoon. What happened in the minutes before he died?

At last the set nears its end. Zachary steps to center stage, introduces Walt and the Asian guy, tweaks a few offhand licks from his guitar, and says, "We're the Zachary Crane band. Now we're going to take a short pause for the cause, but don't go away. We'll be right back."

Walt is wiping his face with a towel as he makes his way back to the bar.

"So, okay," I say, after he's had a chance to drain about half a bottle of beer in one eager swallow. "What's the rest of the story? Rick was mixed up with the Russian mob and . . ."

He dabs at his eyes with the towel. "Damn sweat," he says. "I can't see." He takes another swallow of beer. "Rick's body wasn't the first to turn up in Green Forest Park. Cops found another body there about a month ago. It was a guy who'd been part of a big CD piracy ring . . . seems to have been some kind of a territory battle. The cops got a tip your friend could have been involved—"

"So they think the person that killed this other person killed Rick too?"

"Worse," he says.

"What could be worse?"

Walt's eyes wander past me. In a second, Zachary is standing at my side. "Don't get too comfortable," he says to Walt. "The manager thinks people are leaving and he doesn't want us to take a long break."

"What could possibly be worse?" I say, noticing that my voice sounds kind of desperate and not caring if Zachary overhears the whole thing or not.

"Just a second," Walt says, nodding at Zachary. "We've got some business here." He pulls me a little to the side. Now he looks like a cop again, one of those nice cops that delivers bad news to grieving people on TV shows—sad eyes, serious beefy face. "They think your friend Rick killed the other guy, then the people the other guy was working for killed Rick."

I hear myself gasp. "That's what they think?" I say. "Rick wouldn't kill a person," I say. "I might. You might. But *Rick?*"

"Like I said," Walt goes on. "They think it was a territory battle. There's big money in counterfeit CDs."

Zachary is at Walt's side again. "OK, man," he says. "She'll still be here when you get done. Let's hit. I don't want to get beat out of my money tonight."

CHAPTER 5

"Could we get our check over here, honey?" The question comes from a swarthy middle-aged guy who's busily picking his teeth. Across the table from him a tiny woman with her hair dyed a sooty shade of black is using the back of her spoon as a mirror while she touches up her lipstick.

I blink a few times, like you'd blink if maybe you just stepped off a spaceship into some alien world. Then I remember. I'm at work.

In my mind, though, I'm sitting on a bar stool at the Blues Bar listening to Walt tell me Rick was involved with the mob. And that Rick is a murderer. That can't be. I knew him. I knew him so well.

"Wake up, honey," the toothpick guy says. "We got someplace to go." On the wall behind him, two cowboys on horseback tear after a runaway steer.

I trudge over and plant myself in front of the computer. Rick's not a murderer. He was a wonderful guy and a total blues lover, and he'd want our CD to get done. I can't let this horrible mob idea weigh me down to the point that I don't follow up on the CD.

I slip the check into a plastic folder decorated with a picture of a cowboy smacking his lips over a rack of ribs and head toward the toothpick guy's table. As soon as I get the check delivered—the guy grunts at me around his toothpick as I slide the plastic folder in front of him—I glance around to see if Aldo is anywhere nearby. When I don't see him, I hurry into the break room, grab my bag out of my locker, and paw through it for my address book.

I detour past the kitchen to make sure Aldo isn't hanging out in there pestering Manfred or Vinnie, then I head back down the hall to the phone, where I feed some tip change into the slot and punch in Nathan's number.

I stretch the receiver as far as it will reach and peer around the corner into the dining room. No sign of Aldo, but the toothpick guy catches sight of me and waves the plastic folder in my direction with a frown that makes his eyebrows meet over the bridge of his nose. I hold up a finger and mouth the words, "Just a minute."

The phone rings four times then I hear Nathan's recorded voice telling me he's unavailable to come to the phone right now.

I finish out my shift, drop off my apron and my special Seafood Chalet vest in my locker, and head out past the Dumpsters to my car.

Nathan lives in a penthouse. But it's in South Hackensack, and it's located on the roof of an apartment building that shares the block with a mixture of wood frame houses covered in layers of mismatched siding, and small factories where people who don't speak English manufacture things like valves.

"Maxx, long time no see." Nathan's about fifty, a solid guy with a thick mane of silvery hair. He reaches out and gives me a hug, pulls me into a small room painted a warm shade of brownish gold. Every available surface has some kind of a percussion instrument sitting on it. Small skin-covered drums, huge gourds enveloped in nets of beads, oblongs of wood scored with ridges—all heaped on shelves and tables or arranged along the edges of the floor. "What's up, Maxx?"

"I tried to call you a couple times, but I couldn't reach you. I swung past on my way home from the restaurant and saw that your lights were on."

"Get you something? A beer?" The words come out with the ragged sound of somebody dumping a load of gravel.

"Sure."

He steers me toward the sofa, which is draped with a brightly striped blanket of coarse wool. "Have a seat."

In a few seconds he's back, slipping a can of beer into my hand.

"So it's blues now, huh? Since when?" He lowers himself onto a small leather-covered hassock, raises his beer to his lips, and tips his head back.

"Since I wised up."

"You mean about Sandy?"

"You've got it. People think blues is about being miserable, but it's really about looking out for yourself."

"I hated to see you guys break up though."

"Everybody did," I say. "Everybody but me. Well, me and about fifty chicks who didn't realize a guy that's sneaking out on somebody else to be with them will sneak out on them to be with somebody else."

"Fifty?" Nathan says with a touch of admiration.

"Maybe not fifty, but women *do* go for the guitar players."

"He's doing good now. Still down in Nashville and working all the time, from what I hear." Nathan tips some more beer into his mouth. "So how're things going with the CD? Rick's a nice guy, huh?"

"That's what I'm here about," I say. I take a swallow of beer. "Nathan—"

I must look stricken because even before I say anything else, Nathan's face shapes itself into an expression of mourning.

"Rick's *dead.*" I tell him the whole thing, spilling it out fast

60

because I'm afraid I'll start crying if I pause long enough to realize what I'm saying.

"The mob?" Nathan shakes his head briskly. "Sounds like
some fairy tale the cops dreamed up so they won't have to do
any work."

"But why would *anybody* kill him, really? He was supposed to
show up at our gig Saturday night with the master for the CD,
and he never came. And so I went up to Nyack Sunday morning. I was so pissed off . . . I thought he was hanging out with
Brenda Honeycut . . . the singer?" Nathan nods. "I found a
note from her. I guess they used to have something going on?"
He nods again. "Now I feel awful that I doubted him like
that . . . when all the time he was dead." I close my eyes and
swallow hard. My eyelashes are wet and there's a hot little knot
forming between my eyebrows.

"Brenda Honeycut." I open my eyes to see Nathan shaking
his head sadly. "Rick could've been just what she needed, but
she's such a handful that she drove the poor guy crazy. Now I
hear her career's sort of stalled and she thinks it's his fault."

"She does? Why?"

"She was writing great songs when he was her guy, and now
he isn't and she's not." Nathan fingers his beer. "I guess there
was more going on with you and Rick than the CD?"

"Yeah." I lower my gaze to the floor, where it lands on a
miniature conga drum. "What's Brenda's music like, anyway?
I've heard of her, of course, but I've never heard her songs."

Nathan pulls himself up and plucks a CD from the only shelf
that isn't covered with drums. He lifts out the disc and leans
toward his CD player. "Here," he says, handing me the jewel
case.

The cover shows Brenda Honeycut standing in the yard of a
weather-beaten shack, her band clustered around her. Okay, it's
possible she recruited three giants to back her up. But it's also

possible that they're three normal-sized guys and she's tiny.

"She's really small?" I say to Nathan.

"Tiny."

I picture the driver's seat in Rick's pickup, moved way up like some tiny person had been driving it.

"Seems crass to ask," Nathan says. "But what's going to happen with the CD?"

I shrug. "I never got the master. And now his house is a crime scene and there's no way to get inside. That's sort of what I stopped by for. Do you know any way I can get in touch with that Ben guy? The other partner? Rick might have had backups that he stored someplace else besides the studio. I understand Steve is kind of hopeless, but maybe Ben can help me out."

Nathan sets the CD down, opens a cupboard, and pulls out a small leather-covered address book. He pages through it for a few seconds then says, "Here you go—got something to write on?" He reads off a 212 number and a Manhattan address, Upper East Side.

"Sounds rich," I say, scribbling it in my appointment book.

"He's got his fingers in a lot of stuff, some kind of strip club for one thing." Nathan snaps the little book closed and tucks it back in the cupboard. "And he might not miss Rick all that much," he says musingly.

"Why's that?"

"I heard he had some different ideas for the label."

As I head back down to my car, I realize we never got around to hearing Brenda Honeycut's CD.

The crime scene tape is still up in the parking lot, and there's a phone message waiting for me when I get upstairs. *Maybe it's the cops,* I think. Maybe they found something out—though how could they when I didn't see the car or anything? But it's not the cops. It's from somebody I'd just as soon not talk to.

I push the PLAY button and the voice I hear makes me sink into the big chair and lower my head into my hands while my heart bumps around behind my ribs like a startled animal.

"Hey, Maxx," says a voice I recognize all too well, even though it's a subdued version of its normal swaggering self. "Sandy here. Thought I'd check in and see how you're doing. I might be in New York next week. Give me a call if you feel like it."

"I don't feel like it," I say to the machine as I poke the DELETE button. "I don't feel like it at all. And damn that busybody Nathan Danzig."

I grab a quick tuna sandwich and head right back out for rehearsal, topping up Red's food before I leave. He looks at me like he wonders how he got here.

Mitzi's boyish face is smiling, but it's a worried smile as she watches me walk down the hall. She's sitting on the ratty sofa that, flanked by a coke machine on one end and a trash can on the other, constitutes Feedback's lounge, leaning back in a kind of parody tough-guy slouch with one ankle crossed over the other knee.

"Anybody else here yet?" I say when I reach her.

"Stan." Her brief laugh is more like a sigh. "He's hiding out in there." She jerks a thumb toward the doorway that leads into the office. "He's afraid you're still mad at him about the other night. He said he paid Brownie for a rush job on his amp and everything's fixed now."

Mitzi's all in black tonight, black jeans, chunky black boots, a black T-shirt with a Harley logo on the front.

"I've got bigger things than Stan to worry about," I say.

She nods sympathetically, leans forward, and reaches for my hand. "I know. Michael told me what happened. I know you and Rick were friends too, besides the business connection."

"Is Michael here?"

She shakes her head no. "Not yet. He called me Tuesday."

"He only cares because he's worried about the CD."

Mitzi's eyes wander past me to focus on something further down the hall and a tiny wrinkle appears between her brows.

Michael's all in black tonight too, including a narrow knee-length coat that, despite being fashioned of glossy leather, gives him the look of a nineteenth-century preacher.

"You really messed up this time." His precise voice reaches us from halfway down the hall.

I wait till he gets closer to answer, but all I say is, "Yeah?"

"I've been asking around about your friend Rick and his label. It seems like we're the only people in the whole city who didn't know what was going on there." He slings the gig bag that contains his bass off his shoulder and carefully balances it on the floor in front of him like a shield between him and the world.

"What *was* going on there?" I try not to sound alarmed, even though inside I'm feeling kind of sick.

"You know he had those supposed *partners?*" His already sarcastic voice adds a little extra sarcasm to the word.

"I know about them," I say.

"Ben Darling, the business manager, is a compulsive gambler and that other guy, that Steve?"

"Yeah?" My voice is barely audible, even to me.

"A complete burnout." He shifts the bass so now it's like some weapon he's about to brandish.

Just then Stan appears in the doorway, ducking a little bit like he's not sure his six and a half feet will quite clear the opening. "The room's ready," he says, almost meeting my eyes, but not quite. "And I made sure everything's the way we want it." He nods at Mitzi. "None of those lousy, beat-up cymbals they usually try to give us . . . and I checked the mike."

"That's fine, Stan. Thanks. You don't have to—"

He backs up, still talking as we head through the door, almost colliding with Neil, who has emerged from the restroom, wafting a hint of marijuana smoke with him. We straggle down the hall to Studio F, Stan still walking backward, now talking earnestly about how he changed the strings on all his guitars today.

Once we reach the room, Mitzi climbs up behind the drum kit and fires off a quick volley on the snare. Neil settles himself at the keyboard, kicks off his sneakers, and launches into a snatch of some baroque thing. Stan tunes up and tears into his Albert King imitation. And Michael, his ear cocked to his amp and his thin face twisted into a strange, intent sculpture, plucks his bass strings one at a time.

"Ready, Michael?" I put my hand on his shoulder, but he shrugs it off like a dog shooing a fly with a quick shiver of its skin.

"In case you hadn't noticed," he says scornfully. "I'm tuning up."

"Right, right, right," I say, stepping away from him, taking up my spot behind the mike. At last he nods. "Okay, let's get going," I say. " 'Killing Floor.' Stan, you kick it off."

Three hours later, we wind up with "Sweet Little Angel." I'm sagging with exhaustion, longing to escape to my car and drive back to New Jersey, curious too about whether the parking place I found along Twenty-Ninth was really legal. But while Michael's fingers were roaming over the fretboard of his bass, his brain was apparently busy too, processing and reprocessing the information he'd been collecting all day.

"You're not taking off, are you?" he says as I head out into the hall with a fist full of cash to pay for the session.

"We've been here three hours," I say. "If we don't clear out they'll throw us out."

"That's not what I mean. I think we should have a little band meeting. I think you owe us an explanation of how you could make such a mess out of things and what you plan to do about it."

"It's not a mess," I say. "First of all, I think *you* should have a little respect for the fact that someone we knew and worked with has been killed. Second, I'm in the process of tracking down the master, and then I'm going to call around and find a good price on getting copies burned in time for CityBlues—not because I care that you're upset but because Rick worked hard on that CD and I think he'd like people to hear it."

Michael has to fight to keep from looking surprised, but he manages. Then he says, "Assuming you actually *do* find the master, how are you going to pay for the copies? You gave all our money to your friend."

Over his shoulder I can see Mitzi looking at me worriedly as she tucks her sticks into her backpack. Stan looks worried too, his lanky frame kind of drooping, his fingers actually quiet for once, even though he's still holding his guitar. Even Neil seems kind of stricken.

"I'll get it back," I say, a sudden burst of adrenaline dispelling the tiredness I felt before.

"Good luck," Michael snorts. "Prowling Rooster Records is so far in debt they can't get any credit anywhere, they've got a backlog of CDs they can't burn because nobody'll trust them to come through with the money, and about ten people want to take them to court for unpaid royalties."

"I'll think of something," I say. "I've been in touch with the business manager."

"Really?" Michael says, his voice squeaking in surprise.

"Well, sort of. At least, I know how to get in touch with him," I say.

Michael laughs. "Don't forget he's a complete crook. And full of schemes that probably won't go anywhere. I heard he wants to turn Prowling Rooster Records into a rap label."

By now we're out at the desk and I hand the money to Tony, somewhat comforted by the sympathetic expression on his homely face. He's wearing his usual black leather vest, but over a bulky green hoodie with skulls printed all over it.

"I'll keep that in mind," I say. "I'm going to meet with him in the next few days."

Really? says a voice in my head, as my heart speeds up.

Yes, really, I answer myself. *And besides that, I'm going to take in Brenda Honeycut's gig at the Last Chance.*

CHAPTER 6

I give Ben Darling a call the next morning at about ten. Friday's one of my days off, and I call him from home instead of using that annoying pay phone at the restaurant. But all I get is his machine, so I leave a message and get to work cleaning my apartment, wondering if he'll return my call or try to blow me off.

My activity causes Red to start pacing back and forth in his cage. I feel sorry for him. He hasn't been outside for days, and at Rick's he could go outside whenever he wanted. I wonder if Julio said anything to his cousin yet.

By noon I haven't heard anything from Ben Darling, so I call again—with no luck—before I collect my wash and head uptown for a quick lunch at Roy's and a visit to the laundromat.

It's close to three by the time I get back. No message from Ben, so I try again and get the machine. I don't leave another message though. I don't want him to feel like I'm stalking him, and when I finally reach him, I want my question about the master for the CD to seem like a businesslike inquiry, not a desperate plea.

It occurs to me that since I'm going to Brenda Honeycut's Last Chance gig tonight, I might as well head into the city right now and detour through the Upper East Side on my way to the Village. I might be able to track down Ben Darling in person, or at least figure out when he's actually at home. Maybe he's got talkative neighbors.

Even for the Upper East Side, the building is grand, very grand for a compulsive gambler with part share in an indie record label that specializes in the blues. Of course, Nathan said he's got his fingers in a lot of other stuff, like a strip club. The strip club must pay well.

The doorman looks up from a textbook open to a page of really technical-looking diagrams. He's a cute, young blond guy and he asks, with a slight Russian accent, if he can help me.

"Is Ben Darling home now?" I say, so urgently that he pulls back with an alarmed expression on his face. Despite my resolution to act laid-back about my errand, I worked up a case of nerves on the drive over.

"He should be back very soon, ma'am."

"Like when?"

"He's at gym," he says, leaving out the "the" like Russians sometimes do.

A drift of perfume floats my way. A woman in an expensive suit saunters by on her way to the elevator, favoring the doorman with a languid wave that sets her bracelets jangling.

"When did he go out?"

"Maybe hour ago."

So he was home all day and ignoring my calls. "Is the gym close?" I say.

"Right around block. On Lexington. You go up to corner and turn left."

The reception area of the gym could be the lobby of a small, super-elegant hotel. A voice intercepts me as I hurry across the thick carpet. "Are you a member?" it says. I turn and notice a blond woman sitting behind an ornate desk in the corner. With her well-toned body and glowing skin, she's a good advertisement for her employer, the Lexington Avenue Health Spa.

"Not really," I say. "I just need to talk to somebody. His doorman told me he was over here exercising." I look toward a hallway that seems to lead into the heart of things.

"Only members are admitted," she says, expressing regret by allowing a tiny wrinkle to mar her perfect forehead.

"But I don't want to use the equipment or anything," I say. "I just . . . I just—" Chill, says a voice in my head. He'll come out sooner or later. All you have to do is wait for him. Settle down on that comfy-looking sofa, page through a copy of *Vogue* magazine . . .

But what if there's a back door and he goes out that way?

"I just—is that a restroom?" I inch closer to the hallway. "I'll be right back. I—I ate something that disagreed with me and I really need to—"

I step across the last few yards of carpet and pick up speed. As I move forward, I hear the echoes of machines clanking and voices chattering over some Beatles tune that's been watered down to sound like a jingle.

The room at the end of the hallway has mirrors on the walls and gleaming blond wood on the floor and elaborate, pastel-toned exercise machines accessorized with weights and pulleys. Only a few people are around, and since I don't know what Ben Darling looks like, I don't know if any are him.

Some of the people are working out on mats placed here and there on the polished floor like padded beach towels on a very shiny beach. They're raising their feet, their legs, their pelvises, curving to a sitting position then reclining again. They look too busy to talk, so I approach an overweight middle-aged guy who has heaved his panting, sweaty self off a long vinyl-covered bench, also accessorized with weights and pulleys.

"Do you know a guy named Ben Darling?" I ask, as he mops

his face with a towel. "He's supposed to be here right now."

"Ben?" he says between pants. "Yeah, he's always here, very faithful." He scans the room. "Don't see him now, but that's his trainer right over there." He points toward an attractive woman bobbing up and down along with the other bobbing figures on the padded mats.

Ben Darling's trainer looks like a human greyhound: long slender face, long slender body encased in silvery-gray spandex.

"Is Ben around?" I say as her torso bobs up toward me. "Or did I miss him?"

She holds up a finger in warning, then counts, "Eighteen, nineteen, twenty," bobbing up and down on each number. "Didn't want to lose count," she says, hopping to her feet. "Who're you looking for?"

"Ben Darling."

"He's in the showers. We just finished training." She gazes past me at her reflection in the mirror then looks me up and down.

"You should build up your shoulders," she says. "You'll find that as you get older, there's a tendency to pull in—" She lets her head droop and rounds her shoulders in an exaggerated slump. Noticing my reflection in the mirror, I self-consciously straighten my back. But something else is reflected in the mirror too: the blond woman from the reception room. She's poised in the doorway with a burly guy in a uniform at her side.

"Here's my card," Ben Darling's trainer says. Against a pink background the name "Carrie Carlisle" is embossed in a flowing script. Beneath the name are the words, "Recapture the body you were born with."

"He should be out soon," she says. Meanwhile, the blond woman and the burly guy are advancing across the floor.

"Her," the blond woman says accusingly, aiming the tip of a

carefully manicured finger at me. "She's not a member. She forced her way in."

"I'm leaving right now," I say, my words overlapping with Carrie Carlisle's announcement that Ben has emerged from the locker room.

"Here he comes now," she adds, smiling flirtatiously as she watches him approach.

Ben Darling strolls toward us through an aisle formed by two rows of those pastel exercise machines. He's a gnome-like little man, fifty or sixty, with a bald spot surrounded by a silvery cap of close-cut hair like the fur of some lustrous animal. He's wearing a carefully creased pair of blue jeans and a silky black sweater styled like a long-sleeved polo shirt. Dangling from a hand carelessly raised to his shoulder is a suede jacket so soft and buttery that it might as well be made of silk. He's got the leathery skin of somebody who's spent too much time in the sun, and he looks like he's been somewhere sunny quite recently. He's even a little sunburned.

He regards me curiously. "Hi," I say. "Your doorman said you were here. I was in the neighborhood. I'm Maxx Maxwell, the person who's been calling you all day."

"Ahhh," he gives me a wide smile, showing me his gleaming teeth. "Sorry I didn't get back to you. I've had a lot on my mind." He winks at the blond woman. "It's okay. Maxx is a friend of mine." He touches my elbow and leads me across the floor. He's wearing some kind of aftershave lotion that smells expensive.

When we reach the reception area, he pauses and says, "So we meet at last. Rick told me so much about you. I see he was right."

I'm wearing a jacket. Otherwise I suppose he'd be checking out my measurements about now. Instead, he reaches out to shake my hand. The tan skin of the hand he offers me is marred by several evil-looking scratches that rake across the knuckles and disappear under the cuff of his sweater. Involuntarily, I step back.

"Gruesome, isn't it?" He laughs easily. "My cat is kind of temperamental. She gets jealous when I'm not around." As we head toward the elevator, he says, "So what can I do for you, Maxx?"

"I want to go ahead with the CD. My band put a lot of time into recording it and Rick would have wanted it to come out. We were hoping to have it in time for the CityBlues festival."

"The CD?" He stops and looks at me curiously.

"We were making a CD with Prowling Rooster Records. We paid Rick a lot of money. The master was all done, but his house is a crime scene now and there's no way to get anything out of it—at least no way for me to get anything out of it."

"I'm not sure what you expect me to do." He lays a hand on my shoulder. I guess it's supposed to be a comforting gesture but the way his fingers dig in is kind of creepy. We're standing by the elevator now.

"You're his business partner."

He lifts the hand from my shoulder and waves it as if bothered by something in the air. "Not my project," he says.

"Your name is on the Prowling Rooster Records business card."

A vague twitch of irritation passes across his face. "I really haven't been involved in the day-to-day—" The elevator arrives and the doors glide open. "After you," he says, stepping aside and bowing slightly, but with a mocking air.

"You must have talked to the cops. You must have some idea what's going on . . . when the house won't be a crime scene anymore. And—" It comes pouring out even though I hadn't planned on bringing it up. "—you must have told them Rick wasn't in any kind of mob, that he wasn't pirating CDs. He can't have been—" I feel a lump rising up in my throat and blink away a bit of moisture forming on the edges of my eyelids.

"Here—what's this?" His hand is kneading my shoulder again. "That's nothing for you to get upset about."

"It is, though . . . he seemed so honest, so good."

He shrugs. "I don't know what kind of stuff Rick was up to."

"You were his business partner. I can't believe the cops wouldn't be awfully interested in you too."

"They had some questions," he says, trying for offhandedness but not totally succeeding.

The elevator arrives at the ground floor and the doors glide open. He pulls on the leather jacket and heads for the revolving door that leads out to the sidewalk.

"How about our money then? I'd like it back if we're not going to end up with a CD."

He ignores me and keeps walking.

"You're the business manager," I call after him. "You must handle the money."

His pace speeds up. When he notices me following him, he stops, scowling. "Look, I didn't have anything to do with your CD. I've got a million projects. That wasn't one of them." He holds up a hand and ticks off on his fingers, starting with his index finger. "I've got a club uptown. I've got part share in a restaurant in the Village. I manage a reggae club based in Barbados—got my own place down there so it's handy. Spend a fair amount of time in Barbados." The scowl disappears and he chuckles. "It's a tough job but somebody's got to do it." Suddenly he grabs his pinkie. "Then there's Prowling Rooster Records, but look—" He wiggles the pinkie. "That's the smallest one."

He turns up the collar of the jacket and launches himself into the revolving door. I follow along in the next compartment.

When we reach the sidewalk, we're buffeted by a blast of icy wind. He pulls the jacket around himself and shivers. "I shouldn't even be here. I should be sitting on my patio in Barbados soaking up the sun. But Rick made a goddamn mess and the cops got interested." He snorts in disgust. "Look at this. Five P.M. and it's pitch dark. I hate New York in the winter."

Barbados. That explains the tan, and probably the jealous cat, languishing in a kennel somewhere when he goes away. Looks like he wasn't around when we were making the CD, or even when Rick was killed.

"What about Steve?" I call after him. "Would he know anything about the master."

"Got me," he says without even turning. "He might." He looks over his shoulder and catches my eye. "Ask him. It can't hurt."

"Pretty sad turnout," the bartender is saying to a guy in a snappy silk shirt covered with maroon and navy swirls.

The Last Chance is only about a third full, and Brenda Honeycut is due to go on in five minutes.

The silk-shirt guy reaches for the shot of whiskey the bartender served up. "Sure is," he says with a not-very-happy smile. "But it's not my problem. I'm just a sideman." The smile reveals teeth too perfect to be totally real, and the hair's a little too dark to go with the deep lines at the corners of his eyes. But he's still kind of a cool-looking guy.

"I thought she was a big name," the bartender says.

"Fantastic performer," the silk-shirt guy says. "It's just that—" The smile fades and he breaks off to raise the whiskey to his lips, tip his head back, and drain the glass.

"Just that what?"

"It's been ages since she came up with any new material. Kind of a dry streak—and people always want more. It's a tough business." With the smile gone, he looks tired.

"How come she's not writing new stuff?"

He shrugs. "Ran out of ideas, I guess. Broke up with her boyfriend and it wiped her out." He crooks his arm to bring his watch into his line of sight. "Looks like it's show time." I watch him head for a door hidden in the shadows at the edge of the stage.

All the lights go out except the tiny ones glowing red up on the stage, one for each amp. The taped music cuts off in mid-song. Tiptoeing shapes, unseen, barely heard, move into place among the equipment. I feel a little breathless myself, like it was me up there, about to sing.

The lights come up on stage with a sudden glare that spills over onto the faces sitting up close. They reveal Brenda, poised behind the mike with an acoustic guitar hanging around her neck. She didn't look too bad in the picture Nathan showed me, but in person . . . well, appearance isn't everything, I guess.

She's older than me, maybe even almost forty, and too thick through the middle to be showing the inch or so of bare skin that the low-riding jeans and the high-riding top reveal. She's got boots on her feet but I can't see much of them because the jeans hang down so far that they almost brush the floor. No way to tell if they've got the kind of soles that could have produced those dirt curlicues in Rick's truck, but maybe I can get a closer look when the set ends. She's got a wild mop of hair the color of rust and a wide face with a nose like a random lump of dough plopped somewhere in the middle.

But she can definitely sing. "Caught a train, maybe last year—" She leans toward the mike, turning the words loose one by one, like it hurts to let them go. "Went someplace, maybe it was here—" Her hand churns a desperate burst of sound out of the guitar. "Met somebody, maybe it was you—" She's got a folk-singer voice, but like the real thing, like somebody that learned to sing sitting on the porch of a cabin in the Ozarks, trying to make their voice reach all the way across the valley to the hills on the other side, high and tense, almost nasal, but so real you have to listen. "And I loved somebody, but somebody wasn't true."

Behind her, the band is keeping up a steady rhythm, nothing obtrusive. The silk-shirt guy is stroking chords out of a gleaming black Strat, the drummer's a mellow-looking black guy, and the bass player is a balding middle-aged guy with a pot belly.

She sings a few more verses, punctuated by chords chunked out of the acoustic hanging around her neck. As she sings, her face changes from nondescript to almost beautiful, eyes widening then narrowing, mouth laughing then soft with a syllable that whispers its way to the mike. In fact, her face is so elastic I feel like I can read her thoughts, like it's nothing but a thin veil between the world and her brain.

She sings for about an hour, wrapping the set up with a tune about a lonely night and a long road and a journey that ended up right where it started except she wasn't the same person anymore.

As the final chords die away, there's a spattering of applause, but the audience is so small it's like people are wondering why they turned out for this since obviously hardly anybody else did.

As soon as the stage goes black, I step away from the bar and head for the door I saw the silk-shirt guy disappear through. It opens into a shabby hallway that leads to another door.

I listen outside that door for a minute, wondering what kind of scene I'm going to step into, then take a deep breath and reach for the doorknob.

I'm looking into a shadowy room hardly big enough for the sagging sofa and random collection of chairs arranged around its walls. I recognize the band, and Brenda, of course. The drummer and bass player are lounging on the sofa with cans of soda, and the silk-shirt guy is messing with his guitar. Brenda is talking to a woman in a T-shirt that says LAST CHANCE across the front. An open bottle of whiskey sits on a nearby table. A guy in a Last Chance T-shirt says, "Help you with something?"

"I need to see Brenda," I say.

"I can pass on a message," the guy says. "She's kind of busy."

"I'll tell her myself." I step around him.

"Hey, wait—" the guy says behind me, but I ignore him.

Brenda notices me then, and watches me as I cover the five or six feet that separate us.

"You knew Rick Schneider," I say.

"What?"

She's even shorter than I expected, almost a head shorter than me, and up close like this I can see that the rusty red hair is an attempt to camouflage the dull grayish brown that half an inch of roots make clear is her real color. "Rick Schneider. There's something you might not know—"

"And who're you?" she asks, even though something in her face says she already knows who I am. I can tell from the alcohol on her breath that she's been working on the whiskey.

"Maxx Maxwell." She's eyeing me up and down, taking in my hot-pink angora sweater with the plunging V-neck and my chartreuse velour hiphuggers, her face kind of crumpling, like it did while she was singing a song about watching pretty girls flirt. Little does she know nobody wanted to flirt with me till I discovered the effect that blond hair and a push-up bra has on guys.

Now she's biting her lips, really biting them, and her mouth is a narrow line. She's kind of panting, but through her nose, and a furrow has appeared between her eyebrows. Her eyes look so wild I'm almost scared, but finally her darting gaze lands on the guy who intercepted me at the door.

"Hey, Grady." Her voice is a pathetic squeal. "Who let her in?" She nods at me.

"She walked right past me—"

"Take her away." In the space of three words, her voice grows from an uncertain squeak to a full-scale bellow. "Take her away, away, away." Her hands rise from her sides and her fingers curve and stiffen till they look like talons. Everybody in the room is watching her, the drummer and the bass player rolling their eyes at each other like they've seen outbursts like this before.

"Uh—you're gonna have to leave," the T-shirt guy says, and his hands pantomime shifting something from one place to another.

"But I need to tell you something about Rick. He hasn't gotten in touch with you, has he? And it's because—"

This time the sound that comes out of Brenda's mouth isn't even a word.

"Okay," I say. "I get the message."

But I don't make it to the door before I hear her voice again, more human sounding, calling, "Wait! Wait a second. Get her! Catch her before she goes!"

The T-shirt guy reaches me as I turn around. "You have to excuse her," he whispers. "She's kind of moody."

"You say he tried to reach me?" The desperation in her face reminds me of the expressions that passed over it while she was singing.

"I don't know, but if he didn't, there's a reason." I step back toward her, almost sorry for her now. The T-shirt guy backs out of the way and lets me go.

"A reason?" She looks me up and down again like she thinks I'm the reason. But then she says, "I know the reason. He's dead. Steve told me. I saw him today."

"I'm really sorry, Brenda. I identified the body."

She's glommed onto my arm and she's gripping so hard it

hurts. "They asked you?" She backs toward the sagging sofa, her knees buckle, and she falls, almost missing it but landing with her legs splayed out before her.

Her boots are revealed now, heavy boots like hiking boots, with a curlicue tread deeply engraved into their heavy rubber soles.

I go back to the bar and order a beer. There's another show in about half an hour and I suspect that if the silk-shirt guy needed a shot to gear up for the first set, he'll probably need another one to get in shape for the second.

I stand there sipping my beer till the shadowy door at the edge of the stage opens and all three of the backup musicians make a beeline for the bar.

"You guys sound good," I say to the closest one, the drummer, after the bartender has fixed them up with drinks.

"Somebody shoulda warned you," the silk-shirt guy says with a laugh.

His gaze strays from me and drifts toward the entrance while his mouth shapes a grin and his right hand rises in a cheerful wave.

I turn to look where he's looking and notice, returning the greeting but disappearing into the narrow passage that leads out to the street, a woman who could have posed for the photograph on the wall in Rick's bedroom. She has the same huge, haunting eyes, sculptured cheekbones, and glossy black hair, except instead of flowing to her shoulders, her hair is short, like she's going for a punk look.

"Who's that?" I ask the silk-shirt guy.

"That old boyfriend of Brenda's—the guy who broke up with her? That's his daughter. She and Brenda kind of got to be friends back in the days when Rick was still in the picture."

★ ★ ★ ★ ★

Without even saying goodbye, I plunk my half-full glass of beer on the bar and hurry toward the entrance. As I step into the passage that leads to the street, about ten people arrive at the box office to get tickets for the second show. By the time I weave my way through them and thrust myself out onto the sidewalk, there's no sign of the young woman.

I turn right, toward the heart of the Village, but the blocks are short and every corner offers a tempting vista of restaurants, shops, and clubs. She could have turned anywhere.

He never told me he had a daughter.

What else didn't he tell me? I wonder as I walk back to where I squeezed the Bonneville into a space along Greene Street that barely cleared the crosswalk.

I wonder it all the way up the West Side Highway, across the bridge, and along Route 4 to Hackensack.

CHAPTER 7

Cold blasts of air rattle my windows all night. The cold seeps into my room, and the sound of the windows rattling interrupts snatches of sleep that aren't really sleep. How could Rick have been pirating CDs? How could he have had anything to do with any kind of mob? And most important, how could he be a murderer?

But if the cops keep going the direction Walt says they're going, they'll find somebody that fits their theory, and they'll blame Rick's death on him. And in their minds, that will prove Rick killed somebody too, the guy whose body turned up in Green Forest Park a month before Rick's did. Or they won't find somebody and the case will stay open. Either way, Rick will always seem guilty.

I'm up before it's even light, scrabbling around in my bag for Brenda Honeycut's letter to Rick. She supposedly had a gig somewhere in Westchester the night before Rick was killed, then some kind of a confusing schedule that was going to take her all over the place before she came back for the Last Chance gig. If she flew out right after Westchester, I can cross her off my list, despite the curlicue pattern in the soles of her boots. But who does that leave besides the mob?

I find the letter and smooth it out against my pillow, scanning the page for the Sleepy Time Motel number and turning it over to study the tour schedule. The Chicago gig was Sunday, the 9th. So she'd probably been planning to hang out with Rick all day Saturday—until she found out he wasn't interested anymore. Because of me.

But what if she *was* with him Saturday and that's when he told her about me and they had some kind of a fight and she killed him?

Of course, Rick was big. How could a little person like Brenda beat him up and wrap him in a curtain and drag him outside and all of that? Still, she seemed so out of control at the Last Chance. Sometimes when you're really freaking out, you can do all kinds of superhuman things.

Or maybe she shoots him and then panics and calls her manager. Even though she's not as bankable as she used to be, he figures she'll be worth more to him out of prison than in, so he comes up and together they wrap Rick up in the curtain and slide him into the back of the truck.

I make a cup of instant coffee and carry it over to the big chair, take a quick sip, and grab the phone. It's still dark outside, as dark as if it was the middle of the night, but motels have people on duty all the time, don't they? I punch the Sleepy Time Motel number into the phone.

Instead of the chirpy female voice I got the other time, I get a male voice, a very groggy male voice, but he rallies around with, "Sleepy Time Motel. How may I help you?"

"I'm looking for somebody," I say. "Somebody that stayed there last week. I need to know when she checked out. Her name is Brenda Honeycut—"

"I'm sorry," the voice says. "We don't release information about our guests."

"But she's my . . . uh . . . my sister," I say, leaning forward like the motel person is right there in front of me and I'm trying to be really earnest. The big chair gives a horrendous squeal as my weight shifts. "Brenda sort of ran out on us, and now our mother is ill—"

"Sorry," the voice says. "I can't help you."

"Where are you?" I say. "In case I want to stay there some-time."

"Yonkers," the voice says.

I uncover Red's cage and give him some food and water. He seems to be getting used to me. The look in his beady eyes doesn't seem as suspicious.

Half an hour later, I'm on the road, speeding toward Rick's house. Brenda said she saw Steve and that's how she found out Rick was dead. So Steve must be around now. It's probably a long shot, but maybe he can help me figure out how to get a copy of the master. He's supposed to be part owner of Prowling Rooster Records, after all. And maybe while I'm at it, I'll check out the Yonkers Sleepy Time Motel. Sometimes you can find things out in person that you can't find out on the phone.

I make the turn at the Day'n'Nite Limo Service, curve up a hill, and bounce along the rutted drive that leads past the trailer. I might as well park in the clearing behind Rick's house.

The trees are almost bare now, and the thick rafts of fallen leaves have faded to a color that's no color at all. The crime scene tape is still up, but no cops are around. The tape seems even brighter now as the leaves around it have faded. The air is still and frigid and it smells clean, with just a tiny edge of the sharp smell that comes when leaves start to decay. Bunched along the horizon are heavy clouds like a smear of black ink across a pale sheet of paper.

I park near the truck and stand there looking at it for a minute. The back is full of dead leaves, soggy and slippery. It'd be hard to know if there was ever any blood that could prove my theory. Cops could figure it out, of course, with all that CSI stuff, but it looks like they were so anxious to tie Rick in with this mob thing they didn't even bother to check the truck. The leaves don't seem to have been disturbed at all. The mob probably has its own trucks. Why would it need to use Rick's? That's probably what the cops told themselves.

I open the driver's side door and scoop up a handful of that strange pasta-like dirt, trying to picture the tread on the bottom of Brenda's boots. Then I realize I've been jumping to a huge conclusion—that whoever killed Rick would have ended up with muddy shoes.

There's not much mud around here that I can see because of all the dead leaves, unless somebody did some serious tramping back in those woods. Rick once mentioned that there's some kind of a stream back there. But maybe there's mud at Green Forest Park where Detective Carlson said that jogger and his dog found Rick's body. If there isn't, I can stop thinking about the truck and the too-far-forward-seat and the pasta-shaped mud and Brenda's boots and all of that.

I put the dirt back where I found it, dust my hands together to get the remains off my gloves, and crunch over the dead leaves till I'm standing at the foot of the steps that lead to the door of the trailer. There's no sign of life inside, but maybe Steve sleeps late. I check my watch. It's only nine o'clock. I wouldn't want to have somebody bother me at nine if I didn't have to be up. I'll give a little tap and if he doesn't answer, I'll wait a while and try again. No point in getting on his bad side the first time I meet him.

The little tap doesn't get any response. I head back to my car. Maybe I'll drive down to that doughnut place where I overheard the conversation about Rick and the mob and grab a cup of coffee. But as I get closer to the house and see the crime scene tape again, it occurs to me that even though the tape is still up, the cops are gone. There's nothing to keep me from going into the house and looking for the master myself, like I wanted to do the last time I came up here.

I circle the house till I come to the cellar doors I discovered the other day, haul one of them back till it overbalances and lands on the ground with a thud, revealing the old wooden steps that lead down into the shadowy basement. My flashlight's in the car, but in a few minutes I'm following its wavering beam across the concrete floor—wavering because my hand is trembling, holding my breath against the dank, musty basement smell.

Nothing in the kitchen looks any different, but after I make my way down the long hall that leads past the old dining room and emerge into what once was the studio, I find myself blinking, gaping at the bare room like someone pulled off an amazing magic trick. The table is still there, and the shelves where Rick used to keep his tidy boxes of backup disks, but the gear is totally gone, and so are the boxes. No 32-track recorder, no laptop, no amps, no pedals, no mikes, no mike stands, no nothing. And if those shelves ever held backup copies of Maxximum Blues' debut CD, they certainly don't hold them now.

"I'm not home," the guy yells from deep in the woods, which glow with a golden mid-morning light. Through the scanty foliage that remains on the trees I can see him striding toward me—a long-legged figure like a woodsman: thick, dark beard, unkempt hair, bulky plaid jacket. A lithe russet dog bounds along at his side.

"I'm not home." He says it again, scowling, as he emerges into the clearing. The dog, however, is panting at me happily, its tongue lolling between its grinning jaws.

"Are you the guy that lives there?" I say, pointing down the road at the trailer. He nods, barely. "Steve Bernier?"

"Yeah, but I'm not home. Didn't you hear me?" He bends, pats the dog, whispers, "Let's go, buddy," and heads toward the trailer, dislodging flurries of leaves.

"Hey! Wait! I need to talk to you."

"About what?" he says without turning around.

"Prowling Rooster Records."

"That was Rick's scene, not mine." He picks up his speed and plows ahead, the dog capering happily at his side.

"But wait! Please wait!" I'm running after him as he continues to stride toward the trailer. I don't usually cry, but all the ridiculousness of the past couple days is catching up with me. I feel my voice break as my throat contracts in an aching spasm.

"What happened to the master of my band's CD? Where did Rick's gear go?"

He pauses for a minute. Slowly he turns and his profile comes into view, silhouetted against the trees like he's posing for a painting of Davy Crockett or somebody. His profile could almost be the profile on a medal.

"What do you mean? You were in there?" He gestures toward the house.

"I'm Maxx. Rick was making our CD for us. And he was . . . we were . . ." I swallow hard and command my voice to behave. "I really cared about him." I squeeze the words out and raise a hand to wipe away a tear that's sliding down my cheek.

He mounts the steps that lead to the door of the trailer, unlacing and stepping out of his boots when he reaches the top. "I guess you might as well come in."

The dog edges between us, nosing its master's calves, almost knocking me off balance. The three of us spill into a cozy space that's kitchen, living room, and bedroom all in one. He waves me toward a molded plastic bench that flanks a small Formica-covered table.

The dog is wiggling happily now, sniffing my crotch and flapping its tail against one of the benches that flank the table.

"Cops took everything away," Steve says. "They need it

for . . . whatever it is they're doing." He takes off the heavy jacket and hangs it on a hook that protrudes from the back of the door, peels off his gloves and tucks them in the jacket pockets, one in each.

"So? Will it be tea?" he asks, like I'm there on a social call.

"Did they say they'd bring it back?"

He shrugs. "Ben might know. He spent more time with them than I did." He peers at me like he's trying to read my mind. "What about the tea?"

"Okay," I say, pulling off my gloves and shrugging my way out of my fake leopardskin jacket. He reaches two mugs and a box of teabags down from a cupboard over the sink. I start to feel a little better. There's something comforting about watching somebody make tea.

And weird as this guy is, the setup he's got here is appealing—his tidy kitchen, his shelves with their careful stacks of books and CDs, and his combination bed and sofa with its bright coverlet.

I start to sit but my attention is captured by a painting hanging over the combination bed and sofa. It's a face that I seem to be encountering everywhere lately—in Rick's bedroom on the wall, at the Last Chance on the girl that the silk-shirt guy told me was Rick's daughter, and now here in Steve's trailer—the huge eyes, the high cheekbones, the full mouth with the tiny imperfection in the upper lip, framed by dark, glossy hair.

"Who's that?" I say, still standing.

"My sister. Her name was Claire."

"Was?"

"She's dead now," he says.

"Did Rick know her?" Steve turns away, picks up the kettle, and fills it at the sink. "Did Rick know her?" I ask again. No answer. "She looks just like his daughter."

He puts the kettle on the stove and turns back around. "Rick doesn't have a daughter," he says.

"He doesn't? But I saw her last night—"

"That chick's not Rick's daughter." He twists a knob on a boombox sitting on top of a compact refrigerator, and the cheery sound of an early Beatles tune fills the room.

"You know who I'm talking about then?"

"I know who you're talking about." He says it like he wishes I wasn't talking about her.

"Is she related to you and your sister?"

"You could say that." The kettle gives a shrill hoot. He turns away again, like he's happy to have a distraction.

"Cops swarming all over the place," he mutters, as if to himself. Suddenly, he turns, catches my eyes like he's accusing me, "I threw out a hundred bucks' worth of weed. Dumped it in the stream. Thought they were comin' for me. I'll prob'ly have to clear outta' here. Wonder what's gonna happen to the house."

When he turns back, it's to hand me a mug with a teabag tag dangling over the side. He settles across from me at the table. As soon as he's seated, the dog climbs up and nestles into his lap. "Considers himself a lap dog," Steve says with the first smile I've seen, letting his hand caress the dog's silky coat.

"The cops think Rick killed somebody," I say. "Did they tell you that?"

He doesn't answer, stares instead at the steam rising from his tea. "They don't tell people things like that," he says. "How'd you find out?"

"I know a guy that used to be a cop. They think Rick was pirating CDs and somebody cut into his territory, so he got rid of the guy. But the Russian mob was involved in it somehow, or maybe two mobs, rival mobs, so then somebody got rid of Rick."

"Sorry I don't have cookies or anything."

"So what do you think? You knew Rick really well and you

were part of Prowling Rooster Records. That story's not true, is it?" A strange pleading tone that doesn't sound like me has crept into my voice.

"I wasn't involved in the day-to-day stuff," he says. "I don't know what Rick was up to."

"But you knew him for a long time. He wouldn't do something like that, would he? Besides, who needs to pirate CDs anymore? Any kid with a computer and a CD burner can get whatever they want for free."

"International market," he says, stroking the dog's head. "People in places like Indonesia don't have computers."

"What are you saying? You think Rick really did it?"

He shrugs. "He wasn't a fucking boy scout, you know." He lifts the teabag and watches curiously as it twists on its string, little drips of tea slipping off and falling back into the cup. He looks from the teabag to me. "Or on second thought, maybe he was. We never talked about that." His gaze drifts back to the teabag, still now, and no longer dripping.

"Did you know Rick had some old bullet wounds, like somebody shot at him once?"

He shrugs. "Like I said, he wasn't a boy scout."

"You were his friend and he let you live here for free. Don't you care about his reputation?"

"Maybe I wasn't his friend. Maybe there were other reasons why he helped me out," he says as the dog nuzzles his cheek. "And he's dead now. What difference does his reputation make?"

"That's sort of an unanswerable question," I say. "I guess if you don't get it, you don't get it."

"Very cool CD you guys were working on."

"You heard it?"

He fiddles with his teabag. "Some," he says. "Sounded real good."

"You wouldn't have a copy of the master *here* or anything?" I look around the little space. When I look back at him, he's engrossed in massaging one of the dog's ears. "The cops took all the stuff out of the studio, but maybe there's still a copy around? A copy that wasn't in the studio?"

"He didn't *give* it to me. He only played it for me."

"But can the cops simply carry stuff away? Don't they have to give somebody a receipt?"

"I've been gone. I was—" His voice falters and he pauses for a minute like he's not sure where the sentence is going. "I was up in Worcester roadying for a band one of my buddies is in. Didn't know about what happened to Rick till I got back."

He pushes the startled dog out of the way and jumps to his feet. The next thing I know, he's tossed a folded newspaper onto the table.

"Check it out," he says. "Page two. The band got a nice write-up." He settles back onto the bench across from me and the dog again clambers into his lap.

"Thanks," I say, and skim the article. Then I rub my forehead. "I've really got a lot on my mind right now. When you listened to the CD, were you up at the house or here?"

"I don't know where it is," he mumbles, starting in on the dog's ears again. He studies me for a minute. Despite the woodsman look, he's got delicate features and pale grayish-blue eyes. He reaches for the paper, opens it, and pores over the first page he comes to. "The gig was last Saturday. They swung through here and got me the day before."

He resumes rubbing the dog's ears. "The cops talked to Ben, too. Maybe he knows if they're ever going to give all that stuff back. He took care of the business end of things."

"I talked to him once and he wasn't very helpful."

"I think the cops gave him something, some kind of a receipt or something. You know, they have to—when they take your stuff. Ben pays attention to shit like that. He's quite the businessman." Steve goes on, staring past me as he speaks, his fingers busily kneading the dog's ears. "I mean, I really dug what Rick was doing, trying to keep the label pure and all. Just real blues. I admire that. But I tried to stay out of the way, not bother him. It was enough that he—" He stops and one hand makes a convulsive scooping motion like it's trying to capture some elusive word.

"It's enough that he what?" I say.

He shrugs. "He let me live here. Otherwise . . ."

"Otherwise what?"

He leans across the table, bending to the side because the dog is perched solidly in the middle of his lap. His eyes flash strangely and he says in a voice that's strangling with laughter. "Otherwise I'd have to work, man. I'd have to work." The laughter erupts. A bouncy tune I've been hearing everywhere lately is jingling out of the boombox.

Suddenly, he's on his feet, muttering, "No, no, no." He steps across the floor and clicks the tune off so decisively that the boombox skitters across the top of the refrigerator and falls to the floor with a crash. The dog watches him in puzzlement.

He returns to the table and picks up his mug of tea as if nothing has happened.

"You don't like that song?" I say.

"I like it too much," he says. "Or I did, before they got hold of it. That music was what my youth was all about."

"Rick said that once about a band that he was in."

"Never mind." He eases himself out from behind the table and stands up. "I've got stuff to do," he says. "You done there?" He reaches for my mug.

"Can I get your phone number so I can call you and ask if the cops have brought the gear back?"

"What would I need a phone number for? I don't have a phone."

I pull on my coat and my gloves and head for the door. I'm halfway to my car when he comes running after me. He thrusts the newspaper into my hand. "Read the review. You'll like it. They're a very cool band."

CHAPTER 8

I should track Ben down again, I'm thinking as I continue on toward my car. Maybe he knows when all Rick's gear is going to be returned—or at least maybe he's got some kind of contact information that will let me ask the cops if I can ever expect to get my hands on the master for the CD.

But I want to check out the Yonkers Sleepy Time Motel today, too. And that question about the mud is nagging at me. Green Forest Park is a little ways south of Nyack. I can stop off there, then swing across the George Washington Bridge and make my way toward Yonkers.

So half an hour later I slide my car next to an SUV in the park's main lot and set out on foot along the rutted asphalt road that leads into the park itself. To my left, a lumpy expanse of winter-browned grass stretches up a slight hill toward a stone shelter. To my right, a steep cliff falls away into a ravine jumbled with brush, fallen branches, and sodden clumps of dead leaves.

Soon the road reaches a crest and starts to slope downward again, curving around outcroppings of dark stone with geometric markings of pale greenish moss. On the other side, the brushy ravine has given way to a thickly planted swathe of spiny evergreens with ivy covering the ground under them and twining up onto their trunks. Beyond them is what looks like a vast field of ripe wheat stretching to a distant lake whose dull gray water mirrors the gray sky.

And it's along here, as the road straightens and continues to slope downhill, that I come upon a long strip of yellow plastic tape strung across an expanse of six or seven of those evergreens. On the tape, the words "Police Line Do Not Cross" are repeated again and again until they trail off in a final "Police Line Do N" as the tape folds around the trunk of what could be a small, perfect Christmas tree.

It looks like whoever killed Rick dumped his body behind this row of evergreens, pushing it into the midst of that stuff that looks like wheat, with its tall stalks crowded so densely that you can't see the ground. But there aren't any cops standing guard here either, just like at the house.

I duck under the police tape and ease my way through the bushy evergreens, noticing without really thinking about it how they smell like Christmas morning, pushing them out of the way with my bare hands and realizing I must have left my gloves in the car. Now I'm past the evergreens, easing my way toward that stand of dry stalks, hearing them whisper as their long feathery leaves catch the wind.

I don't really see any spots where the stalks look like they were disturbed recently. But whatever this stuff is, it's so thick that it could hide all sorts of things, which I guess is why the person that killed Rick thought this would be a good place to dump his body.

I check behind me to make sure I'm standing in the area marked out by the police tape, then turn back to stare at the ragged edge where the ivy that creeps around the trunks of the evergreens gives way to the stalks, rich dark green suddenly replaced by pale gold.

As I scan the expanse of stalks, I notice an area to my right where they aren't quite as sprightly, like maybe something heavy was lying on them and they haven't had a chance to spring back up yet. I move toward it, squeezing between a few of those evergreens, tangling my feet in the ivy. I reach the edge of the field and step toward the flattened spot and—I'm sinking. It's like I stepped into a swamp.

I try to jerk my foot out of the soupy mud, but now the other one's caught too and there's no way to get a foothold back on solid ground. I turn and grab for the closest thing I can reach, a cluster of tendrils coiling around the still-upright trunk of a dead tree. My hand closes on a fistful of thorns. The sudden pain is so intense that instead of grasping tighter I let go and let myself fall backward, landing wedged between a couple of bushy evergreens. As I fall, the spiny tendrils rake across the back of my hand.

"Help!" says a startled voice, my voice. I let myself lie still for a few minutes, gazing up at the blank sky, panting in time to the thudding of my heart. When I've calmed down a little, I slowly bend my knees and feel my feet pull loose from the swampy mud. When they're solidly on land, I scrunch myself into a sitting position and examine my hand.

It felt bad and it looks worse. A string of angry pink spots in my palm and, across the back, a nasty scratch about three inches long that's oozing blood. Besides that, my favorite cowboy boots are slimy with a coat of cement-like mud, and the same mud covers my jeans halfway to the knees.

I pull myself to my feet and walk back to my car, trying to ignore the feeling of my soggy jeans rubbing against my calves every time I take a step.

I'll have to make my visit to the Yonkers Sleepy Time Motel tomorrow. I could go home and change and head over there today, but we've got a gig in the East Village tonight. As long as I'm going into the city anyway, I might as well do my Ben Darling errand. We've got an eight o'clock sound check, so I'll have plenty of time to detour through the Upper East Side and catch Ben at his gym again. That sweaty guy I talked to made it sound like Ben shows up at the Lexington Avenue Health Spa every day.

By the time I get home, the mud is dry, and from the knees down, my jeans are as stiff as if they'd been dipped in cement. If that mud had dried in the treads of heavy boot soles and the little dry shapes had popped out, they'd look like that stuff on the floor of Rick's truck, like stuff that could have come from the treads of Brenda Honeycut's boots. He breaks up with her and she's furious—all the more so because her songwriting inspiration left when he did.

This time I intercept Ben as he's emerging from the Lexington Avenue Health Spa. Even with the blustery wind that's buffeting the few bundled pedestrians hurrying along the sidewalk, I can smell his aftershave lotion. He's putting on his gloves, tugging one up over a large bandage that covers the back of his right hand.

"Nice to see you," he says smoothly, with a bland smile that lets his tan contrast with his gleaming teeth. He continues walking as if I'm an acquaintance he happened to pass on the street.

I keep pace with him. "I need to talk to you again," I say.

"Oh?" He says it curiously, like he can't possibly imagine why, and keeps walking.

"You said Steve might know something about the master for my band's CD."

"Ummm?" He speeds up. He's wearing the buttery suede jacket from the other night, but tonight he's paired it with elegant wool slacks.

"He didn't," I say. "He said Rick played it for him but he doesn't know where it is now." We've reached a corner and he's about to plunge off the curb when the light turns red. He stands there, holding his body too stiffly to be as unconcerned as he's trying to act, not meeting my eyes, as three or four taxis hurtle past. The wind is whipping my hair around and I raise a hand to smooth it down. "But he did tell me one useful thing."

His shoulders tighten. He turns toward me, though the light's green now. "And what might that be?"

"He said the cops gave you a receipt for Rick's equipment. So there must be a way to get in touch with them and ask them when they're going to return everything. Or maybe they even told you when they'd bring the stuff back. Even if the master wasn't with the stuff they hauled away, I'm sure there's a backup or two."

The wind is so strong it's making my eyes water. I dab at one of my eyes with my gloved hand but all I do is spread tears all over my cheek. He leans toward me looking worried, like maybe he thinks I'm crying, and intercepts my hand as it's on its way back to my side. He pats it, but we're both wearing gloves so the gesture isn't very intimate.

"I know you spent a lot of time working on the CD. And it must be very important to you."

"It is," I say. "So, did they?"

"What?"

"Tell you when they'd bring all the stuff back."

"No." We've reached another corner and the light is red. "No, they didn't."

"Is there a number I could call? The receipt they gave you must have somebody's name on it. Or a phone number."

"Probably," he says. "But to tell you the truth—" He turns toward me with his arms out as if to show he's not hiding anything. "I'm not really sure what I did with it."

"What?" I'm so amazed I just stand there, even though the light has turned green and people are surging into the intersection all around me. He grabs my arm and pulls me to the other side of the street. "You're supposed to be some kind of a businessman," I say. "You were the business manager for Prowling Rooster Records. And you didn't keep a piece of paperwork as important as that."

He holds up one of his gloved hands and wiggles his pinkie at me, like a brown leather grub. "Remember what I told you? I've got a million projects. Prowling Rooster Records is the smallest one. Half the time I'm so busy I can't think straight." I dab at my dripping eye again. He regards me intensely. "I can't help it. I'm busy. I've got to head up to the club right now and I'll be there till two. Maybe pop out for a bit to check on things at the restaurant, head back to the club in time to tally up for the night. Can't trust the people I've got working there to do anything right without me hanging over them."

"So there's nothing you can do? Nothing at all?"

"Sorry," he says, and darts to the curb just as a cab discharges a pair of women in fur coats. He takes their place in the back seat and waves at me as the cab pulls back into traffic.

Mitzi's laughing to herself as I catch up with her along Second Avenue.

"Do I look like I need to be saved?" She's bundled up in a navy peacoat with a stocking cap pulled down so far I can hardly see anything but her nose and well-shaped but lipstick-less mouth.

"No more than most people," I say. "Why?"

"One of those Jesus people latched onto me down in the subway. An old guy that looked like a street person. I could hardly escape—" She hands me a flyer. "Did you know that when the final days arrive, gay people and lesbians will not be among the elect?"

"I think I might have suspected it," I say.

I glance at the flyer, whose headline reads "The Lord Will Come in Glory Within the Year" and features a picture of Jesus standing on a cloud with rays of light all around him, and stuff it into the pocket of my coat.

"This neighborhood's going to hell," Mitzi observes, stopping so quickly that I bump into her. "Look at that." I look where she's pointing. "A tanning parlor! Who ever would have imagined a tanning parlor in the East Village? And there's another one down the block from where we rehearse."

We walk along in silence for a few minutes, past the Ukrainian National Home, dating from when this was a Ukrainian neighborhood, a vintage T-shirt place, and a new, very upscale restaurant.

"Hey," Mitzi says. "I forgot to mention it last Thursday. I can't make the rehearsal this coming week. Is that going to be a problem?"

I sigh.

She hears me.

"I'm really sorry, Maxx. It's my friend's dad. He's sick—terribly sick—and we're going upstate to see him. She really wants me to be along. I'll be back for the gig on Friday—promise."

I shrug. "Sounds like something you need to do. I'll deal with it." At her worried look I add, "Don't worry."

Club 52 is a new venue for us, a nice big room with a bar along one wall, a pool table in the back, and a row of squashy sofas where people can chill out like they were at home in their own apartments. The bartender, Warren, is a friendly guy with dark-rimmed glasses and a little soul patch under his lip.

The place isn't very crowded but it's early yet. We get set up and do a quick sound check, I tell the band Thursday practice is canceled, then we go our separate ways. Mitzi joins some friends who've shown up at the bar, Neil hurries out the front door—probably to grab a quick toke—while Stan settles his lanky body on top of his amp and starts soundlessly fingering the strings of his guitar. And Michael trails me to the bar, where

I'm going to grab a free beer, compliments of Warren.

"So did you find anything out?" he asks before I even have a chance to take a sip of my beer.

"About what?"

He gazes at me with a pained expression, a slight line between his eyebrows, like someone who's got a bad headache. "The CD, of course. You said you were going to talk to Ben."

"The master exists," I say. At least it existed once, I add to myself, because Steve heard it.

"And?" The line between his eyebrows becomes more pronounced.

"The cops have everything now. It's part of their investigation."

"And?"

"When the investigation is over, everything will come back, and we can go ahead like we planned."

Michael folds his thin arms over his thin chest. "What did we plan? Rick was supposed to take care of everything for us."

"I'll take care of it now." I tilt the bottle to my mouth and take a quick swallow of beer.

"What do you know about burning CDs?"

"The *Village Voice* is full of ads for places that do it."

"Not a good idea," he says with a quick shake of his head, like a sudden spasm. "I don't like rushing into things. Dealing with people we don't know. That's how we got in trouble in the first place."

Neil has returned from wherever he went and is sitting slumped over his keyboard, looking more out of it than usual.

"It'll end up costing much more than we budgeted," he adds, and the arms crossed over his chest tighten like he feels threatened. "Prowling Rooster Records should make good on this."

"I'm not sure there's still going to be a Prowling Rooster

Records. Ben's got loads of other projects and Steve is pretty hopeless. But one way or another we've got to get those CDs. It's almost impossible to get a gig even at a tiny club anymore without a demo and we definitely need them if we're going to get on the festival circuit.

"We've been doing okay with clubs. There's the Hot Spot. The Basement . . ."

"Boris told me he wants to start booking acts with national reputations. We've got that gig on the 21st, but then that might be it for the Hot Spot. And I talked to Willy yesterday and he didn't sound very enthusiastic after what happened the other night." Stan is obliviously fingering his guitar.

"I don't think we should do it," Michael says. "We've already been burned once. I think you should get our money back."

"There's going to be a CD," I say. "Trust me."

Michael turns away and reaches for his bass. "Are we going to play this gig or not?"

CHAPTER 9

The next morning after I make a cup of instant coffee for myself and give Red his food, I track down a number for the Park Police. It seems like trying to get any information out of the FBI would be hopeless. But this turns out to be hopeless too. I get referred from person to person, and when I finally end up talking to somebody who's actually involved in investigating Rick's death, he tells me that no one can possibly know when the "confiscated materials pertaining to the case," as he puts it, will be released.

I spent so long on the phone that I have to rush off to the restaurant without even putting on any makeup, and in a wrinkled shirt left from Thursday. So when I get off my shift, I swing by my apartment to change before heading up to Yonkers.

The Yonkers Sleepy Time Motel reminds me of the places I pass when I'm driving to the restaurant, places that offer day rates and mirrored ceilings. It's a nondescript one-story stucco building, weathered to a powdery gray and streaked here and there with rust stains.

The building looks like it's been here for a long time, much longer than the Sleepy Time Motel chain has existed, like it was recently added to the Sleepy Time empire—maybe so recently that there hasn't been time to make it look like anything other than a place where married guys meet their girlfriends for a quick rendezvous at lunchtime.

On one side of it is an auto body shop, surrounded by a barbed wire fence, and on the other—eureka—is a small structure that looks like it dates from the same era as whatever the Sleepy Time Motel was in its original incarnation. "Cold Beer" reads the neon sign, a bleached-out pink scribble in the bright light of day. "Burgers + Fries," it continues.

If I was staying at the Sleepy Time Motel, I'd welcome the chance to grab a drink or two when I had time on my hands. Since Brenda was hard at work on a bottle of whiskey when I met her at the Last Chance, I suspect she'd feel the same way, if not more so. And maybe she'd rather hang out with other people than sit in her room and drink alone.

Not too many cars are parked outside the beer place this early in the evening, and a Sunday at that, but the place looks open. I pull up next to a faded Datsun and head for the door. What I need to find out is whether she was around on Saturday and didn't get up and head to the airport for her Chicago gig the next day.

The first impression is the smell of stale beer as my eyes gradually adjust from the brightness outside to the dimness inside. Then I can make out a few shadowy figures hunkered up to the bar. I climb up on a barstool, several spots away from the nearest of them, trying to ignore the stares, hoping I can get away before any of my fellow drinkers decide a single woman who comes into a bar at four P.M. on Sunday is fair game.

"What'll it be?" The bartender is a genial guy, maybe in his fifties, looks like an Italian guy who's still got the sideburns and pompadour of his youth, with enough hair to make the pompadour somewhat credible.

"I'll have a Bud."

When he brings it, I ask him if he gets many customers from the motel.

"Sure do," he says. "That place wasn't there, we'd pretty

much have to close up. Now especially with all the crackdowns on drunk driving. Out on a busy road like this? Who's gonna show up and drink all night, have to fight the semis whizzing past you to make it home? But people staying at the motel? If they need a quick drink, all they have to do is walk across the parking lot."

"I'm looking for somebody," I say. "Somebody that might have stopped in last weekend. A small woman with reddish hair."

"Alone or with a guy?"

"Probably alone."

"Women with guys I don't remember," he says with a wink. " 'Cause what're they gonna see in me? They already got a guy. Know what I mean? And even if they *do* see somethin' in me, what're they gonna do about it with the old man hangin' over their shoulder?" He reaches for the two quarters I left out from my change and taps them on the bar in a quick acknowledgment of the tip.

"Women without guys, on the other hand . . ." His fingers hover in the air near the glass he served up with my bottle of beer. "You're not gonna use this?"

"You can take it," I say. The hand that spirits it away reappears with a damp cloth.

"Women without guys . . . sometimes I remember them. Funny you should ask about last weekend. Prob'ly not the person you're askin' about, a classy person like yourself. Woman showed up about midnight Friday—sat here at the bar drinkin' like she didn't care if she never made it out of here on her own feet." He dabs the cloth at the drips shed by my bottle of beer. "I shoulda cut her off, but she told me she was stayin' at the motel. Figured, what the heck? She's not gonna be drivin'. Seemed so miserable, you know what I mean? Like if she wasn't drinkin' she'd be jumpin' off a bridge somewhere."

"What did she look like?" I say.

"Nothin' too exciting." He wrinkles his nose. "Kinda wild hair, reddish. Little, real little. Had to kind of grab onto the bar to hoist herself up onto the bar stool."

"Did you talk to her at all?"

"Said she was some kind of a singer. Just came from a gig over at the Arts Center."

"And she sat here drinking for the whole rest of the night."

"Sat here drinkin'." He nods. "Till she damn near fell off the bar stool. Came back the next day about three in the afternoon and did the whole thing all over again."

"How late did she stay on Saturday?"

"About ten."

"Do you know if she went straight back to the motel after that?"

"Don't see how she coulda' done much else. She could hardly walk."

So, I think to myself as I head back across the George Washington Bridge, it looks like I can cross Brenda Honeycut off the list, unless she slept off the booze for a couple hours then headed over to Rick's. Possible, but not likely.

Who else could have killed him besides the mob? Gradually, as I drive along Route 4, an idea starts to take shape.

As soon as I walk in the door, I carefully transport the framed album cover to my kitchen table from the spot in the corner where I parked it when I first brought it home. I gingerly pick away the shards of broken glass and free the cover itself from the frame. But Main Street closes down on Sundays, thanks to the Bergen County blue laws, so I can't do anything with it till tomorrow afternoon.

The beer I sipped while I pumped the bartender for information wasn't a very good substitute for dinner. I'm ravenous, but

I discover that I'm down to my last can of tuna and my last egg, so I head back out again. I grab an order of Cashew Chicken at the Chinese place, swing by the Superette to replenish my supply of tuna, bread, and eggs, and eat the Cashew Chicken sitting in the big chair and listening to Ma Rainey.

The next day after work—I'm still on the morning shift—I carry the album cover over to Danny's.

"Looks like you've got an EP there." Danny rests his cigarette in the ashtray on the crowded counter of his shop. The ashtray is shaped like a warped record. He reaches for the album cover. Buddy Holly's voice, singing "Not Fade Away," drifts from the speaker on the shelf behind him.

"What's an EP?"

"Extended play. Longer than a single, shorter than an LP. Two or three tunes, four max. Usually some kind of an indie deal—four is cheaper than eight—and maybe the band only has a few original tunes anyway." He flexes the cover and peers inside. "Where's the vinyl?"

"I don't know. The guy that this belonged to kept it framed on his wall. But somebody knocked it down and broke the glass, and the guy is dead. Somebody killed him."

"Holy shit," Danny says. "As in murder?" He reaches for his cigarette and raises it to his lips, his eyes narrowing to slits as he squints into the rising smoke. He takes a deep drag and exhales.

Sad all over again at this reminder, I nod slowly. "The cops think it was. And he was a friend, too. Somebody I really cared about."

"That's a tough deal." He deposits the cigarette in the warped-record ashtray and turns back to me. "I'm sorry." He bends toward the album cover. "Was the somebody that killed him the same somebody that trashed the album cover?" He points to a long scratch and a gouge.

"I don't know. Maybe there's a connection. But anyway this band was really important to him in some way. I don't know why though. And I'd never heard of them before. Have you?"

"Meal? Not really. My thing is the fifties." As if Danny's Elvis hairdo, blond but otherwise authentic, didn't give that away, a glance at the records stacked in Vintage Vinyl's bins would make it clear.

He studies the album cover. "This is probably some kind of a punk deal—the whole indie thing where the point was to work outside the music establishment. No real interest in making money and bands came from nowhere and then vanished again. Check out the outfits. These guys *look* like punks. I'd peg this for the mid-eighties."

"That makes sense," I say. "Rick would have been eighteen or twenty then."

He turns the album cover over and studies the back. "No clue as to who the fedora dudes are," he says. "I guess they were trying to be anonymous—it goes with the matching outfits and the fact that you can't see their faces well enough to tell them apart." Buddy Holly's voice still drifts from the speaker. Now it's "Peggy Sue." Danny looks closer at the back of the album. "It does list the tunes though," he says. "Let's see . . ." He looks up, pale brows raised in surprise. "Hey, too bad you've only got the cover and it's so scratched up. You could have your hands on something pretty valuable."

"I could?"

"Ever hear of 4Guys4U?"

"Not really."

"It's one of those kid bands. Four cute guys, and their music sounds like rock and roll used to sound. Kids that consider themselves intellectuals like 4Guys4U because it's not rap and it's got real instruments." He looks back at the album cover. "I think 4Guys4U covered one of these tunes. And they're very hot right now and that tune is the reason."

I lean closer so I can see what he's looking at. "Which tune?" I say.

" 'Not Something Pretty.' The third one down," Danny says. "Maybe it's a coincidence, but how many songs called 'Not Something Pretty' could there be in the world? Some of these kid bands are real connoisseurs of old vinyl, the more obscure the better, and they're into discovering forgotten songs and bringing them back to life."

"Do they arrange with the original band to pay royalties and stuff, or do they rip off whatever turns them on?"

Danny shrugs. "Depends, I suppose."

"I wonder if Rick found out 4Guys4U was making money off 'Not Something Pretty,' and then somebody came after him to shut him up."

"If he had this on his wall because he liked the stuff on the album, he'd have had to be deaf not to know that there was a cover version of one of the tunes floating around. It's everywhere."

"Like where? On the radio?"

"Well, not the classic rock station. At least not yet."

"How does it go?" My mind is replaying my meeting with Steve. And a thought is starting to percolate.

I let it percolate while Danny looks at his watch, stubs out his cigarette in the warped-record ashtray, and emerges from behind the counter. "I'm starved," he says. "Could you go for avocado on spelt bread with sprouts? Or a bowl of soup made with organically grown vegetables?"

"In Hackensack?" I say.

"Don't tell me you haven't met Jeremy." He grabs the "Back in Fifteen Minutes" sign tucked next to the cash register. "And bring that album cover," he says. "I think Jeremy's just the man you want to talk to."

"Oops. Better change the music. Mr. Fifties is here." Whatever it is that's playing now sounds like a pleasant cross between jazz and Led Zeppelin, but the tall skinny guy behind the counter turns from slicing a tomato and makes a mock dash for the CD player in the corner.

"I can stand it for a little while," Danny says with a grin.

Strolling back toward us, the guy says, "Hear about this new band everybody's so up on? They're called the Beatles. Probably won't last, but—" He cracks up at his own joke.

"Very funny," Danny says. Then, "Jeremy Radcliff, meet Maxx Maxwell. She's gorgeous, she's talented, and she actually lives in Hackensack."

"I'm sorry," Jeremy says, mock serious. He takes my hand and bows over it with a courtly nod of his head. "So—what can I get you to eat?" he says, looking up.

"It's so cold today," I say. "And Danny mentioned your soup."

"Soup of the day is winter vegetable." I nod.

"I'll have the same," Danny says, "and how about a couple of bran rolls?"

We settle at a small wooden table. "Main Street is coming up in the world," Danny says, surveying the cheerful room with its sparkling picture window and yellow-painted walls decorated with framed prints of vegetables.

"I'm trying to think what used to be here," I say.

"It was that crazy guy who sold vintage video games. Open by appointment only. Remember?"

"Sort of."

"Hey," Danny says suddenly. "I'm forgetting the business at hand." He looks toward where Jeremy is ladling soup into two earthenware bowls. "Jeremy, old pal," he calls. "Do you have that CD you played for me the other day?"

"The one you didn't like?"

"Yeah. That one. Will you put it on for Maxx? But start with the 4Guys4U tune."

"Will do," he says. "Hang on though. Your food is almost ready."

He crosses the room with a tray holding two bowls of soup and two crusty brown rolls, arranges the food in front of us, and heads back behind the counter.

The Led Zepplin-jazz cut ends abruptly. A few seconds later a bluesy hook gives way to a bland, almost emotionless voice singing,

>*"Not something pretty*
>*Not something for you*
>*Cause that's much more*
>*More than I can do,"*

while a blend of layered guitars swirls in the background.

The thought that was percolating in my brain bubbles up and spills over. I'm back in Steve's trailer. He's jumping up from the bench across from me and reaching for the boombox on top of the refrigerator. His fingers are grabbing for the volume knob—and the tune that's being so abruptly silenced is "Not Something Pretty."

CHAPTER 10

"Is the soup okay?" Jeremy asks, looking worried.

"Fine," I say, spooning a piece of carrot into my mouth. "But that song—"

"Don't tell me you're stuck in the fifties too?"

"No," I say. "Blues is my thing. Fifty years ago or yesterday, it's still blues. But what's that CD?"

"A compilation. My girlfriend put it together for me. The 4Guys4U tune isn't really my favorite, but apparently it's been placing in the top five downloaded tunes all this month. Somebody's making a bundle. Ninety-nine cents a song—but if a hundred thousand people dig your song—"

"Does anybody know they got it from another band?" I slip the album cover out of my bag and hand it to him. "Look, there, on the back. 'Not Something Pretty.' "

"Hey, where'd you get this?" he says, excited, but with a tinge of irony, like he doesn't want to shatter his cool image. "I know guys who'd trade their grandmothers for stuff like this."

"It's only the cover," Danny says. "That's all she's got. And check out the scratch and the big gouge on the front."

Jeremy turns it over and traces the scratch with an exploratory finger. "Too bad," he says.

"Do you know anything about this band?" I say.

"Meal?" He chews the inside of his lip for a second and lets his forehead wrinkle in a comic imitation of puzzlement. "Not really. Never heard of 'em, in fact." He hands the album cover back.

"But the guys that would trade their grandmothers . . . they'd know?"

"They'd tell you more than you ever wanted to hear," he says with a nod and a laugh.

"How do I find them?"

"Go down to the Village. Or maybe the East Village, for something like this. There's a used-vinyl shop on just about every block." He pokes Danny's shoulder and grins. "You know, like Danny's place, but hipper. And 4Guys4U is playing at Musica Wednesday if you're interested."

"Killed by Death, I'd say." The guy flips the album cover and studies the back. "Definitely a *Killed by Death*–type rarity." He's got pale, earnest eyes framed by Buddy Holly–style glasses and a dusting of freckles across his pale, pudgy face. "Where'd you get it?"

The shop, wedged between a Ukrainian bakery and a tattoo parlor, is on Avenue B a few doors up from Fourth Street. Long rows of wooden bins filled with old vinyl stretch from the front door to the back wall. The customers, which range from aging beatniks to suburban kids hanging out in the East Village, browse from one bin to the next, flipping through album covers that feature spiky lettering and grainy photos of guys with mohawks. Even though nobody can smoke in stores in the city anymore, the air still seems hazy, like the furnishings have absorbed decades of smoke and are giving it back up, a little bit at a time.

"A friend of mine had it," I say.

He motions to a guy at the other end of the counter, a lanky guy with two-tone hair and an earring in his eyebrow. "Hey, take a look at this," he calls.

In a second the lanky guy is at his side. "Meal?" he says, his eyes lighting up as he snatches the album cover out of the other guy's hands.

"Killed by Death?"

"Totally." The lanky guy's looking at me with the same expression on his face that people in New Jersey get when they think the Blessed Mother has appeared on a stump in somebody's backyard. "Where'd you get this?" he says.

"A friend of mine had it. What's this *Killed by Death* business?"

"Classic example of a rare EP. Worth a fortune." He studies the album cover. "You've got the vinyl someplace safe, I assume. Stored upright, not near heat." He frowns, points to the gouge and the scratch. "How'd this happen? Something this valuable should never be removed from its protective cover. Never, never, never."

"Look," I say. "I'm not a collector. And I don't have the vinyl, and I don't know where it is. This belonged to a friend of mine who just died. He had it framed in his office, and the gouge and the scratch got there when somebody ripped it off the wall and broke the glass. It meant something really important to him, and I'm trying to figure out what."

"Selling?" the pudgy-faced guy says. "Even the cover would be worth a lot—"

"It's not mine to sell," I say. "I came in here to see what I could find out about it."

"Meal," the lanky guy says in a mockery of a lecturing-type voice, holding the album cover up as if displaying it for show and tell. "East Village, 1982, one eponymous album—" He lowers the album cover to the counter.

"Do you know who was in the band?"

He frowns and the earring in his eyebrow twitches. "I'm getting to that," he says. "Drums, Jeb Perkins. Guitar, Tim Morris."

The pudgy-faced guy shakes his head. "Amazing," he says. "Just amazing. A walking encyclopedia."

"They had a harmonica player too," the lanky guy says. "That was weird for a punk band, but they had a bluesy feel. I think that's why 4Guys4U latched onto that tune of theirs. The harmonica player was . . . let me think." He glares at the pudgy-faced guy. "You shouldn't have interrupted me, man. You threw me off my stride." He knits his brow and mutters, "Think, think . . ." A wide smile lights up his face. "Steve Bernier."

"Steve Bernier?" I say. "I know that guy." In my mind I see him reaching for the boombox.

"Bass," the pudgy-faced guy is saying. "There had to be a bass player."

"That would be . . . Rick Schneider."

"Rick's my friend," I say.

"The one who's dead?" the lanky guy says.

I nod. "He had this up on his wall the whole time and he never told me it was because he was *in* the band."

I turn the album cover around so it's facing me, and I stare at the faces, each with the same emotionless expression, each shaded by the brim of a fedora, each the face of a guy barely out of his teens. Something about the one on the far right, the outline of the cheek, the chin a little more square. It's Rick, a young Rick. And the one next to him, the one that's almost too beautiful to be a guy. That must be Steve.

"I know you said it's rare," I say.

"Beyond rare," the pudgy-faced guy says. "It's like *Killed by Death*. Only one in existence—well, one and the one you've got. But that's just the cover."

"Did Meal make any more recordings?"

The lanky guy shakes his head. "The band broke up right

after this one." He nods toward the album cover.

"Why?" I ask.

"Somebody got shot."

"Killed?"

"I don't know."

"Why?"

"Something about a woman."

I catch sight of the note on my door as soon as I emerge from the stairwell, and it doesn't help my mood. Nor does the fact that the sports channel guy's got some kind of a game blasting at top volume.

All I want to do is take my shoes off, grab a couple of beers, and collapse in the big chair with some blues on the stereo. It's nearly ten and I've been up since dawn for the breakfast shift at Aldo's.

But when there's a note on my door it's usually because the super's after me about something—singing practice, overdue rent, parking in his special spot—okay, so I probably shouldn't be keeping a rooster in my apartment, and I suppose it's been crowing when I'm not home and some snitch has been complaining about the noise. But Julio's still checking with his cousin, and I don't really have any other ideas about who would like a rooster.

I reach for the note with one hand, twist my key in the lock with the other, step across the room, and collapse into the big chair, trying to ignore the smell coming from Red's cage. I guess that's what the shredded newspapers are all about. I'll have to ask Leon to pass along his old copies of the *Times*.

I drop my bag on the floor next to the chair and start to unfold the note, wondering if maybe the super might know somebody who'd like to adopt a rooster. But as soon as I see who the note's addressed to, I relax.

"Elizabeth," the note begins, the word spelled out in Leon's graceful hand. "Knock on my door when you get home."

As I leave, Red is rustling around in his nest of shredded paper.

Leon opens the door, carrying his copy of *Othello*.

"Still with that?" I say.

"Sure," he smiles a smile that makes his teeth flash white against his dark skin. "It's just starting to get exciting. Come on in." He bows and waves me toward the sofa. "You look a little dispirited, but I suspect an alcoholic refreshment will improve your outlook."

"It's really my turn and I didn't bring anything," I say.

"Dismiss it from your mind," he says. "I'm feeling munificent."

He heads for the kitchen while I settle onto my end of the sofa and lean against the afghan, but he turns back in the doorway. "Were you around when the parking lot was attacked last week?"

"I was *in* the parking lot," I say. "It almost seemed like whoever did it was aiming at me."

He regards me with a worried frown. "Any connection with what happened to your friend?" I shrug. "Did the cops do anything useful?"

"They took a statement. The person was probably shooting from a car but I didn't see the car. I guess they found some bullets or whatever it is they look for."

Leon nods. "They were out there searching long enough. I guess that's what the lights were all about."

"I don't think bullets are really a clue unless they have a gun to compare them with."

He continues on into the kitchen. As I listen to the pleasant sounds of bottles being removed from the refrigerator and glasses clinking, my eyes wander around Leon's tidy room till they come to rest on the *New York Times,* neatly centered on the coffee table.

"Hackensack Police Bust New Jersey Cockfighting Ring," reads a large headline. Next to the article is a color photo of a burly Hispanic guy clutching a rooster. The rooster is looking at the camera with the same irritated expression Red sometimes gets.

"Leon," I say when he returns bearing a tray holding two bottles of Heineken and two glasses. "Look at this." I point to the article.

"Yeah," he says with a sigh. "You'd think the *Times* could find something more edifying for the front page of its New Jersey section."

"But . . . cockfighting? I didn't think of that."

"Oh, it's real," he says.

"I hate to think in stereotypes, but Julio said his cousin might be interested in Red. You don't think—"

"I wouldn't worry." He gives my shoulder a comforting pat and starts to fill a glass with beer.

"I don't need a glass," I say, taking the bottle from his hand and hoisting it to my lips.

"Elizabeth," he says, with a cluck of mock disapproval. "So unladylike." He settles onto his end of the sofa, fills his own glass, and lifts it to his lips.

"But I *am* worried."

"Those cockfighting roosters are specially bred. Nobody'd be stupid enough to think a pet could hold up in a match." A curious expression, half-serious and half-smiling, plays around his mouth. "Maybe Leon's cousin has culinary aspirations instead. Maybe he's picturing a nice pot of *arroz con pollo.*"

"What?" I say, sitting upright. "That would be as bad as cockfighting. How can you say such a thing?"

The half-smile erupts into a laugh. "I'm sorry," he says. "Just an ill-advised bit of jollity."

"Well, I'm not in the mood for jollity. As if I didn't have enough to think about, I've got to do something with that rooster really soon," I say. "I can't keep him in my apartment much longer. His cage is starting to smell. And I'm sure he crows during the day when I'm not around."

"He does," Leon says with a nod. We sip our beer in silence for a few minutes. "Any luck with your breaking and entering?" he says suddenly.

"My what?"

"You were going to try to get back inside your friend's studio and grab a copy of your CD's master."

"Oh." I sigh. "So much has happened. First I couldn't go in because the cops were hanging around, then they went away and I got in but everything was gone because the cops think he was involved with some kind of Russian mob—and that's why he was killed. And his business partners seem to be perfectly happy to believe that, too."

"Do you?"

"Of course not. He was a good guy. And his partners weren't even around when it happened. One of them was in Worcester roadying for his friends' band and the other one was in Barbados or something. And he's got the tan to prove it." I shake my head, wishing I could shake away this whole mess, and decide to change the subject. "You're not reading *Othello* for the first time, are you?" I say, reaching for the little paperback.

"No," he says. "I read it in school. I just like to dip back into Shakespeare now and then. And it helps with the law."

"It does?"

"Sure. It helps me understand why people do things."

"This one's all about jealousy, as I recall. He kills his wife because he thinks she's getting it on with someone else. And that evil Iago puts him up to it."

Leon nods and leans forward to top off his glass. "Iago is jealous too. That's what starts the whole thing off. He really wants to be Othello's lieutenant, but Othello picks Cassio instead. Iago thought he and Othello were friends, and now he's hurt and disappointed."

"Speaking of the law," I say, "What do you know about copyrights?"

"Copyright law isn't really my specialty. I've read a little bit about it, but if your question has to do with music you probably know as much as I do."

"Maxximum Blues doesn't write its own songs—and Rick took care of figuring out who owned what when we did the album. Anyway, some blues are so old nobody owns them anymore."

"Well, fire away," he says.

"I told you about the album cover Rick had on his wall that somebody knocked down?" Leon nods and takes a sip of beer. "Well, I found out it's from an album he made with a group he was in about twenty years ago. And now some hot young kid band has done a cover version of one of the tunes from the album and it's wildly popular. They must be making a fortune on it."

"And you're wondering if they're using it legally?"

"Exactly. They probably got their start like Rick's old band did—kids playing in clubs. Who'd think you were going to get to the point that you'd be making money?" I tip my head back and drain the last drop of beer from my bottle.

"Looks like you're ready for another," Leon says, and climbs to his feet.

"Maybe Rick's band didn't even bother to copyright their songs," I say. "Like I said, they were just kids."

"Hang on," Leon says and heads for the kitchen. In a minute he's back with two more bottles of Heineken. "Copyright is automatic," he says, offering one of them to me. "The very existence of the recording would be evidence in court if somebody from Rick's band wanted to go after this other group."

"Oh, my God." I set the bottle of beer on the coffee table and rub my forehead. "Maybe the record was inside the cover and the person who knocked it off the wall and broke the glass did it so he could grab the evidence."

"It's possible," Leon says.

"But he left the cover behind. That's still evidence. It lists the songs."

"Doesn't count," Leon says. "You can't copyright a song title—and nobody'd be able to prove it was the same song without hearing it."

"4Guys4U is playing at Musica Wednesday night," I say. "Maybe if I hang around the stage door afterward, I can convince somebody I'm with the band."

But when I call for tickets the next morning I discover that the show is all sold out. I'll think of something, though. All of a sudden things are getting interesting. And maybe I'll drive up to Nyack and talk to Steve again too.

Somehow figuring out what happened to Rick is starting to seem more important than tracking down the CD.

CHAPTER 11

The silver trailer is the same silver as the wintry sky. The air is still. The trees are perfectly bare now and the matted leaves cover the ground like a shabby no-color rug.

When I reach the top step, I tap on the door, but my taps are met by silence. "Steve!" I call. "Hey, Steve. It's Maxx Maxwell. Are you home?"

Maybe he and the dog are out roaming through the woods, like the first time I met him. I could go looking for them, but there's a lot of woods back there, a lot of woods to get lost in, though now that the trees are bare I can see something I never noticed before, way behind the trailer: the outlines of another house, a big wood frame house like Rick's. A neighbor.

What I'm looking at is the back of the house. It must face a road parallel to the road that leads into the clearing where Rick's house stands.

I took the trouble to drive all the way up here so I might as well wait a while to see if Steve appears. But I'm freezing. I'm about to retreat to my car where it's warm when a door opens in the back of the neighbor house and a small figure in a red parka emerges onto a small porch. The figure is carrying a garbage bag and heads down a few steps toward a trash can tucked under the edge of the porch.

"Hey!" I hear myself yell, and suddenly I'm galloping through the woods, releasing a rich, spicy smell from the decaying leaves that my boots toss up. Anybody who lives this close might have seen something or heard something or even talked to Rick about something that could help me.

The figure is a young woman and she's still holding the garbage bag as I dart around the last tree and come to a stop.

"I'm Rick's friend. I didn't know there were any other houses back here." I'm half-talking, half-panting as I try to catch my breath.

"I'm Kate," she says. She's wearing an apron under the parka, and she's got one of those faces that's perfect without makeup. "I'm sorry about what happened," she says. "Were you really close to him?" The worried look that suddenly comes over her face seems absolutely genuine. "You know what happened, don't you?" she says. "That he's dead?" There's something motherly about her, even though she looks like she's not much beyond twenty-five.

I nod. "I know."

"Come on in. It's cold out here." She beckons, then looks at the garbage bag and laughs. "Let me get rid of this."

She leads me into an old-fashioned kitchen where a baby gazes at us from a playpen, and something sweet is baking in the oven.

"I'm Maxx," I say. "Maxx Maxwell."

"And this is Joey." She beams at the baby. "Say hi to Maxx, sweetie." Then, back to me, "Would you like something to drink? Something warm?"

"I'd love some coffee."

"Is tea okay? I don't keep coffee around."

Suddenly, we both notice that the baking smell has turned into a burning smell.

"The cookies," she whimpers. "Oh, no." Her hand, like a kid's hand with short nails and ragged cuticles, rises to her mouth.

In the playpen, the baby begins to whimper too. Kate dashes

to the oven, grabs a potholder, and pulls out a cookie sheet. "They're okay, sweetie," she says to the baby with a reassuring smile. "We only lost a couple."

Sitting at the kitchen table, a long rectangle with its top rubbed to a smooth glow by generations of use and polish, we sip tea and nibble cookies still warm from the oven.

"Did you know Rick very well?" I ask, wondering if she really can contribute something to help me in my quest.

She shakes her head. "Dave and I haven't been up here long—that's why we hardly have any furniture. We left the city to get away from all the craziness. He's a writer, so he can do it anywhere."

The baby starts to moan, and Kate discovers he's dropped his cookie. She gives it back to him and kisses him on top of the head. "It's okay, sweetie," she murmurs. She looks back at me. "We never even met Rick, but practically the day after we moved in, this weird guy turned up looking for him—" She interrupts herself to kiss the baby's head again.

"A weird guy?"

"Last summer. We'd barely moved in. Anyway, my husband came home late one night and as he's getting out of the car, he hears singing."

"Singing?"

"Spooky, like it's coming out of nowhere. Out of the trees. And a guitar too, a guitar strumming along. We knew about Rick's studio and everything—the guy we bought the house from told us. But this wasn't like that. Turns out there's an old treehouse—"

Now the baby is crying, face red and cookie forgotten. Kate jumps up. "I've got to put this little guy down for his nap."

While she's gone, I picture a summer night, leaves on the trees making the woods a place to hide secrets, maybe it's humid too, kind of spooky. Then here comes a voice out of nowhere, singing . . .

"Who was singing?" I say when she returns.

"Hmmm?"

"You said someone was singing in the treehouse."

"Oh, yeah. Pretty sad story. Made me wonder why anybody would want to be a musician. The guy said he was flat broke, bumming off friends. So he's sitting up in this treehouse. We didn't even know the treehouse existed because it was summer and the leaves were so thick. It's hard to tell if it's our treehouse or Rick's or somebody else's. My husband followed the sound. Seems the guy was some old friend of Rick's from way back, they even played in a band together—"

"Meal?" I say.

"What?" She looks puzzled.

"Rick was in a band called Meal. Did the guy say what his name was?"

"I don't know. And I don't think he said what the band was called. But he and Rick grew up together. The guy said he and his parents used to live in the house where Rick lives now—" She stops and raises a hand to her mouth. "I mean, where he lived. Rick bought it when the guy's parents moved to Florida." She pushes the plate of cookies toward me. "Have more. Help yourself."

I take one and bite into it. "What did the singing sound like?"

"Kind of nice. Very professional."

"Why was he in the treehouse?"

"Came up here looking for Rick. Said he just got back from Europe and needed a place to stay. He'd been singing in the subway for spare change."

"Rick wouldn't let him in the house?"

"I forget what the deal was. I think it was that Rick wasn't home. The guy figured he'd turn up eventually. They'd hung

125

out together in the treehouse when they were kids. He was excited to be back in the States, said he was sure his career was really going to take off. My husband would remember more. He talked to him for a long time." From somewhere deep in the house comes the wail of a baby. "Oh, poor Joey," she says, jumping up. "He's getting a new tooth and it's really hurting him." She disappears through the kitchen door and I hear light feet tapping on the stairs.

I sip what's left of my tea and discover it's cold, reach across the table for the teapot and refill my cup.

Feet on the stairs and the murmur of a soothing voice tell me Kate is returning. "When will your husband be home?" I ask as she turns the corner into the kitchen, bouncing the baby against her shoulder.

"An hour or so. Why?"

"You said he'd remember more about that guy."

"I guess you're really interested, huh?"

"Rick was a good friend," I say. "Since he died I've been trying to piece together some stuff, track down some people that knew him when he was younger. Maybe this guy is one of them."

"Like a mystery, huh?" she says, settling into her chair and arranging the baby on her lap. "Maybe my husband can help you. Like I said, he talked to him for a long time."

"How about the treehouse?" I say. "Can you show me where it is?"

She snuggles the baby into a little carrier and leads me past a grand but sparsely furnished living room, out the front door, and along the side of the porch. "Look," she says, pointing toward where Rick's house is visible through the trees. "See the big tree that's fallen over, leaning against the other one? Now, just past that, look up."

Sure enough, I see a sturdy tree with a small wooden shed perched on a solid, almost horizontal branch about ten feet from the ground. One of its walls backs up against two sturdy branches that fork off the trunk a few feet higher.

"Yes, it's a treehouse," Kate murmurs to the baby. "Someday you'll climb up there to play with your friends."

"How do you get up to it?" I say.

"I'm not sure," she says. "I think the guy came down to talk to my husband. Or maybe they yelled back and forth." She gives me the worried look. "What are you going to do?"

"I'm curious," I say.

"It's so cold," she says. "And it's getting dark. Be careful."

I make my way among the bare trees, breathing in the sharp, almost smoky smell of decay as my boots disturb the spongy layers of dead leaves, detouring past my car to grab my flashlight. As I get closer to the tree with the treehouse, I notice that lengths of wood nailed to the bark make a rough set of steps.

I circle the tree, looking up at the treehouse, telling myself that it's not going to come down in the next fifteen minutes if it's been up there as long as the weathered condition of its wood—faded to a silvery gray and with darker streaks where nails have rusted—suggests.

Sticking the flashlight in the pocket of my jacket, I take a deep breath. Then I anchor my boot on the lowest step, clutch the step that's more or less at chest level, and ease my way up, grabbing the next highest step with my hands, feeling with my boot against the rough bark of the tree till my foot finds another step and then another and another.

Finally, I've climbed high enough that I can let myself tip forward through the treehouse's door onto the wooden platform that forms its base. I scrabble a few feet using my hands to pull myself forward, then drag my legs through the door, crawl a few feet, and sit back on my heels.

The door and the small window, a hole in the opposite wall, don't allow much daylight into the treehouse. I pull out my flashlight, click it on, and let the beam investigate the small room.

Leaves have sifted in over the years, and blasts of wind have driven them against the walls, where their colorless drifts soften the sharp angles. Something else is here too though, something that the wind didn't bring.

I let the flashlight play over it for a minute before I pick it up, smiling in spite of myself at the first headline that catches my eye: "Neighbors of Dead Man Say He Was Really Not Very Nice." It's a copy of *The Snooze*, the parody newspaper you can pick up in Manhattan every week. So the mysterious guy that turned up in the treehouse last summer was dividing his time between singing and reading *The Snooze*?

This copy of *The Snooze* looks too fresh though, to have been sitting here for four or five months. It looks like it just came off the press. And when I shine my flashlight on the date, I discover that it's the November 10 issue. So somebody—the singing guy or somebody else—has been hanging around in the treehouse much more recently than last summer.

As I pick it up and unfold it, something drops out. It's a single sheet of paper, about six by eight inches, densely printed on both sides, starting with the words, "The Lord Will Come in Glory Within the Year." The text is illustrated with a picture of Jesus standing on a cloud with rays of light streaming from his body. It looks like the flyer Mitzi gave me the other night, the one she said she got from the Jesus guy in the subway. I tuck *The Snooze* and the flyer into my bag.

I'm heading back toward Kate's house, hoping that her husband is home by now so I can ask him about the guy in the treehouse, when I hear a slight crunching sound behind me, repeated at regular intervals, as if someone besides me is out for a walk.

I turn, and through the early evening dusk, I discover a dog trotting happily through the trees, a dog with a smooth russet coat and velvety ears that flop with each step, its long pink tongue nearly skimming the ground. The dog is followed by a figure in a red and black checked jacket, with the unkempt hair and beard of a mountain man. The dog circles back to the figure's side and looks up with all the adoration that its eyes and its flapping tongue can muster. It's Steve.

"What the hell?" the figure says. "What are you doing back here?"

"I need to ask you some questions. Can we go inside where it's warm?"

He shrugs. I take that to mean yes, and follow him and the dog toward the clearing, with the trailer at the edge still glowing slightly even though the sun has disappeared. Steve climbs the stairs first, unlocks the door, and enters.

The door swings further open, and he backs out of the way to let me step inside. The dog bounces past me, then turns and sniffs my legs.

"So? Will it be tea?" Steve asks, like he did the other time.

"Okay." I get rid of my gloves and jacket and sit down, charmed again by his cozy setup. But something is different today and I can't put my finger on what it is. I'm sitting exactly where I was sitting the last time, and as I gazed at that far wall . . . what did I see that's not there now?

He fills the kettle at the sink and gets it going on the stove. *Where to begin?* I ask myself.

He reaches down a couple of mugs and settles a teabag in each.

"So what's on your mind?" he says.

"I know about Meal now. You were the harmonica player."

He doesn't answer, stares instead at the steam coming from the teapot spout. The kettle begins to shriek and he lifts it from the stove and fills the cups, then he swings around and sets the two mugs on the table, along with napkins and a pair of spoons. "I still don't have any cookies," he says. I let the tea steep for a minute then fish out the teabag with my spoon and take a sip. Steve settles onto the bench across from me and does the same. The dog climbs up after him. "How'd you find out?"

"That album cover on his wall. I took it to a vintage vinyl place in the city."

"I don't want to talk about Meal."

"I know why it bothers you," I say. "The band broke up because somebody died. But that's not what I want to talk about. I want to know how the copyrights were handled."

He shakes his head no.

I drink my tea in silence for a few minutes, wondering how to proceed as I gaze around the trailer, admiring how carefully he's arranged his small assortment of possessions. There was a picture on that far wall, I suddenly realize. A picture of that beautiful woman. Now it's gone.

"What happened to the picture?"

"What picture?"

"The picture that used to hang over your bed."

"There was no picture," he says.

"Yes, there was. You said it was your sister. She was really beautiful."

"Maybe I'm already starting to pack," he says. "I'm prob'ly gonna have to move out." He pushes the dog's muzzle aside, but gently, and leans forward. "Don't you want your tea?"

"I drank most of it," I say, "and I have to get going." I want to talk to Kate's husband and I don't want to burst in when they're eating dinner.

I start to rise and the dog jumps off the bench too.

"Mind if I use your bathroom?" I say as I pull the jacket on. Tea has that effect on me, and I already drank a couple of cups in Kate's kitchen.

"Help yourself."

It's like the restroom on an airplane, its side forming one wall of the alcove that contains the table and benches. Inside is a toilet, a sink, and a tiny shower. And something else, something that doesn't fit with Steve's careful housekeeping.

It's the boombox that used to sit on top of the refrigerator, but it's never going to play music again. It looks like somebody threw it on the floor and then jumped on it, over and over and over again.

"What happened to your boombox?" I ask when I come out.

"Sometimes songs come on it that I don't want to hear. Now that won't happen."

"Like the one that was playing when you turned it off the other day?"

"I said I don't want to talk about Meal," he yells, the sudden contrast with his previous manner, almost unnaturally calm, startling me.

"I was Rick's friend too, you know. Maybe I have a right to know things."

"Didn't you hear me the first time? I don't want to talk about Meal." His creamy skin is starting to turn pink.

"Well, I don't want to believe that Rick was some kind of mobster. I think there's a way to explain what happened and why it happened. I've already discovered some interesting things—"

"I don't care what you found out. I don't want to talk about Meal. Or Rick. Or my sister. Or anything." His voice rises and rises. It's like he's building to some kind of climax, like he's some kind of crazed, out of control rock and roller, churning out a few last ear-shattering licks before setting his guitar on

131

fire and tossing it into the audience.

His face is totally red now, at least the part that's visible above the beard and below the shaggy hair. His brows are drawn together, his eyes glinting with fury.

"No more talking about Meal." He's standing now, trembling with anger—or is it something else? The dog is pressed against my legs, as if it's as surprised by this outburst as I am. "Get out of here," he shrieks, "before I get really pissed off. And don't come back. Ever."

I fumble my way out the door and down the steps into the dark.

I'm shaking as I hurry through the woods toward Kate's house, glad I have my flashlight and grateful for even its tiny wavering beam. Instead of climbing the back steps and tapping at the kitchen door, I circle the house. I hardly realize I've actually been running till a sharp pain in my side makes me stop and lean against a tree, pulling huge gulps of frigid air into my lungs through a mouth dry from panting. After a few minutes, I continue forward, leaning heavily on the railing as I haul myself up the steps and onto the broad wooden porch.

"Eat with us," Kate says as she leads me back into a kitchen that now smells like onions frying in olive oil. "I'm making spaghetti. Dave remembered some stuff about that guy he didn't tell me the first time."

Sitting at the table leafing through a small pile of mail and sipping from a glass of wine is a nice-looking man wearing khaki pants and a navy-blue sweater. He looks up, gives me a smile, and says, "Hi, I'm Dave."

"Have some wine," Kate says, putting an empty wine glass on the table in front of a vacant chair and tilting a bottle over it.

"He's been back—or somebody has," I say, sliding *The Snooze* into place next to the now-full glass and slipping into the chair.

Dave leans over and I point to the date. He shakes his head and says, "Poor guy. Maybe he came back looking for a place to stay—didn't know he wasn't going to find Rick." He flips idly through the first few pages. "I love this thing," he says. "It used to be better though. Now it's got so many ads." He turns several more pages. "Hey, look," he says. "Something in it was interesting to our friend." He points to where half a page has been torn out.

"It's the entertainment section," I say. "Maybe some show he wanted to see. Or maybe he's been getting gigs. Maybe it was an ad for his own show."

"I hope so," Dave says. "There was something kind of manic about him. I got the feeling that if things didn't work out like he thought they would, he was going to have a pretty hard fall."

"Did he say anything about the band he played in with Rick? Was it called Meal?"

"You know what stuck in my mind?" Dave says. "I asked him how long he'd been living in Europe and he said almost twenty years. I asked him why he went in the first place—expected him to tell me it was because Europeans love American music and he thought he'd make his fortune there. But he didn't say that. He said he decided to leave the city because too many beautiful women were dying."

"Did you get his name?"

"Tim something."

"Tim Morris." *The guitar player in Meal.*

"That might have been it." He nods. "I think that was it."

133

CHAPTER 12

I hear the phone ringing inside as I fumble my key into the lock. I get to it right before the machine cuts in. But what I hear after I pick it up and say hello makes me start shaking and sink into the big chair. Across the room, Red stares at me with his beady eyes.

"Hey, Maxx," says an all too familiar voice. "How are you doing?"

This time he sounds calmer, almost like his usual swaggering self.

I take a deep breath and say, "Fine, Sandy."

"That's good. Did you get my message the other day?"

"I got it," I say.

"No reason we can't keep in touch, you know."

"What did Nathan tell you?" I say.

"Nothing. He said he talked to you."

"So he had to grab the phone and let you know?"

"No. I called him. About something totally different." Now he sounds kind of hurt, but I know that routine. I don't say anything so he goes on. "I'm in the city. Have you heard of that show that's running Off-Broadway? The rock version of *Othello*?" His voice gains momentum, turns back into the swaggering Sandy voice. "The music is all live. The band sits on the stage. It's going to Broadway, and I've got a shot at the lead guitar part." He stops, but not to wait for an answer now, just to take a breath. "I'll be playing four shows: Thursday, Friday, Saturday, and Sunday—they're trying me out. If they like me, I'm in for the Broadway run." He stops, and when he starts up again he sounds nervous, but just a little. "I've got comps, Maxxie. Lots of comps. Want one? Name a night."

While he's been talking, I've been calming down. Now I say, calmly, I hope, and pleasantly, "Thanks, Sandy, but I really don't want to see you again. I've been involved with someone else."

"Who? Is he a musician?"

"Does it matter? He's someone else. Someone I really cared about."

"Cared? So it's over?"

"He's dead, Sandy. And I really cared about him."

"Dead? What happened?"

"I don't want to talk about it." I feel my throat go tight.

I guess he picks up on the tight-throat sound, because the next thing he says is, "I understand." Of course, he says it in his super-sincere voice, the one he uses when he isn't being sincere at all. He goes on. "But maybe you could use a friend, Maxxie. Couldn't I still be your friend?"

"I don't think that would work out very well. I'd just as soon we forgot we ever knew each other."

"Ouch. That's cold." The super-sincere voice again.

"I didn't mean it to be. It's the truth. You really hurt me and I don't want a repeat of it."

He's quiet for a minute, but it's a strategy he uses. When he's soloing and he knows he's got the audience hanging on every note, he'll stop and let a couple of bars go by before he launches into the next lick.

At last he says, "That makes me think you still care for me a little bit. Otherwise you wouldn't be afraid I could make you feel something again."

"That's not it at all." But I know he's right.

"I think it is, Maxxie. And I understand."

"I don't want you to understand. I want you to leave me alone."

"But—"

"Okay," I say. "We're friends. Are you satisfied?" And in my mind I add, *As long as we don't ever have to see each other again. Because even after everything that's happened, I don't think I'm totally out of love.*

"So . . . the tickets," he says. "Invite somebody to go with you, one of your girlfriends. Leave as soon as it's over. It's the hottest show in the city right now. Totally sold out. People would kill for a couple of comps."

"I . . . it sounds great for you, but I'm so busy with my job and my own band that I almost never go out. I really couldn't use them."

"But if you were going out, what night would it be?"

"I usually work at night." But not now, says a voice in my head, because you're subbing for Martha on the breakfast shift. "And if I'm not at work I'm rehearsing." But you're not rehearsing this Thursday, says the same voice, because Mitzi's going upstate with her friend—and you're free on Saturday and Sunday besides.

"Well, in case you discover you're free, there'll be a pair of comps waiting for you at the box office. They're yours any night you want to use them."

"You really don't need to—"

"They'll be there, Maxxie. They'll be waiting for you. Maxx Maxwell. It's at PlayTime on Forty-Second, right near Eighth."

"How's the case coming?" Leon hands me a bottle of Heineken and pushes a coaster along the coffee table till it winds up in front of me. "Here's a little refreshment to alleviate the strain of your cogitations."

"I went back up to Nyack to see if the trailer guy could tell me whether that kid band is using the Meal song legally, but he got really upset. He doesn't want to talk about Meal at all. He practically threw me out of his trailer. It was kind of scary."

"Too bad you drove all the way up there and didn't get an answer. That's a long trip."

"It wasn't a complete waste," I say. "I've got another mystery person to track down now—somebody that maybe collects Jesus literature and reads *The Snooze*. He was in Meal too." I tell him about the treehouse and the singing guy.

"Well, he's got good taste in reading material," Leon says, and his eyes twinkle behind the horn-rimmed glasses.

"Just because you're an intellectual snob—"

"You think I'm being sarcastic?" he says with a grin. He leans toward the copy of the *Times* neatly centered on his coffee table and slips a copy of *The Snooze* out from under it. Holding it in both hands, he assumes a mock-serious expression, opens it, and says, "I particularly admired this headline: " 'Crazy Man Announces Plans to Stand on Sidewalk, Hassle Passersby.' "

"Sounds like Hackensack," I say.

"I know. That's why it's my favorite." He closes the newspaper again and hands it to me.

"Where'd you get this?" I say.

"It circulates at school. And as for the Jesus literature—" He crosses to his desk, picks up an impressive-looking textbook, and extracts a flyer. "They make good bookmarks," he says. " 'The Lord is coming.' I think I got this one when I was up on Main Street doing errands." He hands it to me.

"It's a different style than the one in the treehouse," I say.

"How about these then?" He flips through a few more books and hands me several more.

"You're going to lose all your places," I say, leafing through them, "and none of these look like the treehouse one anyway."

137

Leon settles back down on his end of the sofa. "Was the copy of *The Snooze* recent?" he asks.

"The same issue as this one," I say. Then something occurs to me. I jump off the sofa and run for the door.

"Was it something I said?" Leon calls after me.

"Hang on," I shout from the hall.

In a minute I'm back with the copy of *The Snooze* from the treehouse. I leaf through it till I find the place where half a page has been torn out, then I pick up Leon's copy and leaf through that till I come to the whole version of the same page.

"It looks like the treehouse guy was interested in a total-body depilatory service," I say.

"So—look for somebody furry," Leon says. "Or check out what's on the other side."

I turn the page and all of a sudden the hairs on the back of my neck stand up, like they do in that quivering moment of excitement when a pattern starts to emerge from a hopeless muddle.

In the spot where my copy of *The Snooze* has a missing half page, Leon's has a half-page ad for 4Guys4U's concert at Musica.

Leon is nodding, as if to himself. "So," he says musingly, "this *Snooze* is so new that whoever left it up there could have been hanging out in the treehouse right around the time Rick was killed. Why didn't the cops find it?"

"The treehouse isn't very close to his house—and the cops got onto that crazy mob idea right away. Since they had that lead to follow up, it probably seemed like searching for clues that pointed in other directions would be wasted effort." I reach for my beer but notice that it's empty. "Got any more out there?"

"I do, but hang on a minute. Weeklies like this often come out before the date actually printed on them. I picked my *Snooze* up last Friday."

"That's the day before Rick was killed," I say. "So this issue was already floating around."

As he slips a fresh bottle of beer in my hand, I surprise myself by saying, "How'd you like to see *Othello?*"

He looks at me with something like respect and says, "Where's it playing? I thought I kept up with the theater news. Or do you mean a film?"

"On Forty-Second, a place called PlayTime."

"Sounds like an Off-Broadway kind of place." He pauses, looking puzzled, then suddenly he isn't puzzled anymore. "Not the rock opera!"

"Yeah. Shakespeare. I can . . . somebody wants me to . . . I could have tickets. Want to come?"

"Elizabeth." He smiles, but it's a chiding smile. "Me? At a rock opera? To each his own, his or her own. I'm a culture snob, I know. But opera—" He bows his head. "And Shakespeare." He pronounces the word like it's a prayer. "And—"

I interrupt him. "Rock. I know. You don't have to say it."

But he cuts in again. "I'm boring. How can you stand me?" He flashes a self-mocking smile. "Pitiable taste in music." He shakes his head slowly. Then, as if he's just realized something, "But you need an escort, Elizabeth. And you want to see it. In that case—the *Times* says it's the hottest ticket in town. I suppose one of your friends, your musician friends—"

"It's okay, Leon. I don't really want to go. I thought you might like it because it's Shakespeare."

"And *Othello* at that. I wonder, will he sing the blues to the fair Desdemona? Or maybe they'll do more of a rap thing."

I shake my head. "I don't know. I don't care, really. Thanks for saying you'll come, but I don't really want to. I just thought you'd like it."

I leaf through the Jesus flyers on the coffee table and study each one more closely. None of them is at all like the flyer Mitzi had. But if she can remember exactly where she picked hers up, it might put me on the trail of the treehouse guy.

When I get back to my apartment, I call Mitzi. She doesn't answer so I leave a message on her voice mail.

As I stare into my closet the next day, I'm thinking about what I found out from Mitzi about the flyer when she returned my call. But will I have time to follow up on it tonight? I'm not sure. I've got another errand first.

I shove a few hangers aside and pull out my leopard print leggings and my black leather bustier. I haven't worn them for ages, but they might be just the thing. When I make the first contact, I'll probably still be bundled up in a coat, but later . . . it's been my experience that you get more cooperation if you look like a chick a guy'd like to look at.

Obviously I'm not dressing for the Seafood Chalet. I already put in my shift this morning. Aldo gets so pissed off when I call in sick that subbing for Martha this couple of weeks is turning out to be a great stroke of luck. I toss the leggings and the bustier on the bed.

A few annoyed squawks emerge from Red's cage as the clothes fly past, reminding me that I haven't checked his food or water all day. I'll be out late—I hope—so I'd better get him taken care of now while I'm thinking about it. I'll leave his cage uncovered till I get home. I feel kind of sorry for him having to spend so much time under my bedspread. No matter what happens tonight, I should be back before it starts to get light.

In the bathroom, I tease my hair up into kind of a fifties-style beehive with tendrils that fall down my neck in the back. I make up my eyes with lots of shiny black eyeliner and extra mascara and finish the whole look off with my reddest red lipstick.

After I've got the leggings and the bustier on, I try a few different pairs of boots, but decide they don't look sexy enough.

So I pull out my old spike-heeled sandals with the rhinestone straps. I used to really dress up for gigs when Sandy and I played in Atlantic City, and the sandals were part of my best outfit.

Slipping my feet into them reminds me of the phone call from Sandy—and that I was all set to drag Leon into the city so I could watch Sandy pose as the great guitar hero. Why can't I purge him from my mind forever? Some guys get under your skin and stay there.

I can't wear the sandals unless I spend half an hour doing my toenails. I pull them off and throw them back in the closet. I'll wear my black cowboy boots. They'll go good with the bustier. And I'll make up for the boots by wearing my red patent leather jacket, even though my legs will freeze. It's got a belt that I can cinch up nice and tight to show off my shape.

The guy behind the ticket-office glass laughs when I ask him if there's any way to get into tonight's concert.

"No day-of-show tickets? Or ones that people didn't claim?" I ask.

He only shakes his head.

"Nothing left at all?"

He shakes his head again.

Back out on the sidewalk, I scan the crowd, mostly twenty-somethings in jeans, shapeless jackets, and stocking caps. There's always somebody whose friend canceled out at the last minute and who'd just as soon replace that unused ticket in their pocket with a couple of bills. And sure enough, here she is, clutching the spare ticket in a mittened hand and calling "Anybody need a ticket?" in a peeping voice that leaves a puff of frozen breath behind.

But a huge black guy in a leather athletic jacket sees her, too.

"Sellin' how many?" he says to the girl as we collide. Armored by the elaborate jacket, he didn't notice the impact.

"Just one. My friend is sick."

"I'll take it," I say.

Like I'm totally invisible, the black guy whips a roll of bills out of his pocket, peels off two twenties, hands them to the girl, and grabs the ticket.

A minute later he's roving along the sidewalk calling, "Tickets. Tickets here. Get your tickets." And just as soon, somebody's handing him three twenties and reaching for the ticket.

Oblivious, two cops stroll along the velvet rope that keeps the ticketed in a tidy line. Above the theater entrance, a sign reads "Scalpers sell fake tickets."

Well, obviously this one doesn't. But people whose friends bailed out at the last minute seem to be in short supply. After ten more minutes of pacing without another chance to get a twenty-buck profit in three seconds, the athletic-jacket guy drifts off down the street. The people shuffling restlessly behind the velvet rope start to file slowly into the theater. I wait till they're all inside and the guy that's been taking the tickets starts to close the door.

"Can you tell me something?" I say.

"Maybe." He looks me up and down.

"Where's the stage door?"

He shrugs, his face twitches, and his glasses slip down his nose. With the glasses, the wiry build, and hair not much longer than two days' worth of stubble, he could almost be some kind of monk. "No big secret, I guess. It's around the side, second door down. The door that says 'Serbian Army Veterans Association' above it." He pushes the glasses back into place with a pale, skinny finger. "You won't get in, though. Everything's locked up."

The bar that faces the side of Musica has huge picture

windows. I'd be able to keep a constant eye on the stage door if the band's tour bus wasn't parked in the way. So I stare at the logo on the side of the tour bus while I sip a shot of Jack Daniel's and then nurse a couple of beers.

When the twenty-somethings start flowing back out of the theater doors, it's time to get moving.

"You like this kind of music?" the guy asks. He's posed near the door of the tour bus under the Serbian Army Veterans Association sign. He's clearly not a Serbian army veteran, but he's a veteran of sorts, probably a veteran of many nights like this. His backstage pass dangles against the Led Zeppelin logo that peeks from the opening of a heavy leather jacket. His abundant hair, a faded shade of auburn and longer than mine, flutters in the chilly wind. His eyes regard me wearily from twin nests of wrinkles.

"Love it," I say, smiling what I hope is a charming smile.

"Really?" His eyes sweep toward the crush of twenty-somethings crowded around the stage door and he takes a deep drag on his cigarette. "You don't seem like the 4Guys4U type."

"You've never seen me at their gigs?"

"I work for Musica," he says. "It's the first time they've played here."

The stage door cracks open an inch or so, and a nervous rustle pulses through the crowd.

"What will happen now?" I ask.

"Nothing." He nods toward the stage door and I notice that the crack has vanished. He draws on the cigarette again.

"How long have you worked here?" I ask.

"A couple years."

"And before that?"

"Look," he says, sighing heavily, which makes him start coughing. He looks at the cigarette in his hand, frowns at it, and tosses it to the ground. "This isn't going to do you any good. It's my job to keep people away from the band."

"They don't like to hang out with their fans after a show?"

"They'll decide who they want to hang out with, not me."

"Okay," I say. "The truth then. I need to talk to them because a guy I really cared about is dead and I want them to know about it because he wrote one of their songs."

He raises his eyebrows but doesn't say anything. After a few seconds, he feels in his pocket and comes up with a pack of cigarettes. But another rustle in the crowd grabs his attention and he hastily tucks the cigarettes away again.

"So—send them a letter." He grabs my arm and tugs me a few feet away from the door of the bus.

The stage door opens, all the way this time, and a few burly guys in Musica T-shirts spill out. Forming a wedge that divides the crowd, they back toward the door of the tour bus.

Following them is a self-assured guy with dark hair cropped to follow the curve of his skull and a little goatee that calls attention to his full, well-formed lips.

Arms wave over the shoulders of the T-shirt guys. Voices shout, words overlapping: "Roger! Roger!" "Great show." "Autograph? Please, please, please. Autograph!" "Roger! Over here! Roger!"

Staring straight ahead, the self-assured guy heads for the tour bus, where the now-open door is still being guarded by my friend.

More of the Musica T-shirt guys spill out of the stage door and link arms with the first batch, forming a human corral into which three more guys, presumably the rest of the band, step one by one. Unlike the first guy, these guys are boisterous and shaggy, laughing and poking each other like they've got adrenaline to spare even after two hours onstage, sporting various combinations of overgrown hair, facial and otherwise.

They're followed by a few older guys in black jeans, black T-shirts, and black leather jackets.

I push myself through the crowd, trying to ignore the feeling that I'm about to be crushed or trampled. When I'm so close that the only thing between me and the nearest band member, one of the boisterous ones, is the burly arm of one of the T-shirt guys, I shout, "Hey, I need to talk to you guys."

The band member's gaze lands on me for a second, then he turns away and says something that makes the guy next to him burst out laughing.

"No, really," I say. "Please." He doesn't even look at me.

The guy at the head of the procession, the self-assured one with the goatee, is about ready to climb onto the bus. I hurl myself sideways, squeezing between the backs of the T-shirt guys and the people in the crowd that have managed to squirm their way to the front. I'm glad now that I'm wearing cowboy boots instead of the spike-heeled sandals with the rhinestone straps.

I manage to grab the goatee guy's arm until a T-shirt guy pulls my hand loose. But at least the commotion gets the goatee guy's attention. He stops where he is and the whole entourage stops behind him, people bumping up against each other like human sheep.

"I've got a message for you from Rick Schneider," I say.

He looks at me blankly but he stays where he is.

"Let's get going, man," one of the shaggy guys says. "I need a drink bad."

The goatee guy turns and raises a pacifying hand. "Hang on, Dory," he says. Then, to me, "Who's Rick Schneider?"

"He wrote 'Not Something Pretty.' "

Suddenly, his lips part and his eyes widen. Just as suddenly the self-assured look comes back. He leans to the side and whispers something to one of the burly guys, turns back to me.

145

"Why don't you hang out with us for a while?" he says in a voice that sounds anything but cordial. "Ride back to the hotel with us."

"Can't we talk for a few minutes here?"

He starts to say something but he's interrupted by the shaggy guy. "Roger, man. Move it, will you?"

Meanwhile, the crowd is becoming even more restless, and the T-shirt guys are having to struggle to keep their arms linked.

Roger pushes the closest T-shirt guy to the side and edges back to open a space between me and the step that leads onto the bus. "It will be better this way," he says, grabbing my arm, not all that gently, and guiding me through the door.

CHAPTER 13

Inside, the bus is like a cross between a hotel room and a squatters' camp. The three shaggy guys push past us and hurry toward the back where they sprawl on a couple of bunk beds that jut from the bus's walls. One of them retrieves a bottle of whiskey from a duffel bag, takes a long swallow, and passes it around. A minute later, the pungent smell of marijuana fills the air.

Instead of beds, the front of the bus has several lounge chairs facing each other across the aisle. Roger motions me toward one of the chairs. The older guys take seats right behind where the bus driver sits.

"Hotel?" the driver says, leaning out of his seat. He's an elderly black guy. The bus door closes with a slight sigh.

"Where is the hotel?" I say, willing my voice to sound calm as something in my chest gives a sudden lurch then starts pulsing. "I'm parked around here."

Nobody answers. The driver gets busy and, with a ponderous shifting of gears and a series of pneumatic wheezes, the bus pulls away from the curb.

Roger walks toward the back of the bus, swaying a little as the driver jerks the wheel and the bus sharply merges with the flow of traffic. I look toward the older guys sitting up front. One of them is leaning back against his headrest and the other is aimlessly paging through a copy of the *Village Voice*.

When Roger comes back, it's to offer me an open bottle of

whiskey. I put it to my lips and take a swallow.

"Like this stuff?" he says with a slight smile. "Have some more." I take another swallow. Smoky fumes rise to my nostrils while the liquor traces a warm path to my stomach.

He sinks into the seat across the aisle from me and raises the bottle to his own lips. "Man, that's good," he says with a long sigh after a swallow that makes his adam's apple bounce in his throat. "You put me on the spot there." He looks at me so hard it's like he's trying to see right through me.

"What do you mean?"

"Rick Schneider. After what we've been through with Meal, I should know that name as well as my own." He takes another swallow of the whiskey, passes the bottle to me, and rubs his head in a gesture that takes his hand over the crest of his skull, across his face, and all the way down to the little goatee. "But touring—? I'm not sure I know my own name anymore."

"What you've been through with Meal?"

He waves his hands like he's trying to fend off some unwelcome intimacy. "Don't ask," he says. "And hand over that bottle."

I take a quick sip and pass the bottle back across the aisle.

"A message from Rick Schneider, huh?" He laughs. "You've been in touch with him by Ouija board or what?"

"Well, it's not really a message," I say, blinking a few times as I feel the whiskey start to take effect.

"What is it then?" Now a little smile starts to play around his well-shaped mouth.

When I hesitate, he hands the bottle back. "How did you like the show tonight?" he asks.

"I couldn't get in. It was sold out." Between the booze I had while I was waiting for the concert to end and these hits of whiskey, my tongue has a little trouble getting around the words.

"So you hung around for three hours—for what?"

148

"I—" My voice sounds like it's coming from somewhere else. My skin feels numb and my brain doesn't seem to be controlling what I do. "Where did you get that song?" I blurt it out without really planning to.

" 'Not Something Pretty'? It's a Meal song, of course. I thought you knew that." He looks toward the back of the bus. "Nando brought it in," he says. He turns back to me and raises his eyebrows. "Oh, I get it. You think we're not legal. Here to bust us for stealing your dead pal's tune?" He looks toward the back of the bus again, "Yo, Nan!"

All of the shaggy guys have collapsed, two face-down on the beds, one of them sprawled in the aisle of the bus with his shoulders propped against a door that probably leads to the toilet.

The one in the aisle raises his head an inch or two and says, "Whatchu need, my man?"

"Where'd 'Not Something Pretty' come from?"

"That's the tune from Calhoun." He giggles. "Hey, it rhymes. I never noticed before." He giggles again. "It's from the Meal EP I found at that little place in Vermont. Remember that gig? Calhoun, Vermont? And that dirty little shop? Turned out the guy didn't know he had it, said he was a big fan of theirs, but he sold it to me anyway."

He reaches under one of the beds for an acoustic guitar, pulls himself into a sitting position, and strums a few chords. "The whole EP is dynamite," he says.

"You have it here?" I say.

He shakes his head. "At home, up in Boston." He strums a few more chords and starts to sing,

> *"She's having my . . . maybe*
> *Here's a lullaby for . . . maybe*
> *It's—maybe—it's gonna be cool when I'm a—*
> *Rockabye maybe—"*

"That's on it too?"

"Guess one of 'em had a kid," he says.

"Which one?" I say. "Who wrote it?"

"They're all copyright Rick Schneider and Steve Bernier," he says. "Like Lennon and McCartney. But who knows who really wrote what?"

"How'd you even find that out?"

"It wasn't easy, let me tell you. But when we signed with our label, some chick took all that over. Labels have people to do stuff like that for you."

"So Meal's getting royalties?"

"Well, somebody is. Rick's dead, from what we heard."

"Who told you?"

"The chick at the label."

"But Steve's getting money?"

"I guess. Unless he's the one that's in prison. Can they get money from outside when they're in prison?"

"One of them is in prison?"

"According to the vintage vinyl dude that sold me the EP."

"Must be Jeb Perkins," I say. "What's he in prison for?"

"Shot somebody. A long time ago. Supposed to be getting out. Maybe he is out." Nando picks the guitar up and starts strumming, singing, " 'It's gonna be cool when I'm a—' " He pauses. "That part knocks me out. You think he's going to say, 'When I'm a dad,' but instead it stops." He looks at me. "How'd Rick die, anyway?"

"Somebody shot him," I say.

In the cab riding back to Musica to retrieve my car, I remember what Mitzi told me. It's late, almost midnight, but maybe not too late.

The cab driver's a Sikh, turban and all, chatting away on a cell phone with a headset, in some peaceful language that sounds like water lapping over stones, laughing every once in awhile, a peaceful laugh.

We're zipping down a block in the thirties, brownstones, a bar at the end, a grocery across the way with a bright flower stand bathed in light and protected from the wind by a clear plastic drape.

"Excuse me—" I lean toward the gap in the window between the front seat and the back.

The driver says something into his headset then turns his head slightly in my direction.

"Take me to Times Square instead," I say. "I just remembered something I've got to do."

Without even slowing down, he swings right at the next corner. I stare at the flower stand as we turn.

Soon we're heading past cascades of neon, billboards as alive as TV screens, deep into the blazing heart of Times Square, bright as a noon bathed in cool white light. Most cars are taxis, surging up Broadway, turning two lanes into three, then back into two, horns like random trumpet blasts in a raucous fusion experiment.

"Where do you want to get out?" the cab driver asks in a version of English that has the same peaceful cadence as his Sikh language.

"Take me over to Port Authority," I say.

Two bucks in the machine, one-use Metro Card in hand, run it through the slot, push through the turnstile. It's bright and busy down here, earnest young white people lugging satchels, middle-aged brown people making a tired trek home from ill-paid jobs, huge laughing black people in careful outfits that say being huge is cool.

The tunnel that leads to the trains resembles an ill-maintained public restroom, with dirty white tile walls and an occasional whiff of urine.

I hear him before I see him. It's a jaunty rhythm, a slow jerky intake in sweet breathy gasps, then, smoother and more forceful, a long exhalation. It's a guy with an accordion. Nobody stops, but on the grimy concrete floor his upturned hat contains a few bills.

I stop and wait through a tune I almost recognize, watching his arms pump in and out, fingers busy on the keys with their shiny pattern of black and white.

It winds down, and before it starts again, I toss a dollar in the hat and say, "You sound good." He nods, then quick before the fingers start their busy search and the pumping resumes, I say, "Do you ever run into a guy down here that plays the guitar?"

"Lots of guys," he says in an accent that somehow goes with the accordion. He waves a vague hand further down the tunnel. "Down there," he adds. "This is my spot."

"How about a guy that preaches and gives out flyers about Jesus?"

His forehead wrinkles. "Flyers? What is flyers?"

"Papers," I say. "Papers with writing about Jesus."

"Down there," he says, waving down the tunnel again. "He don't like stand near music. People can't hear him."

I thank him and head down the tunnel, falling into step behind three women in saris with heavy wool coats buttoned over them. I pass a wiry black guy with a set of steel drums and a skinny blond guy playing a saxophone. When I emerge from the tunnel I'm in a large, open space bathed in a bright, shadowless light and echoing with footsteps, human voices, and the metallic rumble of trains.

It's the spot Mitzi described, the spot where the guy gave her the Jesus flyer. The treehouse guy must play down here, assuming only one Jesus guy gives out those particular flyers.

Tucked against a wall near the mouth of the tunnel is a concession stand with a bright display of magazines and a counter ranged with piles of candy bars. A bored-looking Indian guy hovers near the cash register.

"I'm looking for somebody," I say as I pick up a package of chocolate-covered peanuts and hand him a dollar. He nods politely. "It's a guy that plays the guitar down here. Near where another guy hands out Jesus literature."

"Lots of guitars," he says. "Only one Jesus guy."

"Have you seen the Jesus guy here tonight?"

"Too late for him."

"The guitar player I'm looking for is a white guy, maybe about forty. And he sings too, maybe like pop songs, folk songs, blues—that kind of style."

The polite look turns into a smile. "Maybe I know who you are talking about," he says. "Usually he is standing in the tunnel, right at the end there." He points toward where the saxophone guy is giving vent to a tortured blast that twists through half an octave before it ends. "The guitar player is very good," he says with a nod. "Very good player. And his songs are something unusual, not what you hear every day. He writes them, some of them, himself. That's what he told me."

He pauses to hand a pack of cigarettes across the counter and take a few bills from a guy that mutters, "Don't bother with change. These damn things cost so much, what's a few coins?" before he hurries off.

"When does he usually hang out down here?" I say.

The guy screws up his mouth and lets his forehead pucker. "I haven't seen him for a few days. When he comes, he usually comes in the afternoon, stays three or four hours."

I pull my notebook from my bag. "Could you give him a note?" He nods. I tear out a sheet of paper and write, "Please call me about Rick." I add my phone number and sign it "Maxx Maxwell."

★ ★ ★ ★ ★

Swaying on the bright train, sounds blotted out by the *clackita-clackita* of wheels on the rails, the window view only my reflection as the train races through the black tunnel that connects Port Authority to Grand Central Station, heading back to my car again—and my mind's racing too.

All songs copyright Rick and Steve, the 4Guys4U guy said. So royalties for "Not Something Pretty" go to Rick and Steve. But not to Rick anymore because Rick's dead. So what happens to the money? Would Steve get it?

Clackita-clackita. The train surges, I sway right then left as the wheels sigh to a stop and the doors snap open. Grand Central. I let the small crowd gathered in the aisle pull me along, out the door, onto the platform, follow a black lady Muslim in a floating white chador as my mind hurries on ahead of me.

All songs copyright Rick and Steve. But the treehouse guy writes songs too. What if he wrote the Meal songs but Rick and Steve took the credit?

Or maybe Rick and Steve didn't really write the songs together. Maybe they only copyrighted them together. What if Steve wrote "Not Something Pretty" all by himself and he was pissed that Rick got part of the money? But if he wrote it, why would he turn it off when it came on the radio?

Maybe he hates it now and he's embarrassed. I'm embarrassed about lots of stuff I thought was cool when I was younger. Maybe he didn't want 4Guys4U to cover the song at all—wanted it to remain in the oblivion of a vintage-vinyl bin—but Rick insisted, said Steve would even get money. But Steve doesn't seem to like money.

Still, he seemed so anxious to give me that paper with the article about the band he said he was roadying for. Like he wanted to make sure I believed he wasn't around the weekend

Rick disappeared. Like he wanted to make sure even I knew that he had an alibi.

He followed me out the door to stick it in my hand, but what did I do with it? It's probably still in the car.

I find the Bonneville right where I left it, but before I head back to New Jersey I dig my flashlight out of the pouch in the door and shine it around on the floor. No newspapers.

I open the back door and check the back seat. Nothing. Stooping, I lean into the car and let my hand work its way under the seat. Grittiness gives way to a smoothness that curves into the shape of a folded tabloid, and I pull out *What's Up in Worcester* ("Learn where Worcester meets, greets, and eats").

I focus the beam of the flashlight on articles about a new Thai restaurant and a meeting of the Main Street Merchants' Association. Pages flip; the flashlight pores. Here it is, finally, tucked between an ad for an astral reader and an article about the Hitchcock festival coming to the university: "Blues Still Cool—NYC's Delta Dudes Show Why."

"Last Saturday," the article begins, and the flashlight scrupulously veers up to the top of the page and notes a publication date of November 12. So "last Saturday" was the same Saturday Rick was killed.

The flashlight searches the article for some mention of Steve Bernier, but there's nothing to prove that he was really there. All this copy of *What's Up in Worcester* proves is that Steve somehow got his hands on a copy of *What's Up in Worcester.*

The band's from New York though. And if they're gigging as far away as Worcester, they must be ambitious enough to line things up in the city too. I'll pick up a copy of the *Village Voice* and see if I can track them down, ask whether they know a crazy guy named Steve Bernier, whether he was with them in Worcester on November 8.

155

CHAPTER 14

Handsome in a navy pullover and gray flannel pants, Leon serves up my coffee with a flourish. "And to what do I owe the honor of this early-morning visit?" he says, settling into the chair across from me and giving me a genial smile, a sudden white-toothed crescent in his coffee-brown face.

"If two guys had a copyright on a song that was making a lot of money, and one of them died, what would happen to his share of the money?"

"Oi," Leon says, faking dismay. "Still with the song already." He adds a spoonful of sugar to his coffee and pushes the sugar bowl toward me.

"No thanks," I say. "I like it black."

Leon reaches for the milk. "I should know that by now," he says.

"Anyway," I say, "I found out Rick and Steve hold all the copyrights on the Meal songs. And the first time I met Steve he went out of his way to tell me he'd been roadying for a band up in Worcester the night Rick disappeared—he even gave me a copy of the paper that had a review of the show."

"Interesting," Leon says with a thoughtful frown and a commendatory head nod, like one of those TV talent-show judges acknowledging that an unpromising singer has actually pulled off a good performance. "Methinks the gentleman protests too much. Is that what you think?"

"Something like that. But the whole thing is very confusing

because Rick was helping him out, letting him park the trailer on his property, even giving him food, for all I know. Why would he want to get rid of somebody that was so useful to him?"

"And unless they had some very specific arrangement with those copyrights, Rick's money would go to Rick's estate, not to Steve. If Steve killed Rick, maybe the motive was something totally different, something that didn't have anything to do with money."

"Like what?"

"Well, maybe he wasn't *planning* to kill him. Maybe they were arguing about something." Leon shrugs. "They were arguing and it got out of hand. Maybe that's how the album cover got knocked off the wall."

I nod. "It's true. I have to figure out how the album cover fits in." I raise my coffee cup toward my mouth, but a quick idea makes me decide I want to talk instead of drink. "Back to the copyright thing," I say. "Like I told you, Steve's a very weird, otherworldly kind of guy. What if he doesn't even know how royalty agreements operate? What if he *thought* that with Rick dead there'd only be one name left on the copyright?"

"He'd have to be extremely otherworldly," Leon says with a laugh. "But the alibi thing is mysterious." He nods. "Like he felt guilty about something.

"Umm," I say, sipping my coffee. "I think so too. I *guess*. Unless he was trying to let me know he had some kind of a life besides hanging around in that trailer and taking walks with his dog. I'd be pretty embarrassed if that's all I did."

"Did the newspaper article specifically mention Steve's name?"

"No," I say. "But why would it? He said he was only the roady. But the band is called the Delta Dudes, and they're New York City guys. They must gig around town. I can show up at one of their gigs and ask them if Steve was really in Worcester the night Rick died."

Leon purses his lips and raises his eyebrows. "Those time-of-death estimates aren't always accurate, you know," he says. "Especially if the body's been in a swamp for a while."

"But I talked to Rick earlier on Saturday, and that jogger found his body on Sunday morning. Anyway, Steve isn't my only suspect." I let my lips form a smug smile. "And that brings me to my next question."

"Uh, oh." His left arm bends and a bit of starched cuff emerges from the sleeve of his sweater as he consults his watch.

"You have to be somewhere, don't you?"

"My nine A.M. class beckons," he says. "But I've got a few minutes. Mr. Answer Man is at your service." He gives a courtly bow.

"One of the other people in that band with Rick and Steve killed somebody."

"I didn't realize popular music was such a violent pursuit," Leon says. "Except for rap, of course."

"Rap," I say. "That gives me another idea. The guy that handles the business end of Prowling Rooster Records—his name is Ben Darling—is thinking about lining up some rap acts for the label. What if Rick objected and . . . ?" I shake my head. "This gets more and more confusing."

Leon pulls himself erect. "Mr. Answer Man has two more minutes," he says.

"How can I find out about something that happened twenty years ago?"

"The Internet, of course. And I'll help you out tonight. But now—" He rises. "I've got to go to school." He steps toward the kitchen door. "Stay and finish up the coffee if you want," he says.

"Thanks," I say, "but I've got to get to work. Go ahead. I'll let myself out."

I hear the closet door open in the other room and hangers clank as a coat is pulled out. Then I hear the door to the hall swing open. "Hey," Leon's voice calls back as I'm thinking he's about to be gone. "Tonight's *Othello*. Are you going?"

"Not on your life," I call back. "Absolutely not on your life."

I wonder if Sandy still looks the same, says a voice in my head as I carry my empty coffee cup to the counter.

It occurs to me, as I sit in traffic, that maybe I don't have to wait for Leon to get home. Maybe Walt can help me out.

So before I go to my locker to grab my Seafood Chalet vest, I drop some coins in the pay phone by the break room.

But I end up telling my story to Walt's machine because Walt isn't home—all about Meal and 4Guys4U, and Rick's scars and how one of the guys from Meal went to prison because he killed someone. I lower my voice a little bit when I notice Manfred staring at me curiously from the hallway that leads into the kitchen. And just before I get to my question, Walt's machine beeps to tell me I've used up all my time.

"This is Maxx, continued," I say after I drop in more coins, dial again, and get Walt's recorded voice again, telling me that he's not available to take my call but to please leave a message. "So how can I find out who this guy killed and why, and what prison he ended up in, and—especially—whether they've let him out yet?"

Maybe Walt's already left for Europe with Zachary Crane, I reflect as I slip my Seafood Chalet vest over my own white shirt. Maybe you'll *have* to be patient till Leon gets back from the university.

But I won't be home when Leon gets back, I realize as I walk toward my section of the dining room. I'll be standing in that strange echoing tunnel under Times Square, watching people sweep past me on the way to their trains while Tim Morris plays his guitar. Because I'm going back tonight, early enough to catch him at the time the magazine kiosk guy said he's normally there.

I listen as a woman with a long, stern face and an incongruous little fringe of light brown bangs across her bony forehead places an order for the breakfast special with two pancakes on the side. But the voice I'm hearing isn't hers. It's a voice in my head saying Tim Morris will know things.

I agree. But will he tell them to me?

And meanwhile, right beneath the surface of my consciousness, a new thought is asserting itself. I'm barely aware of it at first, but as I gaze at the mural in front of me, a cowboy scampering across a prairie in pursuit of an escaping calf, the thought becomes stronger.

"Did you hear me?" the woman demands. "I asked whether you can make the pancakes with whole wheat flour."

"Yes. I mean no," I say.

The theater where Sandy's show is playing is practically *in* Times Square.

I get through my shift—really Martha's shift—somehow and swing by my apartment to see if I've got a message from Walt. Just a few more days till payday and I can settle up with the cell phone company and re-enter the twenty-first century.

No blinking lights on the machine means no message from Walt, so I guess I'll have to wait for Leon before I can follow up on whether Jeb Perkins is likely to be out of prison yet.

My stomach growls and I remember that I haven't eaten anything since I grabbed a doughnut on my lunch break. We can eat at the restaurant, but we have to pay for it, so there's no big advantage in eating there. Besides, being around food all through my shift kind of takes away my appetite.

I head back out, on foot this time, in search of something to eat and a copy of the *Village Voice*. Maybe I can track down the Delta Dudes and figure out whether Steve was really away the weekend Rick was killed.

"Nope," says the News and Deli guy down by the courthouse. "I used to carry the *Voice* but nobody bought it."

"How about an egg sandwich then? On a roll?"

"Sure thing." He turns to the grill.

I peel off a glove to pull two bills from my wallet, watch as a foamy yellow puddle congeals into a spongy disk and gets folded in quarters, tidily tucked into a split roll, and wrapped in waxed paper.

Glove back on, sandwich in hand, muffler tugged up to my chin and hat down to my eyebrows, I head for home under a sky as bleak as the sidewalk, featureless gray, quiet, heavy, waiting for snow.

I nibble the last crusty bite of the sandwich out of the waxed paper and crumple the paper into a ball as the library comes into sight. And as I toss the crumpled paper into the library's trash bin, I remember that libraries have newspapers. Maybe this library even has the *Voice*.

A cluster of low-slung chairs sits on a carpet whose pattern somehow reminds me of how my beaten egg looked spilling out onto the grill. Behind the chairs a wall of newspapers beckons, the *Village Voice* broadmindedly sharing shelf space with the *Wall Street Journal*.

I grab the copy of the *Voice* and page quickly to the entertainment section in the back, but the first thing my eyes land on is an ad for *Othello: The Rock Opera*, "now running at PlayTime on Forty-Second Street." I stare at the ad for a long minute, then flap the *Voice* closed and shuffle it back into its place on the shelf. I can track down the Delta Dudes later. It's better to remove myself from this temptation.

To distract myself from the thought of Sandy, I get up. And as I get up, I notice a row of people sitting at a long table. The people's eyes are focused on computer monitors and their hands are making computer mouses glide purposefully around their mousepads.

I'd forgotten. Anything Leon can do on his computer at home, I can do here right now.

Standing behind a big blond counter is a pretty woman with dark hair and a delicate face, too young for the shapeless cardigan that droops from her thin shoulders.

"Hmmm," she says as I tell my story, and her friendly face turns serious. "It would have been in the news." She frowns slightly. "We subscribe to something called ProQuest. It accesses historical newspapers for about the last century and a half."

She steps out from behind the counter, tugging the cardigan around her as she walks. "Come on," she says. "I'll get you started."

When the screen offers me a box to type in what I'm looking for, I spell out the name "Jeb Perkins" and poke the "Enter" key.

I think I had an inkling of what I'd find, but still I'm not prepared.

Once when I was a kid I fell off a picnic table that was higher than I was tall. I landed on my back on a patch of dusty ground and my head clunked on the ground too, and for what seemed like a whole lifetime I absolutely could not breathe. I watched the sun burn a round yellow hole in the sky and felt my lungs try to move.

The first headline makes me feel like that. Finally, I pull my eyes away from it and lean back in my chair. I study the library's walls, the tasteful modern prints hanging here and there, the sign that says children under the age of twelve have to have their parents' permission on file to use the Internet.

I watch with obsessive interest as a skinny black teenager lifts the cover of the copy machine, takes out a book, turns a page, settles the book back on the glass, lowers the cover, and inserts a coin in the slot.

I close my eyes and feel my lungs fill with air then empty . . . fill then empty . . . fill then empty.

Finally, I look back at the screen. Centered above a three-column story, huge letters spell out the words, "Brutal East Village Shooting Spree." Smaller letters below read, "Musician Kills Girlfriend, Wounds Bandmate."

More stories follow, from other newspapers and from later days, interviews with cops, with neighbors, even—from his hospital bed—with Rick, because of course that's who the wounded bandmate was.

One by one I let the stories flow down the screen, except they're really one big story, and in a nutshell it's this:

Claire Bernier and Jeb Perkins were in love and it was 1988 and they were both twenty and they moved in together and had a child, a little girl. Jeb was the drummer in a band called Meal and Claire's brother Steve was in the band, too. In fact, that's how Claire met Jeb. The band spent a lot of time together, and since Claire spent a lot of time with Jeb, she spent a lot of time with the band too.

And little by little Claire began to discover that she was attracted to someone else in the band, Rick Schneider, the bass player, who, along with Steve, wrote most of the band's songs. She couldn't help herself and neither could Rick and soon it was obvious to everybody that she and Rick were in love.

Claire and Jeb broke up and Claire moved in with Rick and

brought her little girl along. Jeb seemed to be taking it okay, and miraculously the band even stayed together. But one night Jeb got drunk, or high, or drunk and high, and he showed up at the door of the place where Rick and Claire were living. They let him in. In fact, they felt sorry for him because he seemed so desperate.

While Claire was getting a round of beer in what passed for the kitchen—the place was an East Village tenement, just one big room with a curtain at one end hiding a sink and a bathtub—Jeb pulled out a gun and aimed it at Rick. Rick was too startled to say anything, but then the curtain swung to the side and Claire stepped out. She screamed and dropped the three bottles of beer she was carrying. They rolled across the floor, which wasn't very level, clanking into each other and spouting out long crests of foam.

Meanwhile, as Jeb pulled the trigger, Claire threw herself against Rick, grabbing his neck and sagging against him as Jeb's first shot hit. As she slipped to the floor, Jeb continued firing, but the realization that he'd hit Claire made his aim erratic. Even though he was no further from Rick than the width of that tiny apartment, none of Rick's wounds were life-threatening.

The stories continue to flow, but there's a break of about a year and the new sequence starts with the headline: "Jury Hears Opening Arguments in East Village Murder Trial."

The trial doesn't last long. Jeb's family hires an expensive lawyer, but all he can argue is that Jeb wasn't completely in his right mind. The fact that he had recently purchased the gun made it hard to claim that he acted on the impulse of a sudden passion. Ultimately—and here's what I was looking for—he was sentenced to thirty years in Ossining State Prison with no possibility of parole for at least twenty.

So the timing works. He could be out. He could have just gotten out. And his first act on getting out could have been to come looking for Rick to finish what he started—and with even more reason than he had in the first place. Because if it hadn't been for Rick, Claire would still be alive.

In kind of a daze, I make my way across the carpet, through the heavy glass door, onto the sidewalk. Outside, the air is heavy and still and my nose prickles with the hint of frost. I check my watch. Plenty of time to stop by the Superette and buy a few groceries.

But staring at the rows of tuna fish I'm seeing kind of a movie in my brain instead, a movie made up of all those news stories strung end to end.

Claire was Steve's sister. If not for Rick, Claire would still be alive, because Jeb wouldn't have come after Rick and shot Claire by mistake if Rick hadn't stolen Claire from him. So that's why Steve said Rick owed him? But maybe he didn't think Rick could ever really pay him back.

I picture Steve's furious face, glaring at me when I tried to ask him about Meal, hear his frantic voice careening out of control, squeezing through a throat rigid with menace. He seemed so laid back at first, but then he exploded. So maybe he exploded at Rick too. But why wait all that time? Did the song showing up in 4Guys4U's repertoire trigger it somehow?

Instead of picking tuna fish off the shelf and carrying it to the cashier, I hurry out the same way I came in. Back at the library I ruffle through the *Voice* again, ignoring the ad for *Othello: The Rock Opera*.

Further back, among the club schedules, I discover that the Delta Dudes are in town this week and are playing tonight at Ye Olde Drinking Hole, first set at 10:30 P.M.

A voice in my head tries to tell me that *Othello* should be getting out about then and that Ye Olde Drinking Hole is in the same neighborhood as PlayTime, but I ignore it.

CHAPTER 15

I'm staring into my closet trying to decide what to wear into the city when the phone rings.

"Caught me just in time," says Walt's voice. "Saturday I head for England with Zachary. But I got your message. And—" He pauses dramatically. "I've got some good news for you."

"Jeb Perkins is still in Sing Sing? Or he got out the day before Rick was killed? I don't know which I'd rather hear." I knew an ex-cop like Walt would be able to find things out.

"Neither. It's even better news than that."

"Okay," I say, lowering myself onto the edge of the big chair. "I'm ready."

"The feds have arrested a suspect in your friend's murder."

"Who?" Faces flash before my eyes: Steve, Ben Darling, even Brenda Honeycut, despite her seeming alibi.

"A guy named Pavel Shashlik. He does the dirty work for the mob that was trying to take over Rick's territory."

"Rick was *not* pirating CDs," I say. And the idea that Walt still doesn't believe me makes me so mad that I jump to my feet. The big chair rocks back on its springs and lets out a squeal. "And that's not good news. It's terrible news. Now they'll think the whole thing is solved and the person that really killed Rick will go free."

"These guys know what they're doing, Maxx. They're not some bozos from a sleepy little town. They're the FBI. And they started off with a pretty good lead. Somebody tipped them off.

Besides, like I told you when we talked at Zachary's gig, it doesn't look like your friend was any angel. Not only are they tracing the first body that showed up in Tallman Park back to Rick, but it looks like he was responsible for a couple of other unsolved murders."

"What?" All of a sudden I feel like I'm in a cocoon that shuts out everything but a kind of urgent misery.

"Tit for tat. And those guys play rough."

"Rick would never kill *anybody*. I told you that." Now I'm just mad. This is too ridiculous to take seriously. Except Walt is taking it seriously. "Would you happen to know who tipped them off?"

"No, but—"

"Wouldn't sending the cops on a wild goose chase be a good way to deflect them from looking where they really should be looking? Wouldn't that be exactly what the person who's really guilty might try to do?"

"The FBI doesn't fall for stunts like that."

"How do you know? They follow up on the tip, work on the case for a while, find a likely guy who's already a crook so nobody's going to feel sorry for him if he gets framed. And it helps if he has a name like Pavel Shashlik. Great, case closed. Back to the doughnuts."

I'm standing by the window now, watching the darkening street. As I watch, the streetlamp on the corner suddenly clicks on, throwing a wide circle of yellow light that spills across the faded asphalt of the street, the cracked sidewalk, and the scruffy brownish-green grass that passes for the apartment building's lawn.

"Okay, okay," he says. "It's not like you've never been right. You were onto something in that business with your friend Jimmy the last time. I couldn't see it. Because—and excuse me if I sound like a sexist, or whatever people call them now—you don't really fit the mold of a lady detective."

"So what about Jeb Perkins?" I say. "Did you find anything out?"

"No, because—"

"I know. You thought the FBI had it all sewed up." I gaze at the street. Are those tiny glints slanting through the streetlamp's light the beginnings of the snow that's been trying all day to come?

"It's really important," I say. "Jeb tried to kill Rick once. And he missed and killed the woman he loved instead. Sitting in Sing Sing for twenty years can't have made him any fonder of Rick."

Walt sighs, a ponderous sigh, but with a laugh at the end to let me know he's joking. "I've only got one more day till the tour starts, and Zachary's been rehearsing us like crazy. But I'll see what I can do."

"We're playing at the Hot Spot tomorrow night," I say. "If you find something out, why don't you come on down?"

Tim Morris is right where the Indian guy at the magazine kiosk said he'd be, at the end of the urine-smelling tunnel that leads from Port Authority to the trains.

He holds me for a second with his eyes, bright behind rimless glasses, an intense look like he halfway knows who I am and why I'm there. But then the same glance gets transferred to the guy standing next to me, a black dude in a purple fur fedora and a long purple leather coat, and I realize it's part of the act. He's working the crowd.

"I'm goin' on my way . . . start my life anew," he sings, then repeats the line.

He's a slight, wiry guy, with a voice that seems too rich and deep to come out of such a slender body. He's doing a Sonny Boy Williamson tune, plucking at his acoustic guitar with his fingers, making high notes chime out like sudden bells against a sturdy bass line picked from the lower strings.

The words are different than the way Sonny Boy Williamson did it, but he still comes around to a mournful refrain, "got no friend anyhow."

The open guitar case at his feet holds an assortment of change and a few bills. As I stand there, a woman darts forward from the small group that surrounds him, tosses a crumpled bill into the guitar case, and joins the crowd streaming through the tunnel toward the trains.

It's the tail end of the rush hour. If you're doing subway gigs, rush hour's got to be a gold mine. He won't stop till the crowd around him dwindles and the stream slows to a trickle.

Meanwhile, I watch and wait. I've finally tracked him down. Now what do I want to know?

A lot of my questions have already been answered. But maybe he's been in touch with Jeb. Maybe he knows if Jeb is out of prison. And what did he talk about with Rick the last time he saw him? Did they talk about the copyright on the song? Is that why he was interested in the 4Guys4U concert? Did they talk about Ben Darling and the financial state of Prowling Rooster Records?

Half an hour later, he winds up a tune about life on the road with a sudden chord that he grabs from the strings and cuts off with a slap.

"Thanks," he murmurs with a genial smile as a few people drop folded bills in his guitar case before moving on down the tunnel. "Whew." He lifts his guitar strap over his head, holds the guitar in his left hand while he massages his neck with the right. He gives me a version of the genial smile.

"You sound good," I say.

"I should. I've been doing this for a long time." He grins. "Never get tired of it though."

"I'm Maxx Maxwell," I say. "I left a note for you—with that magazine and candy guy." I nod toward the kiosk. "Did you get it?"

"Hey!" He grabs my hand with the one that isn't holding the guitar. "I was going to call you. You didn't have to come down here again."

"That's okay. I wanted to meet you."

"Man, Rick was my oldest friend. It's a shame what happened." He shakes his head, his face suddenly mournful, then squeezes my hand. "It's great to meet you. He told me all about you. How'd you find me?"

I tell him about talking to Rick's neighbor, Kate, but not about the Jesus flyer. Let him figure I'd assume anybody singing in the subway would be at the Times Square station.

"That treehouse is a cool place," he says. "I even wrote a song about it once."

"Have you been in touch with any of the other guys from Meal since you've been back in the States?"

"Steve, of course. 'Cause he was living right up there. Rick'd do anything for his friends. But I guess you noticed that."

"What about Jeb Perkins?"

His eyes tighten for a second behind the glasses. "You know about all of that?" he says. "Rick doesn't usually talk about it."

"I found out anyway," I say. "Is Jeb still in prison?"

"Couldn't tell you. Why?"

"He tried to kill Rick once. Maybe he came back to finish the job."

"Is that what the cops think?"

"No." I tell him what the cops think, the mob and all. It's hard to read the expression on his face as I talk.

"I don't think Rick would do a thing like that," he says at last. "Something that ripped off musicians." He glances at the money in the guitar case. "But what do I know? I was away a long time and people change. I always thought he was a good guy though—and a good friend. Not like in the song."

"You rewrote the song," I say.

"Yeah. I've been thinking a lot about friendship lately." Without slipping the guitar strap back over his head, he bends over, balances the guitar on his knee, and picks out the same rhythm pattern he was using when he did the Sonny Boy Williamson song.

"So have I," I say, hearing Sandy's voice telling me he wants to be my friend.

But I pull myself back to the present. "When did you last see Rick?"

He shrugs. "Couple days before he died, I guess."

"Up at his place?"

"Sure. Why?"

"Just curious. What did he talk about?"

"Stuff," he says. "We were still getting reacquainted, you know. We'd been apart for twenty years."

"Did Steve and Rick write all the Meal songs?"

"Not really," he says. "We all tossed in the occasional idea, for lyrics mostly. But Rick was the mastermind that created Meal, so he gave them the Meal vibe. And Steve always had kind of a cool melodic sense."

"But you write songs now."

"I wasn't that interested in it back then. I thought I was a guitar hero. Speaking of which, I guess I'd better get back to work." He slings the guitar strap over his head again.

"Where else do you play?" I ask.

"Only here so far," he says with a little laugh. "This is a tough town to make it in. Tougher than I thought it would be." He plucks a couple of strings, listens intently, and twists a tuning peg. "Got any suggestions?"

"My band's been playing at the Hot Spot, down on Bleecker

Street. The owner digs the blues. We'll be there tomorrow night."

"I'll try to show up. Maybe you'll put in a word for me." He stoops and gathers up the change in the guitar case, leaves the bills. "I could use a gig that pays better than this."

I'm hurrying along Forty-Second, not because I'm about to be late for anything, but because it's so cold. As I'm glancing here and there, catching glimpses of my scurrying, bundled-up figure in the shop windows, I nearly run into a huge sign set up on the sidewalk. I take a step backward to catch my balance and my eyes land on the word "Othello," spelled out in angular letters shaded to look three-dimensional, like a graffiti artist tagged the sign while nobody was looking. I glance at the facade of what I otherwise would have taken for an anonymous storefront stuck between a falafel place and a souvenir shop. Sure enough, the words "PlayTime" are spelled out over the doorway.

I feel a little shiver and look around nervously, half expecting to see Sandy strolling along with his guitar slung over his shoulder. But all I see is a crowd of expectant theater-goers filing through the door.

I stick my nose up against the plate-glass window. In what passes for the lobby, a restless line of people is making its way toward where a thin guy in a black T-shirt is standing behind a makeshift counter. One by one, people make it to the head of the line, talk to the guy for a minute, turn away looking disappointed, and head for the sidewalk again.

I push the cuff of my jacket aside to check my watch. It's not even eight o'clock yet. What am I going to do till the Delta Dudes hit the stage at Ye Olde Drinking Hole? Sit in the bar by myself and drink beer? Walk the streets till I'm totally frozen? My cheeks are already numb.

What harm would there be, really? I won't hang around afterward. I'll just watch the show, if I can get in. Chances are

Sandy didn't even leave the comps. Why would he, when I said I didn't want to come? But standing in the lobby for a while will give me a chance to get warm. And I'm a little bit curious about whether he came through with the tickets.

The guy behind the counter is all ready to tell me the same thing he's been telling everybody else, that there are no tickets. So when I say, "Somebody left comps for me," he has to close his mouth and think for a minute before he opens it again to ask, almost respectfully, "What's your name?"

When he slips the white envelope into my hand and says, "Enjoy the show," I flash back to that feeling I always used to have when I was with Sandy—like he could manage everything that needed to be managed. I blink and try to shake it off.

But I glance at the envelope and another feeling sweeps over me, a worse feeling. The handwriting that spells out my name has to be Sandy's. Nobody else writes like that, careful printing mixed with shapeless scrawls. I check inside. Sure enough, there are two tickets. So he planned on me bringing someone. That means he didn't expect me to get together with him afterward. And if I stay for the show, he won't even know I'm here till it's all over and he finds out I picked up the comps. And by then I'll be gone.

I give one of the tickets to another guy in a black T-shirt. He tears it in half and moves aside to let me step into a room where rows of folding chairs curve around an open space furnished with a few platforms.

At the edge of the open space is a drum kit and a few more folding chairs. Each chair has a music stand in front of it and an amp behind it. A golden-brown electric guitar is leaning against one of the amps, a sunburst Strat. It's Sandy's guitar.

Most of the seats are full. I pull my half ticket out of my pocket then glance around. Do the chairs have numbers on them or what? A young woman in a droopy black dress, like a long slip, appears at my elbow. Her "May I show you to your seat?" is so carefully articulated she sounds like she's auditioning for something. She checks my ticket and leads me to the end of a row about halfway between the stage and the back of the theater, points at two empty seats about ten sets of knees away, leaves me with a program and a smile.

I wade past the knees and settle into one of the seats. When I realize I'm staring at Sandy's guitar and smoothing my hair while my heart bounces around behind my ribs, I turn my eyes up to the ceiling and lock my hands together in my lap. Now I have nothing to do but pick at the itchy scab on the scratch I got when I went to look at where that jogger and his dog found Rick's body.

All around me people are talking excitedly, but the room is so bare that the sound is diffuse, like the light, everywhere and nowhere. Behind me though, a couple of male voices catch my attention.

"Curious to hear this new guy," one of them is saying as I tune in.

"What do you know about him?"

"He's the one Dick wants, if we can get him. Living down in Nashville now."

Nashville? Could they be talking about Sandy?

"Can he get away long enough for a Broadway run?"

"I understand he used to live up here. Maybe he wants to come back."

"What's his name?"

I close my eyes, and my heart stops bouncing for a minute so I can hear the answer.

"Sandy Wilkins."

I turn to get a look at them, hip rich guys in cashmere and Rolexes.

The conversation shifts to something one of their wives has

planned for the weekend, and I'm calming down when back in the shadows behind the stage, a door opens. A guy in a torn T-shirt steps out and makes his way matter-of-factly toward the drum kit as lights come up at the front of the stage. Another guy follows him, and another guy, and the last guy is Sandy. He steps through the door with that easy grace he's always had, dips his shoulder to glance back and flash a quick lopsided smile at somebody hidden by the door, makes his way to the chair that's closest to the sunburst Strat. Suddenly, I feel like I'm going to faint.

He looks the same, with his streaky dark-blond hair and the half-smile that says, everybody's watching me so I might as well enjoy it. He's wearing a pale, collarless shirt that's probably linen. He settles into the chair, swings the guitar up onto his lap like he's done it a million times, and flips the switch on the amp.

The drummer has already hitched himself onto his stool. Now he gives an experimental tap on the snare and says, as if to nobody in particular, "Here's where the band jams while the actors come out. Somebody call one."

Sandy looks at the other two guys with a question on his face, but he doesn't wait for an answer before he says, "Purple Haze" and jumps right into it. An odd, hostile look passes over the face of the other guitar player, but I don't know what it means.

So as the house lights go down, Sandy's guitar fills the theater. Beyond the bright spot that's the band, shadowy figures move onto the platforms. Brightness spreads over the whole stage, and Othello is standing there, a black guy in dreadlocks and a leather vest, and nobody except me is still staring at the musicians anymore.

I only know it's Othello because right away a couple of other guys, black like Othello and dressed in leather too, are rapping at him, calling him Othello and getting on him about demoting somebody in his gang, somebody named Iago, and telling him that Iago really wants Cassio's job. And Sandy is staring at the chart on his music stand and churning out a groove that sounds like it came off a record jerking under the fingers of a D.J.

Then a white guy comes in, an older white guy wearing a rumpled suit and a tie, and it seems he's some kind of sociologist and Othello has just married his daughter, Desdemona. He accuses Othello of turning her onto drugs in order to steal her affections. But Othello says she fell in love with him while she was helping her dad with his research, tape-recording Othello while he talked about his life and all his exploits.

Then Desdemona is there too, blond and dressed in white—white bell-bottoms and a little midriff-baring top. She and Othello are singing a duet like a soul song from the fifties. They're balanced at the edge of the top platform. The lights make her hair blonder, and they shimmy over his dark, emotion-creased forehead, over his dark bare chest, over his dark arms with their swelling muscles.

The singing stops, but the music goes on. A guitar takes the place of voices. First comes a deep throb, then a run of notes that trails off into a moan. Sandy's fingers slide up the fretboard, grab a string, push it up, and hold on. The sound soars into the air above him, hangs there for a second, fades away.

All of a sudden, he realizes I'm there. His hand falters on the fretboard, and a strangled yelp comes out of the amp, not on purpose. I'm probably the only person in the theater who notices though. Everybody else probably thinks it's supposed to be that way. In fact, behind me, one of the rich-guy voices says, "Wow. Cool sound."

Every once in a while, when there's a break in the playing, Sandy looks up from his music stand. He glances here and there like he's checking out the audience in a general way, then his gaze comes to rest on me. I can't tell at that distance if we're making eye contact, if he knows I'm looking back at him. But sometimes when the music starts up again, his eyes jerk back to the chart like he hasn't been paying attention to what's happening. When that happens, the other guitar player gives him a sinister scowl.

The second half of the show starts with a scene where Iago gets Cassio drunk, passing him a bottle of cognac and teasing him when he doesn't want more than a sip. Finally, though, he *is* drunk and there's a big scene where he kills somebody and Othello throws him out of the gang while Iago stands around looking happy.

Next there's a big confrontation between Othello and Desdemona, about whether she was getting it on with Cassio the whole time and that's why she's upset that Cassio's in trouble. Othello is singing and Sandy's playing his heart out, and the other guitar player is frowning so hard he looks like his face is frozen.

Now Othello's standing over Desdemona with a knife in one hand and a pillow in the other. She's sleeping, and there's a half-empty bottle of cognac on the floor beside her. He's singing about why he's going to kill her. As he sings, he raises his arms like he's some kind of a priest, then the drummer lets fly at the crash cymbal, and after the reverberations stop, there's complete silence.

A tiny, careful embroidery of notes comes out of Sandy's amp, as soft as if he's playing an acoustic guitar. The people around me lean forward. Othello's voice joins the guitar, but just as soft. He's hanging over Desdemona with the knife in his hand, holding it away from him at an awkward angle, and, with the other hand, pushing the pillow down over her face.

When the song ends, the applause seems to startle him. But suddenly he bends lower over Desdemona, moves the pillow away and kisses her. Turning his head away like he can't watch, he puts the pillow back over her face and throws himself on top of it. Her feet twitch for a minute and then go still.

Sandy's half-sitting and half-standing, forcing notes from his guitar that soar like a desperate voice. It's hard to know who to watch, because now Othello's waving the knife in the air. With a bellow that cuts through even Sandy's playing, he clasps both hands around the knife hilt and pulls the knife toward him with a look on his dark face like he's greeting a lover.

Then he collapses on Desdemona. The spill of light across the stage shrinks till all that's bright is the two bodies, a black one and a white one, like a two-tone cross dividing the top platform into quarters. Then the theater goes dark.

Everybody is on their feet cheering before the lights come back up. The cast is drifting onstage one by one, joining hands, smiling and wiping their foreheads, and Othello and Desdemona are alive again.

While the cheering is still at its peak, Othello gestures toward the band and all the actors look in that direction and start clapping too. The drummer points at Sandy and winks at the audience while the other guitar player frowns. Finally, Sandy stands up like he doesn't really want to, but there's a big surge of cheering when he does it. He gives the lopsided half-smile, bows, and sits back down. He looks hot and tired and relieved.

Finally, the audience calms down and the actors leave the stage and the house lights come up. It takes me a few minutes to work my way out to the aisle because the people sitting at the end of my row recognize some of their friends in the seats behind them. I'm edging my way past the last couple of chairs when I hear Sandy's voice call, "Hey, Maxx! Wait!" My heart bounces once, and my legs start to quiver.

CHAPTER 16

He's standing on the stage, holding his guitar by the neck with a loop of cable in his other hand. The bass player is there too, shaking hands with a thin woman draped in a dress that's just panels of dark gauze.

I wave and smile, like I'm a friend, a friend in a hurry to get somewhere, not like I'm trying to escape before the quivering in my legs makes it impossible to move.

"Maxx. Don't leave." Now he's heading up the aisle toward me, still carrying the guitar, and with the cable dragging along after him. The people standing near me step back, but linger around to watch, like they're fascinated by him.

"You got here." He's reached me now. Up close he looks tired. Patches of darkness show under his eyes, and his lips are dry, like he's been biting them. The linen shirt is almost translucent with sweat. "You came alone, didn't you?" He has the sincere look in his eyes, and the tiny crease between his eyebrows that sometimes goes with it.

"I have to be somewhere," I say.

He nods. "Hang on while I grab my gig bag." He points at the stage and starts backing down the aisle.

"I didn't mean I have to be somewhere with you," I whisper to myself. But all of a sudden, my body feels hollow. Without thinking about what I'm doing, I follow him to the stage and sink into one of the chairs the band used.

"Are you okay?" He bends toward me. His eyes look even

179

more sincere.

I nod. "I really can't stay. I have to be somewhere." I hardly know what I'm saying. I'm staring at the shirt, the way it's so damp it kind of clings to his body. And I'm noticing how the hand that still holds the loop of cable is trembling.

"I have to grab my gig bag." He repeats the words. "I'll buy you dinner. Are you hungry? I'm starved."

"Sort of. But I've got money. Besides, I have to be somewhere."

He smiles now. "Hey, I can afford it. I worked tonight."

Before I can say anything else, he's gone. I sit there in a daze. It could be two minutes or two hours. All I can hear is roaring, but it's coming from inside my own head. When he comes back in a leather jacket, smiling and with his gig bag over his shoulder, I follow him out of the theater and into the freezing night.

As we head along the sidewalk, we pass a guy bundled in a heavy leather coat and with a heavy wool cap pulled down to his eyebrows. He's lingering near the "Othello" sign, talking to a couple of women.

"Hey," Sandy says, pausing in front of him. "Good job tonight." The guy gives him a savage stare and turns away.

"What was that all about?" I ask when we're far enough away that the guy won't hear me.

"Poor bastard," Sandy says with a shake of his head. "That's the other guitar player from the show. He hates my guts."

"Why?"

"I took over the part he thought he'd be doing. Jealous, I guess. And to make matters worse, the musical director's an old friend of his."

We're at the corner now, waiting for the light to change, while traffic hurtles past us.

"Where to?" Sandy says. "You said you have to be some-where."

"Ye Olde Drinking Hole. It's about six blocks from here. I need to talk to somebody that's playing there tonight."

"Band business? Nathan said you've got your own band now."

"Nathan is a busybody. And you really don't need to come with me."

"Does this place have food?"

"I think so."

The light changes and Sandy grabs my arm. "Let's get mov-ing before we freeze. I could go for a burger or two."

I feel a little bit better now, calmer, though I can't help glancing up at Sandy as we hurry across the street: the profile like something on a Greek statue, except with a twist to the mouth that brings it to life. But he's behaving himself, acting like we're just friends. Maybe he's right. Maybe we *can* be friends. And I'm not so distracted by him that I've forgotten why I'm determined to talk to the Delta Dudes.

Steve's face rises before me, red with fury, mouth agape, as he refuses to answer my questions about Meal and yells at me to disappear. But another image hovers behind that one: Steve when he's not yelling, a Steve whose wild hair and shaggy beard seem intended to compensate for the fact that with tidy hair and clean shaven he'd look as gentle and dreamy as his beauti-ful dead sister.

So, what if the Delta Dudes tell me Steve had nothing at all to do with their Worcester gig? That will mean he could have been in Nyack the night Rick was killed, and that for some reason he thought it was important to fake an alibi.

The Delta Dudes are in mid-song when we show up, a funked-up version of "Mustang Sally," and the place is so

Peggy Ehrhart

crowded we end up on a balcony that runs along the side of the club.

Sandy takes a deep swallow of beer and leans back against a paneled wall decorated with publicity photos of aspiring actors and actresses, decades of them, judging by the variety of hairstyles.

"Man, am I glad that's over," he says. "That was the hardest score I've ever learned. And that crazy guitar player." He tips the bottle to his lips again. "Grow up, man. It's not personal."

"Hey, you know what?" I say. "It's like *Othello.*"

"That's the whole point," Sandy says with a laugh. "Updated, you know. What'd you think of Othello's dreads?"

"No, I mean that guy and you. It's like you're Cassio and he's Iago. You got the job he wanted. He thought his friend would come through for him, but it didn't happen. And now he's jealous—jealous and really hurt."

Sandy raises his eyebrows and gives me a teasing look. "Deep. You're turning into an intellectual."

"My next door neighbor reads Shakespeare for fun."

The burgers arrive and by the time we're mopping up the last trails of catsup with the last shreds of fries, I hear a voice down below say, "We gotta take a short break now, because the drummer needs a beer. But before we go, I'd like to introduce the band."

By the time I make it down from the balcony, the Delta Dudes are about ready to head for the bar. The guitar player is in the act of leaning his guitar up against his amp when I ask him about Steve and the Worcester gig.

"Checkin' up, huh?" The hand holding the guitar stops in mid-gesture. "Know that tune?" Now the guitar is balanced against his thigh and he's strumming it unplugged and singing off key: " 'Checkin' up on my baby . . .' " He's a chubby guy with a baby face and shaggy blond hair, the rawhide vest he's tugged over his flannel shirt his only gesture toward blues couture.

He looks me up and down, nods in approval, and winks. "Stevie's taste is improving," he says.

"Well, was he in Worcester when you guys played there?"

"I don't know if I should go along with this," he says with another wink and a grin. "Us guys have to stick together." He straightens up and lets the guitar rest against the amp.

"I'm not his girlfriend," I say. "That's not why I'm asking."

"You're sure?"

"Positive," I say.

"Then I've got an idea . . ." He pauses and gives me another grin. "Are you free tomorrow?"

"Oh, *please*." He's so goofy I can't help laughing.

We're joined by a guy I recognize as the Delta Dudes' bass player, blond too, but tall and rangy, with an amused twinkle in his eyes. "I can't believe it, dude," he says to the guitar player. "You've actually got a fan?"

"This is Maxx," the guitar player says. "And here's something else you won't believe. This gorgeous woman is actually afraid that our friend Stevie B. is stepping out on her. She's checkin' up." He nudges the bass player. "Come on, sing it with me: 'Checkin' up on my baby—' "

"I told you that's not why I'm asking," I say, laughing again.

"He's got the big bucks now though," the bass player says, pretending to be serious. "Maybe he's got more chicks than he can handle."

"That's right," the guitar player says, slapping his forehead. "I forgot that our little Stevie is rich."

"Big bucks?" I say. "You mean his share from that song?"

"Not just his share," the guitar player says. He and the bass

183

player look at each other and let their eyes get wide in mock alarm.

"He's holding out on her," they say in unison.

"He ended up with more than his share?" I say. "How? Why? What happened?"

They let their faces get serious.

"You know about Rick, I guess," the guitar player says. I nod.

The bass player cuts in: "Well, Rick and Stevie go back a long, long way."

Now it's the guitar player again: "And Rick always felt he owed Stevie something . . . because . . . well, because . . ."

"I know about Claire," I say.

"So when that money started coming in from 'Not Something Pretty,' Rick signed it all over to Steve."

"Steve told you that?" I say, prodded by a suspicious voice in my head. The voice has pointed out that if Steve killed Rick to get money, he could make up any story he wanted to explain where the money came from.

"No, Rick told me," the guitar player says. "He was worried about Steve, you know. Worried that if people didn't look out for him he wouldn't survive."

"And you guys look out for him, too," I say.

They shrug. "We're not saints," the bass player says, "but we try. We toss him a job once in a while, let him feel like he's still somebody."

"So how about it then? The Worcester gig? Was he roadying for you?" They nod. "And he was with you all weekend?"

"We drove up on Friday," the bass player says. "Drove back on Monday."

"He was sleeping in the back seat the whole way, zonked out on weed," the guitar player adds.

184

"What a jerk." The bass player laughs.

"Totally." The guitar player joins him.

"Get what you needed?" Sandy asks as I lower myself into my chair.

"Pretty much."

"What are you up to?"

"Nothing."

"I don't believe you." He narrows his eyes and studies me but doesn't say anything else for a couple of minutes. Then he adds, "Did you drive over to the city?" I nod. "I dig this band and I hate to walk out on them," he says, "but I'm about beat. Would it be any trouble for you to give me a ride to my hotel?"

"Where're you staying?"

He tells me. "I've got a pretty nice room," he adds, looking toward where the band members are wandering off the stage. Then, quickly and looking back at me, "It wouldn't have to be just a ride."

"We're *friends* now, nothing more. Remember?"

"Do I have to?" He smiles, but it's the everyone's-looking-at-me smile this time and it's almost a smirk.

"You're not as irresistible as you think," I say. "I'll drop you at the corner." I'm on my feet before I planned to be, then I'm striding down the stairs toward the door.

We walk to my car as if we've made a pact of silence. Once he's in the car, though, with his gig bag stowed in the back seat, he turns to me and says, "I know you think I'm the cockiest son-of-a-bitch on earth. But I'm not. And I really need you to come back. I didn't know that what I had with you went so far beyond what I could get—" His voice trails off. "That's not the right word. It makes me sound like what you think I am. Please give me another chance." He rubs his face. "Man, I worked so hard on that show."

185

"I found somebody else, remember? Somebody I really cared about."

I start the car without saying any more. Then I have to concentrate on my driving while I figure out how to get headed east. By the time I know where I'm going, one of those silences has fallen that can't be ended except by superhuman conversational efforts—or by reverting to the topic that brought it on in the first place. I'm not feeling very superhuman, so I let the silence stretch out.

"Here's your stop," I say and look over at Sandy. He's asleep, with a little frown locked between his eyebrows. "We're there," I say, and touch his shoulder.

"Huh." His eyes open and he looks startled. "What's going on?"

"Here's your corner."

He sighs and closes his eyes. "I haven't been sleeping so good," he says. "The show, and I didn't know if I'd see you . . ." His voice trails off, and he's asleep again.

A bus is bearing down on me from behind with an alarming pneumatic whoosh. I can't sit here any longer because I'm in a bus zone. I pull back out into traffic but I can't make the next turn because it's one way the wrong way. A cab veers toward me as I try to change lanes and I almost sideswipe him before I get my foot on the brake. Something's happening at the next corner that's got the intersection clogged with honking cars and a fire truck.

A lot of other people are trying to head east, too, so a glance down the next street where a right turn is possible makes it look like I'll be sitting in traffic for an hour if I chance it. And I've already used up about all of my New York City driving mojo for the night. I look over at Sandy, who's now sound asleep, sigh, and head for the George Washington Bridge.

It's a long drive back. Sitting there in the dark, following a stream of taillights up the West Side Highway toward where the bridge hangs over the river in a graceful glittering swoop, I think about lots of things. One of the things I think about is *Othello*. And friends, and how people depend on them.

He sleeps all the way back to New Jersey. I pull into the parking lot behind my building and look over at him. A splash of light from the big light I've parked under pales and flattens his face like the light from a spotlight, deglamorizing him, like an up-close spotlight does. The corners of his mouth are tugged down, and faint acne scars sprinkle his cheeks and forehead.

More of the light slides down the back of my building, making the yellow-brown bricks shimmer like it was noon. But the street is quiet and still and all the windows are dark in the houses. It's late.

"Hey, Sandy. We're there." I touch his shoulder.

He opens his eyes. "Maxx? Where am I?" He seems puzzled.

"You fell asleep. So we're in New Jersey. Can you move?" He closes his eyes.

"I haven't slept in two weeks." His eyes stay closed, but his right hand slips into the opening of my jacket and lands on my breast. "Do you still wear that fancy bra?" he murmurs.

I pull the hand out and give it back to him. "That's all over now," I say. "I brought you back here because you were asleep and there was a bus bearing down on me and I couldn't find any place to turn right."

He nods. "Okay. I'll behave."

I watch while he opens his door, shifts his feet onto the ground, and slowly pulls himself upright, holding onto the car door. Once he's standing, he lets go and reels for a minute almost like he's drunk.

He steadies himself and turns to fumble with the back door. "My guitar's back here," he says.

I try my door and for some reason the lock lets me unlock it. Then I step out onto the asphalt.

From the street comes a muffled pop. A fraction of a second later, something strikes my car with a sharp ping.

"Sandy! Get down!" I squeeze the words out as I duck behind the car door, hug my knees, and try to make myself as small as possible. I'm not breathing, but the smell of car exhaust is in my nostrils anyway.

"What the hell is going on?" Sandy's voice seems to come from right above me. I peek up to see that he's thrown himself back into the car and wormed his way across the seat.

"Wait and don't talk," I say. "The last time the person only had six bullets. And whoever it is doesn't seem to be a very good shot."

"The last time? I'm sorry to be so repetitious, but what the hell is going on?"

"Shhh."

Pop! Ping! The ping is close, but not too close—maybe three or four cars away.

"That's two," I whisper.

"I'm not going to lie here cowering," Sandy says. "I'm going to call the cops."

"Do it," I say. "By all means." I hear another pop. "That one missed," I say. "You can tell because there was no ping."

"Shit," Sandy says in a small voice. "My cell phone's in my gig bag."

"Yeah?"

"My gig bag is on the back seat."

"By the time you reach it, whoever's doing this will be done." I'm still crouched in the tiniest ball I can make myself into, clutching my knees and shivering.

"What if they learned how to reload by now?" Sandy says. I hear scuffling as he creeps back across the seat.

"What are you doing?"

"Going after my cell phone. Then I'm going to make a run for the edge of the parking lot and disappear around the side of your building."

"Don't do that. You'll be right in the light."

I hear another *pop-ping,* close enough to make me shut my eyes and duck, then another in quick succession.

"He knows we're in this car and he's coming closer," Sandy whispers. "I'm not going to lie here and let somebody I don't even know assassinate me. I suggest you come with me."

A hand touches the top of my head, makes its way down my neck, and fastens itself around my upper arm. Stifling the impulse to scream, I say, "Sandy? Is that you?"

"Come on," he says, tugging on my arm. "Pull yourself back into the car. The shots are coming from your direction."

"It's safer if we hold still. He's only got six shots."

"Two are left." I hear more scuffling. A zipper slides open with a metallic purr. "Got it," Sandy's voice says. Then a second later, almost desperately, "Fuck this thing. The battery's dead."

From quite close, closer than before, comes a boom that sets up booming echoes all around. Right above me, I hear a sharp crack that makes my head jerk upright. A shower of something like pebbles lands on me. Chilly pebbles, I realize, as some of them trickle down my neck.

"That was your car window," Sandy's voice says. "Don't do anything. I'm going for help."

For a whole minute, maybe more, things are as silent as a winter night can be. I picture Sandy, gliding among the cars between my car and the edge of the parking lot where the entrance to the shadowy alley that runs along the side of my building yawns. I picture him dashing from the cover of the last car, frantic to reach the alley's darkness as the parking lot's spotlights pick out his dark form against the gleaming bricks of the building's back wall.

I hear a pop, but it's coming from a different direction this time, more like behind my car than from the street. The ping, if there is one, is mixed in with a sharp clang and a heavy metallic clunk. A few seconds later I hear sounds from the direction of the alley, sounds that resemble a manic drummer attacking every drum in his drum kit at once and following up with a grand finale on the cymbals.

At the end there's a startled yelp.

I close my eyes and let my head sag toward the edge of the car seat, feeling the cold slickness of the old vinyl against my cheek.

That was the sixth shot. If only Sandy could have been patient. But guys can't sit and wait for things to end. They have to get out there and do something, even if it means getting themselves shot.

Still stooping, I feel for the flashlight I keep in the saggy pouch fixed onto the inside of the car door. I creep around the edge of the door and lower myself into a crawling position. In my mind, I see Sandy splayed against the trash cans that line the alley, a neat bullet hole drilled through the leather of his jacket and, between the leather and his skin, also drilled with a neat bullet hole, a dark red circle forming in the white linen of his shirt.

I crawl between the front of my car and the back of a Mazda, between an old Honda and a not so old Jeep, between the tidy gray Toyota I recognize as Leon's and the fancy BMW that belongs to Hiram's snotty girlfriend. I'm still shivering, partly from the cold, partly from other things.

There's no more shooting now. Is it my imagination, or did a car engine come alive somewhere down the street? Maybe it's about to carry the shooter and his gun away. Who else would be out now? It's late for normal traffic in this neighborhood.

I pull myself partly erect and peer over the roof of Leon's car toward where I thought I heard the sound of an engine. A nondescript car is pulling away from the curb in front of one of the aluminum siding houses, gaining speed with a squeal of tires and quickly turning the corner. No chance to make out the license number.

I stay on my feet and turn toward the entrance to the alley, afraid of what I'll find as I turn the corner.

"Sandy?" I call in a voice that's half-whisper, half-lament.

No answer. I take a few more steps. "Sandy? It's okay now. The person is gone." I'm talking to him because it seems like if I don't it'll be like I'm sure he can't answer.

I stop at the edge where the building's shadow starts. I bend my head to peer around the corner, click the flashlight on with my thumb and let its beam cautiously creep down the alley, dancing here and there over asphalt that still hosts in its ragged cracks spikes of green too sturdy to be killed by the November weather.

Here's Sandy's foot. The flashlight beam picks out the leather of his elegant boot, works its way up to the crisp denim of his jeans, washed enough times to be a soft, rich blue.

CHAPTER 17

"Maxx?" a groggy voice murmurs.

I let the light dance to his face, spilling over onto the garbage bag that his head is resting against.

"Are you in pain? Where did he hit you?"

"Why didn't you tell me this alley was full of trash?" he says.

"Are you bleeding?" I step toward him and kneel on the chilly asphalt. "Where does it hurt?"

He pulls himself to a sitting position and lets himself slump against an overturned garbage can. "I wrenched the shit out of my back when I fell," he says with a groan. "Other than that, I think I'm okay." He flexes one leg, and then the other, lifts his arms experimentally.

"When I heard that last shot and then you screamed, I thought he'd hit you," I say.

"No such luck." He leans on the garbage can and starts to pull himself erect, but it rolls a few feet. He loses his balance and lands on the asphalt. "Shit," he says with another groan. "Will you pull me up, Maxx?"

A few minutes later, we're stepping into my apartment. "I guess I'm not sleepy anymore," Sandy says, blinking in the light from the lamp I've switched on. "That's one thing you can say for getting shot at. It wakes a person up." He glances around, murmurs, "Funky. I dig the wallpaper." His eyes come to rest on Red's cage. "What's with the chicken?" he says.

As if in answer, Red clucks a few times.

"It's a rooster, and I'm trying to find it a home," I say.

"Doesn't it crow?"

"I put the bedspread over it when I go to bed."

His gaze wanders further and he catches sight of the phone. "Let's get the cops over here, and while they're on their way, you can tell me why somebody's been following you around with a gun."

A car engine roars in the street below, quiets abruptly as tires squeal on the pavement. A sharp crash pulls our eyes to the window. Something hurtles through the glass, scuds across the floor, and lands near the base of the big chair. Long cracks appear in the window pane, running outward from a jagged hole in the center like the rays on a kid's drawing of the sun. As we stare, a triangle of glass formed by two of them tilts outward and falls to the floor, breaking up into several smaller triangles.

The thing resting near the big chair is a rock with a piece of paper tied around it.

"Don't touch it," I shout as Sandy bends to pick the rock up. "It might have fingerprints."

"I don't think I can get down that far anyway," he says, rubbing his hip. "I really messed myself up when I took that fall into the garbage."

He straightens up and reaches for the phone. "What's the address here?" he says.

I tell him then hurry to the kitchen to grab my rubber gloves.

As Sandy tells the 9-1-1 operator what's going on, I pull on the rubber gloves and pick up the paper-wrapped rock.

"Where'd you learn that?" Sandy says curiously.

"Learn what?"

"The rubber glove bit? What on earth have you been up to since you moved to Hackensack?"

"I didn't learn it anywhere," I say. "It seems like common

193

sense." I carry the rock out to the kitchen and switch on the light over the kitchen table. Easing the string off, I unpeel the paper, unfold it, and smooth it out. It's a sheet of notebook paper that's been folded crosswise over and over again so that, unfolded, it resembles a kid's version of an accordion. Groaning, Sandy massages his hip and lowers himself into a chair.

The writer of the note didn't actually need a whole sheet of notebook paper because the note is composed of only a few words, printed with a not very sharp pencil.

"Your mistake was getting mixed up with Rick Schneider," the note reads. "You will pay." This last part is underlined three times.

"Who's Rick Schneider?" Sandy says.

"He's that guy I told you about. I loved him, but he's dead."

"And that's what all this is about?"

I shrug. "You're looking right at the note."

"How'd you meet him? Seems like he hung out with some dangerous people."

"It started when I decided that if my band had a CD we could get better gigs."

We're interrupted by a buzz that signals somebody's at the downstairs door. "Cops," I say, dashing for the button to click the door open.

Sandy follows me out of the kitchen. "Don't buzz back," he says. "Maybe it's not the cops. I'll go down."

But it is the cops, a lady cop this time.

I hear her before I see her. I'm standing in the doorway of my apartment and from the stairwell comes the sound of a nasal voice whose cadence is more Brooklyn than Hackensack.

"So," the voice is saying, "I tell them, 'What is this? Why is it always me for the petty stuff? You guys can get off your butts once in a while too.' But the vandalism, the graffiti, the urinating in public—who has to go out? Me. The only woman in the department. And every time we get one of those leaf day complaints, who gets nominated to go door to door and tell people not to rake their leaves into the street until after five P.M. the day before pickup? That's right. Me. 'What is this?' I tell my so-called colleagues. 'Some kind of prejudice? Why don't I get to respond to the real calls?' "

Sandy's head pops into view in the doorway at the end of the hall, and the rest of him appears as he climbs the remaining steps. When he catches sight of me, he gives me a look of mock distress and shakes his head.

Following him out of the stairwell is a sturdy woman with short, dyed-red hair. She strides toward me with both hands on her hips, swaggering ever so slightly. Like sausage casings, her shiny dark blue trousers skim her hefty thighs without a crease or a wrinkle.

"Rock through the window, huh?" she says as she gets closer. "Does the super know? He's not gonna be happy."

"More than a rock through the window," I say. "It's a rock with a threatening note attached. And somebody shot at us down in the parking lot, but that happened last week too and you guys never did anything about it."

I step aside to let her in the door. Sandy follows, still shaking his head.

"Shot at you, huh?" she says, looking around the room. "Backup's on its way about that, but you're sure it wasn't a car backfiring?" Her eyes pause when they reach Red's cage. "Super know you've got a chicken in here?"

"It's a rooster, and he's leaving soon," I say. "If it was a car backfiring, it backfired six times in a row, and I could hear bullets hitting things, and one of them broke my car window. And a friend of mine who lived up in Nyack was murdered a couple of weeks ago. I think the same person who did that is trying to kill me too."

"Nyack is a long ways from here," she says. "Let's see this rock."

"It's in the kitchen."

She takes a few steps, but stops and rubs her hands together. "Brrr," she says. "It's cold in here. You got something you can put over that window to keep the draft out? You're gonna freeze your pipes—then you'll really have a mess."

"Where's the super hang out?" Sandy says. "He should be able to patch it up till the glass can be replaced."

"It's two in the morning," I say. "I don't want to bother the poor guy now."

"Go ahead," the lady cop says, giving Sandy a little shove toward the door. "That's what they're paid for."

"He's in the basement," I call as Sandy disappears into the hall. "Across from the furnace room."

"That your boyfriend?" she says. "Quite the hunk." She nudges me with her elbow and winks.

"He's just a friend," I say.

In the kitchen, she contemplates the rock and the note, hands planted on her sturdy hips. "So who's Rick Schneider?" she asks.

"He's the guy that was murdered."

"Nyack police working on this?"

"Park Police and FBI. A jogger found his body in Green Forest Park."

"Any suspects?"

"They think the mob did it."

She looks at me appraisingly. "Was your friend involved with the mob?"

"They think he was pirating CDs, but he wasn't."

"Last I knew, throwing rocks with notes attached through people's windows wasn't really the mob's style," she says.

"What's with the rubber gloves, anyway?"

"I didn't want to mess up any fingerprints that might be on it."

"Rocks don't take fingerprints too well."

We're interrupted by the click of the door opening and then by other sounds.

"Is that a chicken?" the super says, as sirens screech up the street then whine down into silence below.

An hour later we're back from the police station, where we gave statements in a repeat of the scene that happened the last time, but with Sandy standing in for Hiram and his girlfriend. The cops have the rock and the note. The crime-scene tape is up again and, illuminated by searchlights, detectives are searching among the remains of the season's dead leaves for bullets or whatever it is they look for.

While we were gone, the super covered the window with several layers of cardboard and duct tape and returned to his hideout in the basement.

I take two beers out of the refrigerator.

When I come back with the beer, Sandy's still standing in the middle of the floor.

"Go ahead," I say, handing him a beer and nodding toward the chair. "Have a seat."

He looks around the room. "There's only one chair," he says.

"There's only one of me. I don't usually have company."

"I'm not going to take your only chair," he says. "I'll sit on the floor. You take the chair." I've seen Sandy's gentlemanly act before and I know what he's up to. He starts to lower himself toward the floor but stops with a groan.

"You messed yourself up when you fell," I say. "Why don't you go ahead and lie down on the bed?"

"There's only one bed," he says. "What if I fall asleep?"

"I'll think of something."

"No," he says, shaking his head. "I can't take your bed. I'll stretch out on the floor."

He leans on the big chair while he lowers himself gingerly to his knees, flops over, and stretches out full length.

"Well, I'm not going to sit in the chair while you're down on the floor," I say, settling near him with my back leaning against the side of the bed.

He raises himself on one elbow and takes a swallow of beer. "I was pretty surprised when I came home that day and discovered you'd moved out," he says. "Why didn't you tell me what was going on?"

I shrug. "I guess I was afraid you'd make me change my mind."

"How come you did it?"

"I think you know the answer to that question," I say. "Rebecca? Or was it Rachel?"

He sighs. "It wasn't serious, you know. It was just that sometimes I thought you were more interested in the band than me. All we ever talked about was gigs and set lists and arrangements. It was kind of cool to be with somebody that . . . that . . ."

"That worshipped you?"

He nods. "Okay. That worshipped me."

The silence lasts long enough for us both to finish our beer, drinking with a kind of intense concentration, like the reason we're not talking is because we've got something else really important to do. The only noise in the room is coming from Red's cage—busy bursts of clucking and the whispery sounds of wings being half-opened and closed again.

Sandy drains the can of beer and tilts it to his mouth again in one last attempt to find something to do that will take the place of talking. Finally, he sets the can on the floor. "That bird is kind of noisy," he says.

"Want another beer?" I grab the empty can and climb to my feet.

"Sure." I can feel his gaze on me as I walk to the kitchen. As I disappear through the door, I hear him say, "You're still gorgeous, you know." I don't answer. As I open the refrigerator and reach for the beer, I hear Red squawk.

When I get back, Sandy's pulled himself up into a sitting position and he's staring into Red's cage. "He's scratching around now," he says. Red squawks again. "And he's gotten louder. I think it's because he's hungry." He points to one of the metal cups clipped to the mesh of the cage. "Is this where his food goes?" One hand reaches for the sack of chicken feed next to the cage and the other reaches for the latch on the cage's door.

"Yeah," I say. "It is. But don't—"

It's too late. Before either of us can react, Red has burst from the cage with a triumphant squawk and a flurry of wings, and he's half-jumping, half-flying across the room.

"Oh, shit. I'm sorry," Sandy says, cowering next to the big chair with his arms shielding his head as Red whizzes past his face.

I set the two cans of beer on the table. "Hold still until he lands," I say. "He hasn't been out of the cage since I brought him here, so he's probably disoriented."

Red perches briefly on the arm of the big chair, launches himself again in a flying leap that takes him nearly to the front door, where he scuttles along the floor till he reaches the corner.

"Okay," I whisper to Sandy. "He's landed. I need something to grab him with. Can you sneak into the bathroom and get a towel? But don't do anything conspicuous or he'll get nervous."

Behind me, I hear the floor creak and look over my shoulder to see Sandy crawling toward the bathroom. Meanwhile, Red is clucking busily to himself in his shadowy corner, his head twisting this way and that, his eyes glinting as they catch the lamp-light.

In a few minutes Sandy glides up next to me and hands me a towel. "Make sure the door of the cage is open," I whisper, "and put some food in there so once he's back inside we don't have to mess with anything for a while. Water, too. I think he's out of water."

Sandy glides away as silently as he came. But before I can swoop down on Red and bundle him into the towel, he launches himself into the air and careens toward me with a noisy flutter of wings. As I bob away and crouch, he lights down briefly on the bed, but he takes off again with an enthusiastic burst of flapping that sets a cloud of stray feathers adrift.

"Duck!" I shout to Sandy, and he plunges to the floor. I expect to hear some disgruntled muttering, but instead I hear a snicker, then another, and another. Still crouching, I inch along the side of the bed till I'm next to Sandy. The snickers turn into chuckles, then into outright laughter. It's contagious. Pretty soon I'm laughing, too. We clamber to our feet as Red vanishes into the kitchen.

"We're never going to catch him if we're laughing," I manage to gasp out.

"Yes, we are," Sandy says. "I'm not going to let a chicken terrorize me. Give me that towel." He grabs one end of it. He's been laughing so hard that his face has turned kind of pink.

"No," I say, keeping my grip on the other end. "I'm more used to him than you are."

"I can do it," he says. "I want to do it." He tugs so suddenly that the towel slips out of my hands. I lose my balance and tumble backward onto the bed. "You okay?" he says, pulling me up.

"Fine," I say. "Give me that towel."

"No," he says. "I've got an idea."

"Yeah?"

"Yeah. He's in the kitchen now. You go in there and I'll stand in the doorway with the towel and you chase him toward me."

"Is everything ready? Did you put the food in the cage?"

"Water," he says. "I didn't do the water yet." As he steps toward the kitchen door, Red bursts past him with a triumphant squawk and heads for the big chair. "Oh, shit," Sandy says, and he dissolves into laughter again.

Eventually we chase Red into the shower. Sandy stands in the bathroom doorway waving his arms and trying to look forbidding, though he's shaking with laughter, while I finally succeed in wrapping a towel around Red, despite his annoyed squawks.

At last we bundle him into his cage.

"I can't stand it," Sandy says, gasping for breath. "I haven't laughed this hard in months—or maybe even since you were still around." He grabs his beer, tilts his head back, and takes a long swallow. "Whew!" he says, shaking his head. "Laughing like that—" He pauses to fight off a giggle. "It's as bad as having the hiccups, but I think I'm finally okay." He drinks some more beer. "You're still the coolest chick I know," he says, gazing at me.

I'm still laughing. "I can't stop," I say. "How ridiculous was that?" I grab my chest with both hands. Tears are squeezing from my eyes, flowing down my cheeks. "If I laugh myself to death, will you find somebody to take care of Red?"

"Don't laugh yourself to death," he says, only partly joking. He leans toward me and puts his arm around me. "Here, drink some beer. That'll help you."

I try to take a swallow, but sputter it out right in his face.

"Maybe this will help then." He leans toward me and before I know what's happening, he's kissing me. "It's been a long time," he says, kissing me again, his hands feeling all over my body like he wants to make sure I'm really there.

"Please no." I push him away and force myself to step back, even though being so close to him again brings back the longing I felt when he stepped out onto the stage tonight.

"I understand," he says, stepping back too. "I really do." He rubs a hand over his face. "Or at least I'm trying to. I missed my chance and now there's another guy." He looks at the floor then back up at me. "A dead guy." He rubs his face again then sniffs his hand. "I've still got beer all over my face."

He heads for the bathroom. I finish my can of beer, not feeling so much like laughing anymore.

Sandy emerges from the bathroom. He looks serious, too. "I'll sleep in the chair," he says. "It's your place so you should get the bed."

I lie down on the bed in my clothes, but I can't sleep hearing him breathing and knowing all I'd have to do is touch him and I'd be right back where I started. And feeling bad about Rick, too. Am I crazy? Knocking myself out to save Rick's reputation but letting Sandy hypnotize me like he used to?

I end up in the kitchen, sitting on a stiff little wooden chair with my head on the table, cradled on my folded arms. Somehow I sleep, at least for the few hours of darkness that are left, and more deeply than I have in days. It's a desperate kind of sleep, though, full of dreams that leave me with the same grim feeling I got when Walt told me Rick was a murderer.

When I wake up, the room is bright with a chilly-winter-morning brightness. I don't feel very proud of myself, even though Sandy ended up sleeping in the big chair and I ended up at the kitchen table. Yeah, it's noble of me to be so loyal to Rick's memory, but I'm no closer to figuring out who killed him. And besides, what's really noble about resisting a guy I was already determined to forget?

I pull myself to my feet and stretch, feeling creaky. In the next room, Sandy is still asleep. He's twisted into the big chair, covered with the blanket I found on the top shelf of the closet where Mr. Rush must have stashed it for extra-cold nights. Sandy's long sighing breaths are interspersed with little snorting gasps.

I'm in the kitchen spooning instant coffee into one of Mr. Rush's mugs and boiling water in Mr. Rush's kettle when I hear the big chair creak. The sound of footsteps across the floor is followed by a gurgle as the toilet flushes. I reach for another mug.

"Man, oh man, oh man." Sandy appears in the doorway, tilted to the side and rubbing his back. "Sleeping in that chair would probably have done me in anyway, but on top of my adventure with the garbage cans last night—" He sinks into a chair. "Got any aspirin?"

I get him fixed up with the aspirin and we sip our coffee in silence for a few minutes.

"So where's this CD?" he says.

"What CD?"

"You said your band made a CD." He looks so miserable I almost feel sorry for him, the pain in his back distorting his normal grace as he perches at an odd angle on the chair. And he's got a little line between his eyebrows that makes their cocky tilt seem more like a frown.

"It disappeared," I say, "and I don't want to talk about it."

"But all this—" He waves toward the other room and I figure he means the rooster and the broken window and even the fact that the parking lot is now a crime scene. "All this happened because you were making a CD?"

"Sort of." I gaze into my coffee cup.

"Too bad it didn't work out," he says.

"I can take you back to the city tonight," I say to change the subject. "My band's got a gig at the Hot Spot."

"What time's your sound check?"

"Not till eight. But I could go in earlier."

"Maybe I can get Terry to send a car for me," he says, shifting his weight and groaning. "I think he wants to go over some stuff this afternoon." He sips at the coffee. "I'm going to be in Manhattan for as long as *Othello* runs. We could get used to each other again. Just as friends, you know?"

I'm saved from having to answer by a knock on the door. I open it to find Julio standing in the hall, with a sort of miniature Julio next to him—same olive skin, narrow face, John Lennon glasses, but about a head shorter.

"This is my cousin Edwin," Julio says. "He's a social worker. I tol' him about the rooster."

"What would you do with it?" I ask Edwin.

"Have you ever heard of the Semana de Campo program?" he says.

"Not really."

"It's for city kids in the summer," Julio cuts in. "From Paterson, and like that. It's out by the Delaware Water Gap. They have a farm."

"Come in," I say. "Come in." Red clucks nervously as I lead Julio and Edwin toward his cage. "Red," I lean down and catch his beady eye. "Meet your new owner."

CHAPTER 18

The Hot Spot's about three quarters full—not bad considering the air outside has a hushed stillness that says snow is coming. I'm wearing boots in deference to the weather. Not a pair of my cowboy boots though. I dug out a pair of spike-heeled laceups in a dark burgundy red and paired them with black fishnets and a fake zebra fur miniskirt. I finished the look off with a form-fitting black top that has a long sleeve on one side but leaves the other arm and shoulder bare.

As the cymbal crash that ends the first set dies away, a guy, slender and not too tall, detaches himself from the crowd at the bar and heads toward us. At first I don't recognize him, but he skirts the edge of the stage, and the light from one of the spotlights spills onto his face. I realize it's Tim. He's dressed like he was that night in the Times Square subway—jeans that look like they came by their threadbare look from heavy use, not a designer label, and a faded plaid shirt.

"Nice set," he says with a smile. "Good crowd, too. I like this place. Think you could steer me toward the guy that does the booking?"

"It's Boris," I say. "He's probably hanging out in his office. Do you have a demo or something?" My fingers stray to that itchy spot on my left hand, and I give it a good scratch.

Tim's eyes get hard for a second. Or maybe it's the way the light is hitting his glasses. "I've played all over Europe," he says. "That's my demo." His glasses slide down his nose and he grimaces as he tries to twitch them back into place. "Steve here tonight? I'd like to see him." He squints into the lights and scans the house.

"Not that I know of," I say. "Did he tell you he was coming?"

"I haven't talked to him lately."

Suddenly, the PA comes to life as the sound guy puts on some James Brown thing. I step down off the stage and raise my voice to cut through the stuttering bass and guitar. "I don't think he comes into the city much," I say. "He seems to like his solitude."

"Poor guy." Tim shakes his head. "What's going to happen to him now? He's a pretty hopeless case. Too bad Rick didn't have time to make some kind of arrangement for him."

"Well, at least he won't starve. At least not for a while."

"How so?"

"Rick signed all the money from 'Not Something Pretty' over to him."

"I didn't know that." His nose twitches as his glasses start to migrate again.

"Look," I say. "We've got to play again in about ten minutes and I need a beer. If you want to talk to Boris, his office is down there." I jerk my thumb toward the passage at the edge of the stage that leads to the restrooms and Boris's cluttered and smoky den.

As I step toward the table reserved for the band, an arm comes out of nowhere and lands across my shoulders. A voice that sounds like it belongs to a cop says, "I've got some information for you."

"Walt! Thanks for coming."

He nods toward where Mitzi's already taken a seat and is greeting a woman who looks just like her, short hair, well-scrubbed face.

Walt's mouth widens into a smile that makes his ruddy face

gleam. "First I thought, a girl drummer? What's that going to sound like? But she's okay. She's really okay."

"We still miss you though. When did you say you're taking off for Europe?"

"Tomorrow. I should be home packing, but I wanted to let you know what I found out."

"About Jeb?" We've reached the band's table now, but the only band member sitting at it is Mitzi. Stan is perched on the edge of the stage fingering silent licks on his guitar and Michael is hanging out by the bar. Neil has vanished, as usual, probably tucked away in some corner smoking a joint. "Is he out of prison?" I ask.

"Not exactly," Walt says. "But he's not in, either."

"Was he out when Rick was killed?"

"Nope," Walt says. "He's not your man." Mitzi looks up as we pull out chairs. "Nice job," Walt says, reaching for her hand. "I'm Walt Stallings."

"Thanks," she says with a level gaze. She pushes a bottle of Bud toward me. "I knew you'd want this," she says and turns back toward her friend.

For a minute all I'm thinking about is the heft of that cold, sweating bottle in my hand and the way the first long swallow of beer chills my throat all the way down.

"Ah, that tastes great," I sigh and put the bottle down and look at Walt. "What do you mean, he's not out but he's not in?"

"Jeb Perkins is dead," Walt says so quietly that I can barely hear it because now the sound guy has "Purple Haze" blasting over the PA. "He died in prison about five years ago."

"Wow." In my mind I'm crossing his name off my list and realizing nobody's really left. "What did he die of?" I say as Jimi Hendrix's guitar moans and shudders.

"Apparently he got in a fight with another inmate and one thing led to another."

Mitzi looks at her watch, pushes back her chair, and starts to rise. She's decked out tonight in a black turtleneck and cargo pants. "About time to get started again," she says.

I tip the beer to my mouth for another long swallow and stand up. As I turn toward the stage, I notice that Tim is emerging from the passage that leads to Boris's office. He's scowling.

"How'd it go?" I say as he gets closer.

"That guy's an asshole," he says and his scowl deepens. "An absolute fucking asshole." He brushes past me, kicks a chair out of the way, and heads toward the door.

Up on the stage, Michael is hovering over Mitzi as she tightens a nut on her cymbal stand. As usual, he's all in black; black jeans with a carefully pressed crease and a black T-shirt that hugs his meager chest. He's talking intensely about something, but I can't tell what because Jimi Hendrix is drowning out his voice.

Once I've climbed up on the stage though, I can hear Mitzi say, "You know what you need, Mike?"

Michael frowns and his precise voice cuts through the music. "You know I hate to be called Mike."

"Okay, *Michael*. You know what you need?"

He sighs and tightens his lips into a flat line with a little twist at each corner. Mitzi continues. "You need to lighten up."

Out of the corner of my eye, I notice that Neil has taken his place at the keyboards and kicked off his sneakers.

Michael continues to frown. "Why am I the only person in this band that ever does any research?" he says.

Stan glances up from the guitar he's tuning. Blinking through a few strands of wiry hair that have strayed from his ragged ponytail, he says, "Gossip is research?"

"It isn't gossip. If we'd been paying more attention to what was going on at Prowling Rooster Records, we wouldn't have lost all that money."

"It doesn't matter what's going on there now," Stan says with a shrug. "It's too late to do anything." He jerks his guitar cable out of his tuner and plugs it into his amp.

"Not true," Michael says. "Ben's got a plan that might actually make money. And if that happens, we can go after him for what they owe us."

"Where'd you hear this?" I say, interested in spite of myself.

"Never mind." He turns away. The tight line of his lips has turned into a smug smile.

"Come on, *Michael.*" This is Mitzi. "Don't be like that."

He ignores her.

"Please?" Mitzi punctuates the word with a rim shot.

"Nobody was interested before." He picks up his bass and thumps out a few exploratory notes. "Are we starting this set on time or not?"

A barmaid appears at the edge of the stage. "You guys want anything before you get going?"

"I'm all set," Mitzi says.

"Anybody else?"

Michael slips the strap of his bass over his head and settles it into place with a twitch of his narrow shoulders. "Cranberry juice," he says. Neil's in his usual daze and Stan's got a bottle of water sitting on his amp.

"I guess the rest of us are fine," I say. "Thanks."

"Wow," Mitzi says to the barmaid as she turns to leave. "Have the tips improved here or what?"

"Not that I know of." The barmaid laughs. "Why?"

"You look like you just got back from Bermuda or someplace."

The barmaid fingers a cheek. "Oh, this? You don't need to go on a cruise to get a tan. Check out a tanning parlor. The city's full of them. Twenty bucks an hour. You have to be careful, though. You can even get a sunburn."

"Maybe Michael shouldn't lighten up," Stan murmurs.

"What?" Mitzi says.

"People are paying money to get tans."

"Is that a joke?" Mitzi says, "Or are you just weird?"

Michael lets his gaze wander from me to Mitzi to Stan and back again. "Do you really want to know what I heard?" he says.

"I do," I say. "But we've got an audience waiting out there."

Ignoring me, Michael turns to Mitzi. "Ben wants to completely revamp Prowling Rooster Records and he's on the trail of a hot young hip-hop group—three women. If he gets them to sign, the label could really take off, but he's got to grab them like in the next twenty-four hours because somebody else is after them too. The only problem is Steve. He thinks the label should stay all blues. But the rumor is that Ben's determined to take over no matter what he has to do—"

He's interrupted by the barmaid. "Cranberry juice?" she says, handing a glass of red liquid to Michael.

A few minutes later we launch into "The Thrill Is Gone," and the set is underway.

If anything, the Hot Spot is fuller than it was when we started. Every single chair is taken and the crowd around the bar is so dense that anybody heading to or from the door has to squeeze through a mob of people.

Most of the faces are turned toward the stage, and Stan's solos are getting so much applause that when they end and I start singing again, half the verse gets drowned out. Boris has emerged from his office and is lingering along the wall, nodding in time to the beat and smiling his crooked-toothed Slavic smile.

As I scan the faces, I pause at one particular face, strangely familiar. It's a woman, jammed in among the crowd hanging out around the bar. She's so short that she's bobbing this way and that to try and glimpse the stage through the constantly shifting mass of people. Her hair is a wiry, coppery mass and her face is nondescript, with a nose like a random lump of dough.

It's Brenda Honeycut, Rick's old girlfriend. What's she doing here?

Now it's near the end of the set and we're doing our theme song, "Swing It on Home."

" 'Wish I was an apple,' " I'm singing, " 'hangin' on a tree . . .' " I lift the mike off the mike stand and step back for the chorus: " 'Swing it on home . . . swing it on home . . .' "

My gaze strays to the hand that's holding the mike and freezes there for a minute. A long drop of blood is running from my knuckles toward my wrist. I've been scratching the itchy spot on my hand all night, the remains of my encounter with that thorny vine at Green Forest Park. Below me, the tan barmaid hovers over a table, with a tray full of beer bottles.

Something clicks in my brain and I realize that I've got to get to a phone really quick.

"Michael, I've got to use your cell phone for a minute," I say as soon as he's finished settling his bass into its stand. I've already dug the phone number I need out of my bag, grateful that I automatically tucked that business card away even though I couldn't imagine at the time that I'd need it for anything.

He frowns. "Is it band-related business?"

"Not exactly, but it's really important."

"I don't have unlimited minutes, you know. I have to pay for every call."

"I'll give you some money. After Boris pays us tonight, I'll give you five dollars."

He bends over to reach into the bag he has stashed behind his amp. "That's probably more than you really have to—"

"Please, Michael, give me the phone. This is really important."

He hands it over with a sigh and I hurry off the stage, zigzag among the tables, and push my way through the crowd standing around the bar. The taped music is too loud for a phone call, so I end up out on the street. I huddle close to the building, wishing I'd grabbed my jacket. It's pretty cold out here, especially with one bare arm and shoulder. I hold the business card up to the light coming from the neon Budweiser sign in the Hot Spot's window and punch the number into Michael's cell phone.

On the other side of the doorway from where I'm standing, a rangy cluster of smokers are grabbing quick cigarettes between sets.

It's ringing. A couple strolls by arm in arm, bundled up against the approaching snow. The phone's still ringing. I'm expecting a robotic voice to come on and offer me the chance to speak to my party's voice mail when a tiny burp takes the place of a ring and I hear a perky voice say, "Hello?"

"This is Maxx Maxwell," I say. "I met you the other night at the Lexington Avenue Health Spa."

"I can't place the name."

"I'm blond, tall. You gave me your card—"

"It's after midnight," she says.

"I'm sorry, but it's really important. Did I wake you up?"

"I just got in." A drift of cigarette smoke wafts my way, along with a burst of laughter from the crowd on the other side of the door. "I remember you now," the voice on the phone says, "and I understand. When you decide to take action, it's so exciting that you want to do something right away. You actually look okay now, but it won't last. And you could be absolutely spectacular. When do you want to get started?"

"That's not what I'm calling about," I say. I'm starting to shiver. I snake my free hand under the bottom of my top searching for any little bit of warmth.

"It's not?" The voice sounds less perky. "Well, in that case, it *is* after midnight."

"I need to know something. Ben Darling—the guy who works out with you. You had just finished a session with him the night I met you at the gym. I got the impression he was really into exercise, but has he been out of town at all, like the week before last?"

"Checking up on Ben, huh?" she says, laughing a little. "I didn't realize you were involved with him. But I understand that, too. And I know what guys are like. We knock ourselves out to look great for them and what do they do? Run around behind our backs with a chick that's twenty pounds overweight and has bad hair besides."

"It's not that," I start to say, but then stop myself. Let her think what she wants.

The smokers are stomping their butts out on the sidewalk and starting to wander back inside. Time for the next set and Michael's probably getting antsy.

"Woman to woman?" she says. "He's been at the gym every day this month. I don't know if that's what you want to hear or not. If it isn't, I'm sorry. And if you ever decide you want to start working out, give me a ring."

"He wasn't down in Barbados?"

"Oh, he does have a place there, but it's been a while since he did any traveling."

I've got to call Steve quick. I assumed Ben had just gotten back from Barbados because he was bragging about his place there and he was so tan. But now I realize you don't have to leave the city to be tan—even in November.

So what's Steve's number? My bag's inside.

Wait a minute—Steve doesn't have a phone.

The last set feels like some kind of blues marathon, each tune an endless series of chord changes, solos, bass riffs, drum licks.

I'm singing, but I hardly know what the song is. A voice in my head keeps repeating, *You've got to get up there. You've got to get up there. It might already be too late.*

There's the strip club though, says another voice. Ben said he always hangs around the strip club till closing to check on that night's take—but it probably closes at two, like the Hot Spot.

As I step back from the mike after we wrap up "Bending and Weeping," Michael edges over and gives me a big-eyed stare.

"What are you doing?" he whispers. "You sang the same verse three times."

At last the set is over. I tell Michael to get the money from Boris and make sure everybody gets their share and keep five dollars out of mine for the phone call, and I jump off the stage, grab my jacket, and run for the door.

I hurry past clubs spilling people onto the sidewalk now that the night is winding down, caught up in the surging crowd, the sudden smell of freshly lit cigarettes hanging in the heavy chill air.

Now I'm hurrying past the NYU dorms and along the block that dead ends into Bowery. Here's my car, wedged between two other cars that leave me barely inches to maneuver my way out.

The Bonneville's color is deadened to gray in the shadows, with one darker gray door, and—as of this morning—three layers of plastic sheeting taped over the driver's side window. Sandy came downstairs and helped me do it. My car and all the cars belonging to the other people in my building were lined up along both sides of the block. The parking lot was empty, cordoned off by a long streamer of that yellow crime-scene tape.

I try the driver's side door but the lock is acting up again, so I pull the passenger side door open and slide across the seat.

Why do I even care about Steve? I don't know, but I do. I can't let Rick's killer kill again, even though the last time I saw Steve we didn't part on very good terms.

As I stick my key into the ignition, give it a quick twist, and step on the gas, I seem to see Steve's face looking at me, distorted by anger as I back toward the door of the trailer.

The engine whines feebly then falls silent. I twist the key again. More whining, but a little less feeble. I pump the gas. Finally, the engine catches with a sound like a sudden racking cough.

Rick cared so much for Steve. He must have seen something there, under all the weirdness. You have to forgive the guy for his quirks. Who wouldn't have a hard time getting over something like that? His sister killed and his best friend wounded, and the killer—once his friend too—winds up in prison. Music was his whole life and that's what music led to. So how can he get any joy from being a musician after that? How can he enjoy hearing the Meal songs again?

I twist the steering wheel sharply to the right and inch forward till I tap the back of the car that's hemming me in from the front. Now I twist the steering wheel to the left and back up till I tap the car behind me. Repeat the process again and again and again.

At last I'm free and sailing toward the corner. Soon I've joined the late-night traffic heading up the West Side Highway. In my mind, I picture Ben Darling on his way too, determined to make sure that what he wants for Prowling Rooster Records is what happens—like he did when Rick resisted his ideas.

I'll get there first though. I have to. And I'll stick Steve in my car and take him back to Hackensack. After I know he's not in danger anymore, we can figure out what to do next.

That horrible scratch on Ben's wrist came from the same place I got mine—not from his cat like he said. It came from that thorny vine at Green Forest Park, right next to the marsh where he dumped Rick's body.

The beams of my headlights seem to pull the car forward through the dark tunnel of bare trees that leads up to Steve's trailer and, beyond it, to Rick's house. The car bounces over the rutted road, exhaust pipe occasionally scraping the frozen ground. The road curves slightly and as it straightens out again, Steve's trailer comes into view, glowing a pale moonlike silver where my headlights catch its flanks.

As the headlights move across its surface, I see something that makes me catch my breath, and I wonder if I should turn around and head for the cops instead.

The door is ajar. It's three in the morning and the temperature has to be in the twenties, if even that. Why would the door be open unless somebody had forced his way in? Or forced his way out?

I shut off my headlights with a sharp click, and the sudden darkness makes me more aware of the fact that my breath is coming in shallow pants and my skin feels sweaty even though I'm freezing.

I shift the car into reverse and start backing up, slowly though, because there's no moon and the light that bleeds into the sky from the bright lights of Manhattan doesn't reach this far.

As I hear the crunch that tells me I didn't twist the steering wheel in time to avoid one of the trees that lines the road's curve, I hear something else—and I see something.

I shift back into drive to try to free myself from the tree I hit, but as I step on the gas the wheels only spin. I must be hung up on a stump. I try jerking the steering wheel and gunning the engine, but the car just strains and whines.

Meanwhile, a flashlight beam is heading steadily toward me.

And whoever's guiding it, tracking the beam across the bare dark ground, is yelling something.

I take my foot off the gas and let the engine go quiet, and then I can hear the voice more clearly. It sounds a lot like Steve, and he seems to be saying, "Hey! Need some help there?"

Just to make sure, I turn the headlights back on. Caught in their glare is a tall figure with an unruly beard. He's dressed in a bulky red and black checked jacket, and a smooth-furred dog that glows amber in my headlights is capering at his side.

As Steve approaches my car, he seems curious, even concerned, like a friendly guy coming out to help a stranger—that is, until I roll my window down and he points the flashlight at my face.

He's passed through the beams of my headlights by now, and with the flashlight in my eyes I can't see anything anyway, but the voice isn't friendly anymore. Instead it's snarling, "I told you to stay away from here. What are you doing back?"

"Please," I say. "Do you think I drove all the way up here in the middle of the night to hassle you? I found something out that means you could be in danger."

I'm so cold that my teeth are chattering. I hug myself and bend over till my head is almost touching the steering wheel.

"Me?" He laughs. "I'm not important enough."

"You had an argument with Ben Darling about Prowling Rooster Records. You're a part owner, right? So he can't take it off in some whole new direction unless you agree, or unless you're out of the way. He's been bragging that he's got a chance to sign a hot new hip-hop group, all girls, but they're going to escape if he doesn't move really fast—like right now."

"You're nuts," he says. "I'm not in any danger from that asshole."

"I'm not nuts. Rick got killed. Stuff like that really happens." My teeth are chattering so hard that I'm almost stuttering. My breath shapes a foggy cloud in the beam of Steve's flashlight.

He leans forward and shines the flashlight into my car. For a minute or two he doesn't say anything. Then I hear a sigh. "If you freeze to death out here, the cops will come around again." He jerks on the car door. "Come on in the trailer. I'll make you some tea." He jerks on the door again. "Unlock this thing, will you? I'm trying to be a gentleman."

"It doesn't work," I murmur through frozen lips. I slide across the seat, shove the passenger side door open, and let my feet drop onto the frozen ground.

We hurry toward the trailer, me almost running to keep up with him, awkward in the spike-heeled boots. "Why were you out wandering around, anyway?" I ask as we trot along.

"Dog heard a noise outside. Wouldn't calm down till I let him check it out."

We've reached the trailer. He gestures toward the steps. "Go ahead," he says. "Ladies first."

Once we're inside, he lowers himself onto one of the benches that flank the kitchen table and bends toward his boots. He loosens their laces and kicks them off, first one, then the other.

"No," he says, leaning back with a comfortable sigh and letting one foot massage the other. "I'm not worried about Ben Darling. He's harmless. Ben Darling didn't kill Rick."

As the boots slide across the floor and hit the wall of the trailer, the impact jars something free from the tread—little squiggles of compacted dirt, so well shaped that they look like strange dark pasta. A weird sound, like a cross between a cough and a gasp, comes out of my throat. I'm staring at the little brown pasta squiggles like all of a sudden they hold the answer to everything.

I remember leaning into Rick's truck, fingering a handful of dirt that looked like this, convinced it had something to do with Rick disappearing.

"You okay?" Steve says. I hear him shift forward, and out of the corner of my eye I see that he's staring where I'm staring. After a few seconds I feel his eyes on me, and I turn to look at him. He's peering at me curiously, looking worried and almost kind of tender.

"That's just dirt," he says. "I know you chicks dig tidiness, but you look like you've seen a ghost."

"No," I say. "Not a ghost." In my mind I picture Steve shooting Rick, wrestling Rick's body into the pickup, driving to Green Forest Park. I lean on the edge of the table to pull myself to my feet, leaning harder as I feel my head grow light and I start to sway. "I should go," I say. "You're right. It was silly to drive up here. Ben Darling's no threat."

"Hey, hey, hey. Hang on a minute." He reaches toward me and my heart gives a sudden alarmed thud. "Something's got you upset."

I edge away from him, backing past the door that leads into the little bathroom and coming up smack against the trailer's front wall. In a second he's grabbed me and he's holding me tight, one big hand clamped around each arm.

CHAPTER 19

"What is it?" He frowns and studies my face. "You look absolutely terrified."

"No, I'm fine," I say. "If you let me go, I'll be on my way."

"If I let you go, you'll fall over. You might get hurt. And like I said—" A tiny grin comes and goes, almost hidden by his shaggy beard. "I don't like cops coming around."

"Please." I squirm in his grip and my voice comes back to me like a barely audible squeak.

"I get it." He laughs. "Something happened that made you all of a sudden think I'm scary." He drops his hands to his sides. "What was it? The dirt?" He backs up and pokes at one of the squiggles with a sock-covered toe. He looks back at me. "Hey," he says. "Will you at least sit down before you keel over?"

I lower myself onto the bench.

"So it *is* the dirt, huh? Is that supposed to be some kind of a clue? If you spent as much time tramping through the woods after a dog as I do, your boots would get muddy too." He gazes at my burgundy spike-heeled laceups. "I wouldn't advise doing it in those, however."

"Did you ever drive Rick's truck?" I say.

"All the time. He didn't mind. Rick was a good guy."

"Did you ever move the seat?"

"Sure. My legs are much longer than Rick's were." His eyes leave me and move toward the dog, pawing at the door and whining. "Easy there, buddy," he says. "We went out once and you didn't find anything."

"Somebody moved the seat way up," I say.

"Why would I do that? Like I said, I've got long legs."

"If a tall person moved it back so they could use the truck, they might try to put it back like it was when they got done. But they might move it up too far."

He frowns. "I did always try to put it back like it was," he says absently. Then he looks at me. "Done with what?"

"Taking Rick's body to Green Forest Park."

His body stiffens. "You think I did that?"

"No," I say. "I guess I don't."

"What if a short person did it?"

"I thought of that too, but the night Rick was killed, Brenda Honeycut was sitting in a bar next to Sleepy Time Motel in Yonkers and drinking herself silly. I don't think she could have sobered up and gotten herself over here in time to kill him and then catch her plane. She had a gig in Chicago on Sunday."

"Whew," he says, leaning against the stove. "You've really been thinking about this, haven't you?"

"Yeah, and apparently it hasn't gotten me anywhere at all," I say. "So I'm going to leave now. But listen—if Ben comes up here to talk to you about taking Prowling Rooster Records in a new direction, be careful. That's all. Be careful."

He steps toward the door and reaches for the handle. "Okay," he says. "But you're sure you don't want that tea?"

"I wouldn't enjoy it. Honestly. I just want to go home."

As he opens the door, the dog lurches forward and tries to wiggle past me, an excited little whimper squeezing out of its throat.

Steve grabs its collar. "Easy there, guy. It's just a raccoon."

As I head down the steps, the light from the open door spilling onto the ground, I hear something too, a slight rustling from the far end of the trailer. Otherwise, the night is as still as if the ground was already covered with snow.

"You get raccoons up here?" I say, turning to look at Steve.

"All the time. They're rummaging in the garbage."

I reach my car, pull open the passenger side door, and glance back toward the trailer to see Steve, silhouetted against the light from the open door, giving me a genial wave. I slide across the frigid seat, twist the key in the ignition, switch on the headlights, and step on the gas. As the engine chokes its way to life, the trailer door closes and Steve disappears.

I shift into drive and the engine strains, but nothing else happens. I step down harder. The engine whines, the wheels spin, and the car stays where it is.

Then I remember. I'm stuck on a stump.

I feel around in the pocket on the inside of the car door for my flashlight. As I step out of the car, a sudden sharp crack makes the night not silent anymore. The crack is followed by a hollow echo.

I drop to the ground and pull the car door toward me as far as it will go. "Steve! Steve!" I yell though I can't see the trailer from where I'm crouching. "Call the cops. Someone's out here with a gun and they're shooting at me!"

No answer. He probably can't hear me, but surely he heard the gunshots.

"Steve!" I call again, louder. "Help! Help! Steve!"

Steve's voice reaches me at the same time that I hear footsteps pounding over the frozen ground. "I don't have a phone," he's saying. "Sorry. I don't have a phone."

Duh! That's why I had to drive all the way up here.

Another shot rings out, but from a different direction, like it's coming from near Steve's trailer. Was that what the footsteps were all about? The shooter looking for a better angle? Or are there two different people out there with guns, both shooting at me? Or shooting at each other?

More shots, like a volley, back and forth. That answers one of my questions. There are definitely two people. But even if they're not after me, all these bullets flying around don't know that. My only chance to get out of here would be to crawl up into my car and see if I could make my way out to the main road without turning on my headlights—except I'm stuck on a stump.

A lull, quiet again, with that special about-to-snow stillness. Then rustling between the trailer and Rick's house, the sound of feet thumping. Silence again. Are the guns empty? My legs are cramped from stooping and my arm is getting stiff from clutching the door—or maybe I'm slowly freezing into an ice sculpture of a crouching woman.

I twist my spine and wiggle my shoulders, trying to ease the horrible tightness in my back. Silence still, total, except for a tiny creak as my vertebrae rearrange themselves. But then, suddenly, as if the sounds of my vertebrae set it off again, a sharp crack comes from the direction of the trailer.

Near me, too near, a woman's voice murmurs, "Oh, my God," and I hear a sound like something heavy and soft toppling over. "Oh, my God," the voice says again. "I'm going to die."

I let go of the car door so I can feel for the flashlight's switch. The door springs away from me with a sharp creak, and I'm suddenly so unbalanced that I land on my rear end and bang the back of my head against the hinge.

"Ooof." I take a deep breath and turn on the flashlight. As its beam sweeps toward the edge of the woods another shot echoes in the silence.

I hear moaning and let the light move away from the woods and toward the road. First there's only dirt, brown with a dusting of tiny frost crystals. Then I see a body wearing faded jeans, sturdy laceup boots like a hiker might wear, and a black leather

223

jacket, buttoned up snugly. Perhaps the jacket is restraining the flow of blood that has convinced the wearer she's dying.

Now the flashlight's beam has reached the head. Reddish, brownish, grayish hair, so wiry it stands straight out in a frowzy corona, surrounds a round, middle-aged face with a nose like a shapeless lump of dough.

The eyes open and colorless pupils strain in my direction, though the head doesn't move. "Please help me," says a wan voice.

It's Brenda Honeycut.

"How?" I say. "The guy that lives here doesn't have a phone and my car's stuck on a tree stump or something."

A groan starts but then catches in her throat as she holds her breath. "Really hurts," she gasps. "Hurts when I breathe. That's probably bad."

"I'll run up to the trailer. Get him to help with my car—"

"No." The hand nearest me flaps. "Might shoot you."

"Maybe you could control yourself," I say.

"Other guy I mean." A moan turns into a gasp. "Cell phone. It's in my pocket."

The sharp crack of another shot tells me that shining the flashlight around wasn't a good idea. I switch it off.

"Don't go away," the voice moans.

"I'm not," I whisper, "but the flashlight can't be on."

I set it next to the front tire so I can find it again and lower myself into a crawling position. Slowly I creep toward Brenda, inching forward on my elbows and knees, trying to stay as flat as possible. My leather jacket protects me somewhat, but my fishnet stockings and fake zebra fur miniskirt don't insulate my legs from the freezing dirt.

At last my hand touches something that isn't cold. My fingers identify it as denim. I let my hand crawl up till it reaches the edge of Brenda's jacket and pat my way toward where I imagine a pocket might be. I'm holding my breath as my mind forms an image of a neat hole in the leather, with a slow ooze of blood forming around it. Even now my fingers seem to be wet with something thick and slightly sticky.

"Which pocket?" I murmur.

"Inside." I can barely hear her. "Sweater inside."

My hand pats its way to the buttons and I inch forward till I'm crouched over her in a position so intimate I can smell the humid flowery scent of some perfume or lotion, along with a heavy, metallic smell that must be blood.

I take a deep breath, carefully tug each button out of its hole, and peel back the two halves of Brenda's jacket. But when I reach inside, I have to stop and pull my hand away. What I felt in there was so warm and wet that in my mind a deep purplish stain starts to spread and spread. I realize my eyes are closed, like that would blot out what my hand felt.

When I open them again, I'm looking at Rick's house. Is it my imagination, or is there a light on inside?

I pat my way over the front of Brenda's sweater, feeling for a pocket or the bulge of a cell phone.

I hear another shot. A long pause. My hand pats the sweater. I try to ignore the wetness that's gumming my fingers together.

As I feel the cell phone under my fingers, a voice calls from beyond the trailer. "Are you finally dead, you bastard? If you're not, shoot me back. Go ahead. I'm out of ammo." Pause. The voice sounds familiar, but the last time I heard it, I never thought I'd feel anything but pity for its owner. "Hey," the voice goes on. "Can you hear me? I have to say, I'm surprised you fought back. I always thought you were one of those turn the other cheek guys—"

The speech is interrupted by the wail of a siren, by flashing, whirling lights so sudden and bright that I feel as blind as I was in the darkness. But when my eyes adjust, I notice that there's a light on in Rick's house now. Steve must have run over and called the cops.

Between the cop car's headlights and the dancing, blinding lights on its roof, the space outlined by Rick's house, the trailer, and my car is now as bright as a floodlit stage. I rock back onto my heels, letting the bloody cell phone slip to the ground, wiping my hand on my furry miniskirt. I look toward where the shots were coming from, the shots that hit Brenda. All I see is tree trunks, flattened by the bright lights till they look like cutouts silhouetted against the shadows of the woods behind them. No sign of a wiry figure with a gun.

When I look back at Brenda, what I see cuts off the breath I'm about to take. The whole right half of the ratty beige sweater she's wearing under her leather jacket looks like it's been dipped in a vat of dark red dye. I grab at the two flaps of the jacket and pull one of them over her torso, then the other.

A cop, a black guy, crisp and stern in his dark uniform and face-shadowing hat, is pushing authoritatively toward me, right hand poised over the holster at his hip. On the opposite side of the car, another cop, a white guy, is climbing out.

"You the one that called?" the black cop says.

"No, I think somebody called from the house up there." I nod toward Rick's place.

"What happened?"

"A guy in the woods back there had a gun. She had a gun." I gesture toward Brenda. "Neither of them knew they were shooting at the wrong person."

The black cop leans toward the white cop and mutters something in a low voice. The white cop pulls his gun and strides off toward the trees.

The black cop scans the ground, scoops up Brenda's gun, and backs toward the cop car. A voice fuzzed by static crackles through the chilly air.

"An ambulance is on the way," he says, striding back toward us. He bends down on one knee and leans toward Brenda. "How bad is she?"

Her eyes are closed now, and her nondescript face is colorless in the sweep of the cop car's lights.

"There's blood all over the front of her sweater. She told me it hurts when she breathes."

He slides his hand inside the collar of her jacket. "Still has a pulse," he says. "Ambulance should be here in a minute. Hospital's right out along Route 303." He pulls his hand away.

Brenda twitches and her eyes flutter open. They study the cop for a minute and then settle on me. "I like your band's CD," she says.

"Rick played it for you?"

"I saw him the day before he died. That's when he told me about you." She closes her eyes again, breathes out with a little grunt, and grimaces. "I stole the CD. I thought it would really fuck things up between you." Her hand fumbles at my knee and I reach for it. She squeezes my fingers. "Thanks for staying here," she whispers. "Sorry I shot up your car and threw that rock."

"That was you?"

"Any idea what this was about?" the black cop says.

"She thought she was shooting me. She followed me up here because she thinks I stole her boyfriend. Well, maybe I sort of did, but he's dead now."

The shriek of another siren and more of those startling lights, like strobe lights, announce that the ambulance has arrived. It pulls up behind the cop car and the siren modulates to a lower key before it trails off in a gurgle. A couple of paramedics bound out and head toward us, one of them carrying an impressive-looking case embellished with a large red cross.

Meanwhile, the white cop has emerged from the edge of the

woods and stepped into the glare of the cop car's headlights. He hurries toward us, a squinty frown, from the light in his eyes or from something else, twisting the upper half of his face.

"No sign of anybody in the woods," he yells to the black cop as he gets closer. The frown settles into a ferocious scowl. "Call for backup?"

The black cop nods.

"Dogs too?"

The black cop mumbles something and the white cop starts walking toward the cop car.

As the paramedics squat on either side of Brenda, the black cop stands up. He bends his back into an exaggerated arch and flings back his shoulders. "Stiff," he mutters. He looks toward Rick's house. "Wait! Did you check the house?" he calls to the back of the white cop.

The white cop turns, his ferocious scowl still in place. "I thought you were gonna do that," he says.

"This woman's in bad shape," the black cop says. "But somebody should check the house. There's a light on."

Behind me I hear gentle murmurs from one of the paramedics, faint fragmentary answers from Brenda. I turn to see the other paramedic wheeling a low gurney across the frozen stretch of ground between the ambulance and Brenda, wisps of his breath trailing him like pale scarves in the glow of the ambulance's lights.

Meanwhile, both cops are now striding toward Rick's house with their guns drawn.

"The guy in the house isn't the guy you want," I say. "But I think I know where you can find him."

CHAPTER 20

Both of the cops fasten their gazes on me, the white one scowling, the black one looking friendly but skeptical.

I head toward my car.

"Hey! Where're you going?" the white cop yells.

"I need my flashlight."

"Look, ma'am," the black cop says. "You'd better just give us directions."

"You won't find him," I say. "The place where he's hiding doesn't have an address."

I lead them past the trailer, letting the beam of my flashlight dance along its shiny silver flanks as the cops' parallel beams march sternly ahead. Beyond the trailer, I turn sharply and head into the woods. Our flashlights skim the ground, darting between tree trunks. Tiny crystals of ice glow as they drift through the searching beams. And now and then my cheek is brushed by the faintest icy feather stroke.

We walk in silence. In my mind I'm replaying the scene from the other night, leaving the theater with Sandy, and that other guitar player glowering as we walked by, the guy who thought he'd get the lead guitar part because the musical director was his old friend.

Two of the flashlight beams suddenly halt while mine strains on ahead. I turn to see that the cops have halted too.

"There's nothin' back here," the white cop says. "Is this some kind of a trap or what?"

"No trap," I say. "It's right up ahead. Look."

I let my flashlight's beam flicker through one last stand of trees and climb the solitary trunk in the clearing beyond.

It skims over rugged bark, making its steady way upward, till finally it comes to rest on a wooden surface that's not as ragged as the trunk. I let the flashlight outline the details—the floor resting on the giant, almost horizontal, branch; the window, a hole sawed in a sheet of plywood; the roof, slightly peaked, like the finishing touch on a human-sized house of cards.

"A treehouse?" the white cop says. "What is this?"

"Hush," I say. "Listen."

The voice is barely singing. It's more like a whisper: "I'm goin' on my way . . . start my life anew . . ."

I wonder if he'll have time to get to that crucial, sad line he sang in the subway.

Beams waver as the flashlights are shifted from right hands to left. I hear a rustle and a snap as guns are drawn, then two sharp clicks.

"Where's the front of this thing?" the white cop asks.

"Walk around the tree," I say.

"You stand back there," he says, aiming his flashlight toward the stand of trees we've just come through. "And switch your flashlight off." As I hesitate, he makes his flashlight sweep back and forth between us and the trees, like it's herding something along. "Go on," he says. "One individual already got shot tonight."

I back away from him.

"Light off," he shouts. "Off." I keep backing up till I collide with a tree trunk. The snow's coming heavier now. Each blink shakes ice crystals off my lashes. My legs are freezing. I hadn't planned on a stroll through the woods when I dressed for the Hot Spot gig.

The cops make their way around the tree, and they take up a

position facing the front of the treehouse.

"Police," the black cop shouts, sounding like James Earl Jones. "Throw down your weapon."

The singing gets louder but nothing else happens.

"Go up after him?" the white cop asks.

The black cop ignores him. Instead, he yells, "One more warning, then I shoot."

The song starts over again and the singing gets even louder. "I'm goin' on my way . . ." It sounds almost desperate.

The voice is interrupted by the crack of a gun. A flashlight beam rises from the dirt, momentarily dazzles me, and seems to explore something about eight feet off the ground.

"You can save your bullets," says a voice from the treehouse. "I'm out of ammo."

"Throw your weapon on the ground and climb down," the black cop calls.

"I don't want to."

I hear a bullet crunch through wood. Somewhere above the treehouse a branch snaps.

The echoes have barely died away when another sharp crack is followed by cursing from the treehouse. A few twigs fall to the ground and a frantic rustling among the frozen leaves turns into the sound of animal feet skittering over the earth.

"You don't need to do that," says the voice from the treehouse. "I told you I'm out of ammo."

"Then come down," the black cop yells.

"I want to talk to Steve."

"Where would we find him?" the white cop says, his voice mellowing like he's trying to remember something he learned in a hostage negotiation course.

"He lives in the trailer," says the voice.

The cops confer in low voices, but I can't tell what they're saying. Now steady snow is drifting through the beams of their flashlights and I'm brushing flakes off my cheeks every few minutes.

One of the flashlight beams detaches itself from the other and makes its steady way toward me, followed by the sound of heavy boots crunching over the frozen remains of dead leaves.

"Hey," I whisper as the flashlight beam comes closer.

The moving light stops and so does the crunching. "Yeah?" I recognize the voice of the black cop. The voice sounds skeptical.

"He shot that woman by mistake," I say. "Steve's the guy he was really trying to kill."

"What makes you think that?"

I tell him quick, not the way Leon would have explained it. When I'm done, he grunts and the flashlight beam traces a large circle as he turns and the boots start to crunch their way back toward the treehouse.

Low voices again as the cops confer. Now one of the flashlight beams abruptly angles itself toward the treehouse. "Steve will come if you throw your weapon down," the black cop yells.

Silence.

"I said, throw your weapon down if you want to talk to Steve."

Silence.

One of the cops shoots.

More silence.

Then a volley of shots. I can't tell whether both cops are shooting now or just one.

"Okay, I get the point," says the voice from the treehouse. Before waiting for an answer, the voice goes on. "Look out below."

Is he going to jump? But no. With a small, heavy plop, something lands on the ground near where the cops' flashlight beams still capture that steady fall of snow.

One of the flashlight beams ventures in the direction of the plop, and soon I can see a gun glinting there on ground that's now covered with a fragile layer of white.

One of the cops heads in my direction again. I stop him as the beam of his flashlight tells me he's near.

"Hey!" I say.

"Yeah?" I recognize the black cop's voice. Skeptical again.

"Steve hates cops. No offense, but he does. He won't come if you're the one that asks him."

"Oh, really?" Almost amused.

"He'll say he doesn't have to and you can't make him. You can't, can you?"

"Technically, no."

When I get back out to the road, the light's off in Rick's house so I don't go there. Instead, I turn toward the trailer. It glows silver as my flashlight sweeps over it, seeming to rise out of the silvery-white ground. The air is warmer, somehow, now that the cold has cracked into tiny lustrous flakes.

As I climb the steps, I hear the dog barking inside. Before I can even raise my hand to knock, the door opens an inch and my flashlight catches a sliver of Steve's face peering out, his eyes, trapped in its beam, almost the same silvery color as the trailer.

He doesn't say anything, just pulls the door back and lets me step inside.

"Tea?" he says. "Your hat is all covered with snow."

"Thanks for calling the cops," I say. "I know you don't like them."

"What happened?" The dog nuzzles his thigh and looks up at me. Steve's hand lands on its head and feels for an ear.

"It's still happening. You have to come with me." He takes a few steps back. The dog retreats too. "He's up in the treehouse and he won't come down until he talks to you."

"What do you mean? Who's in the treehouse?" Melting snow

is dripping off my hat onto my nose. I brush it off with my glove. "Here," Steve says, handing me a dish towel.

"An old friend of yours," I say. "He came here tonight to kill you, but he shot Brenda Honeycut instead." Steve is still fumbling with the dish towel. "Come on," I say. "Where's your coat?" I head for something that looks like a closet set into the wall between the kitchen and the bed. The dog growls as I go by.

"Why would anybody, let alone an old friend, want to kill me?"

"I think that's what he wants to tell you."

"Okay." He flaps his arms in a clumsy shrug. "I give up." As he pulls on the black and red checked lumberjack coat and steps toward the door, he says, "I suppose cops are still hanging around."

I don't say anything. He eases the door open and holds the dog back while I slip through. "Easy," he whispers, bending down. "You'd better stay here, boy. I don't want you to get hurt."

We tramp through the now-snowy woods, following the tracks I left on my way out, dark prints from my spike-heeled boots with a skim of white from the snow that's fallen since then.

"Why am I doing this?" Steve says, not really to me, but I answer anyway.

"Because Rick was your friend."

The light sound of our boots on the snow takes over from our voices.

"You went to a lot of trouble over this," he says as my flashlight picks up the cluster of trees right before the clearing. "Why?"

"Rick was my friend, too. And I knew he loved the blues so much—and he loved music so much—that he'd never get mixed up in a scheme to pirate CDs. He wouldn't want to cheat a musician. I can't imagine how the cops came up with that whole deal."

"Ben told them. Well, he got one of his mob friends to tip them off."

"Ben?" I stop and stare up at Steve, even though I can't see anything outside the flashlight's range. "Why?"

"Ben really *was* pirating CDs. But he got in much deeper than he planned and it got scary. So he thought steering the cops toward Rick, who was already dead, would explain things, and he could gradually extricate himself and everything would settle down and he'd be okay."

"How do you know?"

"He told me. And you were right. He *was* twisting my arm about what direction Prowling Rooster Records should go, but he's not stupid enough to kill anybody. He's slimy, though. Too bad Rick trusted him with the business end of things. That's how Rick was—the music was all that was important."

One of the cops' flashlights wanders restively in our direction, blinds us for a minute, and returns to the ground to start a steady advance in our direction.

"Is this the individual?" says a voice I recognize as the white cop's.

"What am I supposed to do, man?" Steve says with an edge of irritation in his voice.

"He wants to tell you something." The cop starts walking back toward the treehouse and Steve follows him. I bring up the rear.

"Hey!" Steve calls suddenly, so loud his voice echoes among the bare trees. "I'm here now. What the fuck's going on?"

"You'll find out," comes the voice from the treehouse. "Hold a flashlight up to your face so I can see what you look like." I shine my light on Steve's face, wild hair and beard now frosted with flakes of snow. "Yeah, I guess it's you. Look up here," comes the voice. I aim the light at the treehouse window and Tim's face appears there.

"Tim?" Steve says, his voice sounding more emotional than I've ever heard it. "Why, man? Why would you want to kill me? I never did anything to you."

"Yes, you did. If Rick hadn't been so busy looking after you, he'd have had a minute to spare for me." Tim's face has slowly twisted into something so grotesque it looks almost demonic, and his voice has risen in pitch so much it hurts my throat to hear it.

I take the light away and aim it at the ground. The voice still comes in the darkness. "When I got back from Europe, I thought he'd help me, help me get set up here, book some gigs, make a recording." A hint of boastfulness manages to creep in, despite the misery. "I was hot there, man, filling big clubs. I had a real following."

"But you came back," Steve says, like he can't help wondering why somebody would leave that behind.

"It started to dry up. It was like I could get so far, but not far enough. It was like people liked me, but didn't *love* me. Then I came back, and I realized that Rick liked me too, but he didn't—" A choking noise takes the place of the rest of the sentence. "We had an argument, in his office up at the house. He kept a gun around. I guess because he felt like he was in the middle of nowhere out here. I suppose I was pretty out of control and he thought he'd better defend himself, but I ended up using the gun instead, wrapped him up in a drape, tossed him in the truck, didn't know where I was going, really."

Silence. The snow falls harder.

"Rick was your friend too, man," Steve says.

"He didn't give me any fucking money from any fucking song." Tim's voice sounds savage. "I'm singing for tips in the subway, I'm desperate, and who's he taking care of? Who's he giving money to?" I hear a scuffling in the treehouse then a ponderous thump as Tim tumbles into the circle of light cast by one of the cops' flashlights. The other cop cocks his gun with a sharp click.

The flashlight cop thrusts the flashlight into the other cop's free hand and steps toward Tim, who's bent in a crouch. As the cop reaches out for him, Tim rolls past him, scrambles to his feet, and, as the beam of my flashlight follows him almost against my will, darts into the woods.

"Stop!" shouts the cop with the gun. "Stop or I'll shoot."

"Shoot me, man. Go ahead," Tim calls over his shoulder, before the gun cracks and he falters and sags to the ground.

Epilogue

The man sitting near the back of the theater watches the stage restlessly. Below the huge banner that reads "CityBlues— Nobody Does It Like New York," a band is wrapping up their set.

"I got a little red rooster." The singer whispers it, like it's a secret between her and the microphone. She pauses while the guitar player tweaks a few notes from his strings.

"I got a little red rooster." Her voice is louder now, and notes blend into notes so that the brief phrase seems to tour the whole scale.

She's tall and almost gangly, except for the shapely breasts that fill out her silver-spangled halter top. The halter leaves a few inches of midriff bare above form-fitting white jeans tucked into silver cowboy boots.

Her hair, too blond to be natural, is pulled into a tousled pouf on top of her head; her eyes shaped with dark eyeliner, lips generously covered with bright red lipstick. But as she sings, her face twists into shapes of longing and misery at odds with her glamorous appearance.

The man in the back row has eyes only for her, though the other band members bear watching too. The guitar player is a tall, skinny guy in an oversized T-shirt and ripped jeans. His guitar hangs so low that, as he bends over it, his unruly mane of dark hair hides his face. The bass player, all in black, is as small and tidy as the guitar player is rangy and rumpled. At the keyboard, a medium-sized guy with shaggy brownish hair leans over the keys, his fingers punching out jagged drifts of sound under a nose bent almost to touch them. Under the keyboard, a pair of sneakers have been kicked aside and his restless feet are wearing only socks. Behind the drum kit sits a small woman whose steady look suggests a teacher, perhaps, alert to what's happening in every corner of her classroom. But instead of a desk, she's perched behind an assortment of drums and cymbals, and instead of a ruler, she holds a pair of drumsticks, expertly touching a drumhead here, a cymbal there, as she keeps an ear cocked to the rest of the band.

Now the blond woman is introducing the band, promising one more song as the man near the back of the theater squirms with impatience.

Finally, the set ends and, along with the rest of the crowd, he surges up the carpeted aisles and through the ornate doors that lead to the lobby. Now he's hovering near a table stacked with CDs, gazing particularly at the one bearing a picture of the band that he's been watching. Finally, he picks it up.

"Wanta' buy that?" asks the young woman stationed behind the table. "It's really good." She has unnaturally black hair and an earring in her nostril.

The woman behind the table is hoping the man will buy the CD, or at least linger by the table for a while, because he's so handsome, even though he's old, maybe almost forty.

He's got streaky dark-blond hair long enough to look cool but not like a hippie. And when he glances up and murmurs that he's already got a copy, she notices that his eyes are a striking shade of green.

The eyes rest on her only briefly, though. They shift almost immediately to something else, something off to the side. And as his hands go to return the CD to the pile, she notices that they're trembling.

The thing he's watching turns out to be the singer from the band that just finished, the skinny blond woman with the really obvious push-up bra.

"You didn't have to come," she says.

"I've got plenty of time to make it to Forty-Second Street before the curtain," he says. "I wanted to see your band." He leans forward to give the blond woman a sudden peck on the cheek. "You guys sound good. The CD sounds good, too."

"Thanks," the blond woman says. "Thanks very much."

ABOUT THE AUTHOR

Peggy Ehrhart is a former college English professor who lives in Leonia, New Jersey, where she plays blues guitar and writes mysteries. She has won awards for her short fiction, and her stories have appeared in *Futures Mystery Anthology Magazine, Crime Scene: New Jersey 2, Murder New York Style, Crime and Suspense Anthology I,* and numerous ezines. As Margaret J. Ehrhart, she has also published widely in the field of her academic specialty, medieval literature. She is a long-time member of Mystery Writers of America and Sisters in Crime. As a guitar player, she has performed with The Last Stand Band, Still Standing, and other bands in the New York Tri-State area. She is married to Norm Smith and is the mother of Matt Smith. Her first full-length mystery, *Sweet Man Is Gone,* was published by Five Star/Gale/Cengage in 2008. *Got No Friend Anyhow* is her second Maxx Maxwell mystery.